COLD REVENGE

ROBERT VAUGHAN

WOLFPACK
PUBLISHING
— EST 2013 —

Cold Revenge
Print Edition
© Copyright 2022 Robert Vaughan

Wolfpack Publishing
5130 S. Fort Apache Rd. 215-380
Las Vegas, NV 89148

wolfpackpublishing.com

Paperback ISBN 978-1-63977-273-5
LCCN 2021952515

COLD REVENGE

RAND COLBY STOOD ON THE PLATFORM OF THE RAILROAD station in Rushville, Nebraska, holding the telegram which told him of Nora's arrival. She was coming from Boston—a girl from the East who had never been out west, but was willing to leave her home and family for the man she loved.

A band was gathered on the platform that day to welcome back the Rushville Volunteer Fire Department, which had participated in a ladder race in Kansas City. Though the band was for the Fire Department, it seemed perfect to welcome Nora Stanfield.

"Nora!" Rand called, as he saw her stepping down from the train, hesitating just a little as she saw the crowd at the station. "Nora, over here!"

The young woman turned toward his shout, and all anxiety left her face in the smile that followed.

"Rand!" she called, running toward him. They embraced in the midst of the crowd, and the band played and people shouted, and in the streets, children set off firecrackers.

"For me?" Nora asked after the embrace, and she looked at the celebration.

"Absolutely," Rand said, laughing. "It's not every day one can get a beautiful young woman to leave Boston society and come to the wilderness."

"Ah, but I didn't come to the wilderness, Mr. Colby," Nora said, smiling at him. "I came to the arms of Rand Colby, the dashing young man who has stolen my heart."

"From your father . . ." Rand said. "Is he still angry?"

"Your grandfather Leland had a talk with him," Nora said. "He told father how he had made the mistake many years ago, when your mother married your father. He said he shut her out of his life forever, then by the time he realized how wrong he was, your mother had died, and he was never able to make it up to her."

"I know," Rand said. "She died with that pain in her heart."

"I'm glad you came to Boston to visit your grandfather," Nora said. "If you hadn't, I never would have met you."

A string of firecrackers exploded behind them, and Nora squealed in alarm and jumped into Rand's arms. He laughed and pulled her to him.

"I'm going to have to look those boys up and pay them for that," he said.

"Wait until you see my wedding dress," Nora said. "It's absolutely beautiful."

"If you wear it, I know it will be beautiful," Rand said.

"Oh, but I'm going to have to have it taken in a little bit. Do you know anyplace I can have that done?"

"Mrs. Clough has a dress shop close by," Rand said. "I'm sure she could take care of it for you. When do you want to do it?"

"Right now," Nora said.

Rand laughed. "What? Right now? But you just got here."

"I know," Nora said. "But I want everything to be just right for our wedding, Rand, please. I don't want anything to go wrong, so can we get this taken care of now? Besides, I want to try it on again."

"All right," Rand said. "If it's all that beautiful, I want to see you in it anyway."

"No, you mustn't!" Nora said.

"Why not?"

"Because it's bad luck for the groom to see the bride in her gown before the wedding."

"Well, we certainly don't want any bad luck now, do we?"

"Oh, there are my things," Nora said. "The wedding gown is in the black valise."

Nora held on to the valise while Rand arranged to have the trunks delivered to the boarding house where Nora would stay until they were married, then he pointed out the dress shop.

"I'll run in there and get it taken care of," Nora said. "Then you can take me out and show me the farm."

"I'll be happy to," Rand said.

"Oh, it all sounds so exciting. And to think that your grandfather actually wants you to give up all this and come work for him."

"Did he tell you that?" Rand asked.

"No," Nora said. "Not in so many words. But I know that's what he would like. He'll never make an issue of it, though, because he feels he made that mistake with your mother, and he doesn't want to make it again."

Rand laughed. "You know my grandfather much better than I do. Sometimes I wonder if you might not be a spy sent out here to keep an eye on me."

"Are you going to send me back?" she laughed.

"Not on your life," Rand said. "Listen, I think I'm going to run into the general store and take care of a few things, while you're tending to your dress. Do whatever you have to do, but don't be too long. I've waited long enough and I don't want to wait any longer."

"All right," Nora said.

As Nora went into the dress shop with the valise containing her wedding dress, Rand crossed the street to the general store.

"Did you get it?" he asked.

The store clerk smiled. "One box of lemon drops," he said. "You don't see many of these outside the big cities."

"You're going to have to keep a supply on hand now," Rand said. "Nora loves them."

"I saw her walking into the dress shop," the clerk said. "She's just as pretty as you said she was."

Suddenly there was a series of explosive pops.

"Those darn kids and their firecrackers," the clerk said, as he put the lemon drops in a sack. "You'd think our fire department won the ladder race. They just finished third, from what I understand."

"Holdup!" someone shouted. "Help, somebody, the bank's just been robbed. There was a killin' at the bank!"

Rand moved quickly to the front door and saw four horsemen riding at a gallop from the bank. One of the men was wearing a hood, but the other three were unmasked, and Rand stared at them, making a point to remember what they looked like.

Suddenly the four men started shooting wildly, and those who had come out onto the street to see them had to dive for cover. Rand dropped down to one knee, and his hand went automatically for the pistol he normally carried, but there was no pistol there, because he had thought it inappropriate to be armed when he met his bride-to-be.

The plate-glass window in Mrs. Clough's dress shop crashed in, and Rand remembered that Nora was there.

"Nora!" he called, running across the street, despite the fire of the retreating outlaws. One of the bullets kicked up dust right in front of him, but he didn't slacken his pace. "Nora!"

Mrs. Clough was standing just inside the doorway of her shop with an expression of shock on her face.

"Mrs. Clough, where's Nora?" Rand called. "Is she all right?"

"She . . . she . . ." Mrs. Clough stammered in a strained voice. She pointed toward the back of her shop.

"Nora!" Rand called in an agonized voice. He ran to the back of the shop where he found her lying on the floor, wearing a white wedding gown with a red spot on her bodice. Then, Rand saw, with a sickening realization, that the red spot wasn't part of her dress. . .it was blood. She had been shot right through the heart.

"No," Rand said quietly. He knelt on the floor and picked up her hand, but it was lifeless, already growing cold. Nora's eyes were closed as if she were sleeping, and inexplicably, there was a smile on her face. She had died instantly, unaware of pain, unaware of danger, aware only of her joy, and that joy, Nora took with her to her death.

BOSTON, MASSACHUSETTS:

It was the most difficult three days of Rand Colby's life. Nora lay in a coffin in the baggage car ahead as Rand was bringing her back home to Boston, and to her father.

He had sent the telegram informing Grant Stanfield of Nora's death, and how she had died. He had told him that he would be bringing her home, and what time the train would arrive. He left Rushville before Stanfield would have time to reply. He was afraid her father would tell him not to come with her.

When the train rolled into the Allston Depot, Rand saw a tall, gray-haired, dignified looking man standing on the depot platform. The expression on his face was a cross between anger and sorrow. The sorrow, Rand could relate to, the anger, he would have to deal with.

Rand remained in his seat until everyone who was going to, had left the car. Then, with a resigned sigh, he stood up and stepped out to face Nora's father.

"You brought her home?" Stanfield asked.

"Yes, sir. She's in the baggage car."

"Baggage," Stanfield said. "I send my daughter to you, and you bring her back as baggage."

"Mr. Stanfield, I . . ."

Stanfield held up his hand to interrupt Rand in midsentence. "No, don't say anything. I've made arrangements for the funeral. You can speak to me after Nora is in the ground."

"Don't be too upset with him," Rand's grandfather said later that same day. "Since Mildred, died Nora was all Grant had left. And now that she's gone too, he feels lost."

"Yeah? Well tell me, Grandpa, just how the hell does he think I feel?"

"I just think you should know that you aren't the only one hurting."

Rand nodded. "Yes, sir, I know that. And the truth is, I guess part of the hurt is because I feel guilty."

"Nonsense, you've nothing to feel guilty about."

"It's like Mr. Stanfield said. He sent his daughter out West to marry me, and I brought her back in a coffin. Oh, Grandpa I . . . I." Rand closed his eyes tightly, in a vain attempt to stop the tears.

THREE DAYS LATER, after the funeral was over, and after everyone had left the cemetery, Rand stood over the grave looking down at the mound of flowers. He remembered her happy smile the last time he saw her. And he remembered that she had died with that same smile still on her face.

Rand was surprised to feel a hand on his shoulder.

"Son, I'm sorry." The voice was gruff with sorrow, and Rand turned to see Stanfield standing there. "I had no right to be upset with you. I know that you feel her loss as deeply as I do. And rather than my having any hard feelings toward you, it would be better if we shared our sorrow." Stanfield extended his hand. "I hope you will accept my apology."

Rand took Stanfield's hand. "There's no need to apologize for grief."

The two men held the handshake for a long moment.

"I'm going to get them, Mr. Stanfield. I'm going to get every son of a bitch who did this, and I'm going to see that every one of them pays for what they did, either at the end of a rope or the end of my gun."

2

ST. LOUIS:

CARRIE HOLLIDAY WAS EMPLOYED BY THE NEW LIFE Orphanage where she worked as a governess. It was no mere coincidence that she worked there, for when she was a baby of six months, she had been left at the home. The man who left her told the home authorities little of Carrie's origins. He did not identify himself, but said Carrie's parents had died of swamp fever in Southeast Missouri. He brought her to St. Louis and left her, promising to return when he was able. That had been in the spring of 1851. It was now summer of 1873, and in those twenty-two years, the mystery of Carrie's past had never been solved, for the man had never returned.

"CARRIE, CARRIE, WATCH ME, CARRIE!"

The young boy's call interrupted Carrie's musing. "What do you want, Billy?"

"See how high I can swing!" The tow-headed youngster who had made the bid for attention, stood up in the swing and began working it, pumping with his feet and hands to make it go higher. It slipped back and forth beneath the dappled sun and shade of the great oak tree, and he grinned broadly as he saw Carrie looking at him.

"Oh, Billy, that's high," Carrie said. "I don't think I've ever seen anyone go that high."

"I went that high!" a red-headed, freckle-faced boy put in immediately. He, like Billy, was nine years old, and he, like Billy and every other boy of the New Life Orphanage, was in love with Carrie.

It was a warm Saturday afternoon and as all the chores were done and there was no school work to do, most of the children were playing. They were on the spacious lawn of a stately old house which was the New Life Orphanage, the only home Carrie had ever known, and she loved it dearly. She especially loved its commanding view of the broad Mississippi River.

The heavy bleat of a steamboat whistle caught her attention, and she looked toward the river. A giant three-tiered stern-wheeler was moving down river, aided in its transit by the five-mile-per-hour current which swept powerfully, inexorably, south. A long wake rolled out from the low, rounded bow, while the river frothed and boiled from the churning, splashing paddle at the stern. The children of the home ran to the low wrought-iron fence and waved to the boat, and from the wheel-house, the pilot waved back, then pulled on a rope that sent a white plume of steam, followed by the deep-throated bleat of the whistle that rolled out across the water.

It was always this way. The river-boat captains had saluted the children of the orphanage for as long as Carrie could remember, and for as long as she could remember, she had never watched one of them pass without some sense of nameless, mysterious longing. She liked to imagine that she was on one of the boats, steaming down-river toward places she had never seen, places that had romantic sounding names, like Cape Girardeau, Cairo, Osceola, Memphis, Natchez, Vicksburg, Baton Rouge, and New Orleans, or upriver, then through the Missouri and to the great West.

"He waved at me!" the red-headed child said.

"He waved at all of us," Billy insisted. "Carrie, didn't the captain wave at all of us?"

"Yes," Carrie said, "he waved at all of us."

RUSHVILLE, NEBRASKA:

"We know the names of three of the outlaws," Sheriff Harold Wallace said. "That would be Perry Hoyt, Ely Slack, and Nate Campbell. They were recognized by eye witnesses. The fourth was wearing a hood, as you recall, so we don't have any idea who he was."

"Harold, I want you to appoint me as a deputy. I will work without pay, but I'm going after those bastards," Rand Colby said.

"I can appoint you deputy sheriff, Rand, but your authority would be good only here in Sheridan County," Sheriff Wallace said. "And none of those boys are still in Sheridan County, or they would have already been strung up."

"Well, I'm going after them, with or without authority."

Sheriff Wallace smiled, and held up a finger. "I've got an idea, if you are agreeable to it."

"What's that?"

"While you were back east, those same four men robbed a train. Well, we think it was the same four, we know it was the same three and the fourth was wearing a hood, just like he did when he robbed our bank. I'm pretty sure, if you're interested, the Union Pacific would be willing to put you on as a railroad detective."

"But wouldn't that limit me to just the Union Pacific Railroad?"

"No, and that's the beauty of it," Sheriff Wallace said with a smile. "The United States Department of Justice grants commissions to railroad detectives, which means your authority will be nation-wide. Would you be interested in such a proposition?"

"Yes," Rand said, resolutely. "I very much would. As soon as I sell my farm."

"You're going to sell your farm?" Sheriff Wallace asked in surprise. "Why would you do that?"

"Because I intend to make finding these four bastards my full time job," Rand said.

LARAMIE, WYOMING:

After a fruitless month of looking for clues, Rand found himself in Laramie, Wyoming. He had ridden into town for no specific reason, other than to have a few days off the trail. There was a train sitting at the depot, while passengers were boarding. The locomotive was venting steam in loud puffs, and Rand saw the engineer leaning against the window, smoking a pipe. Crossing the track, he rode down Thornburgh Avenue, a wide street with houses on each side at the beginning of the street, then business buildings as he rode deeper into the town. He rode past the Custer Hotel, the Laramie National Bank, The Elkhorn Barn and Livery Stable.

He heard a woman's laughter from a building just

ahead. The name of the building was the Holliday House, and it looked to be a combination saloon and hotel.

After so many days on the trail, the thought of a beer seemed good to him, so he stopped in front of the establishment, looped Diablo's reins around the hitching rail, then stepped inside.

"Hello, cowboy. Are you thirsty?" a pretty girl asked.

"Nah, I'm just usin' my mouth to grow cotton, is all," Rand replied with a grin.

The pretty girl laughed. "You're funny. My name is Polly. I'll show you to the bar."

"Careful, Mister. Once Polly gets her hands on a man, she don't let 'im go," someone called out, his comment met with laughter from many of the others.

"Hal, this man wants to buy a drink. Or maybe, two drinks?" she added, suggestively.

"Two drinks it is," Rand said. "I'll have a beer, and give this little lady whatever she wants."

"Thank you," Polly said. "Shall we take a table?"

"If you don't mind, I'd just as soon stand here at the bar, so I can take a look around," Rand replied.

"Well, I, uh, thank you for the drink," Polly said and Rand lifted his beer to her as she began moving through the saloon, smiling and flirting with the other customers.

"Haven't seen you in here before." The man who spoke to Rand was of average height, slender, with gray hair and a gray moustache. Unlike the denim trousers and flannel shirts worn by most of the patrons, this man was wearing a brown tweed suit with a white shirt and a red string tie.

"No, sir, I don't reckon you have, seeing as this is the first time I've ever been here."

The man extended his hand. "The name is Charles Holliday. I own this establishment."

Rand took his hand. "Rand Colby." He lifted his beer mug. "You serve good beer here, Mr. Holliday," he said with a smile.

"What brings you to Laramie?"

"I'm a railroad detective," Rand said. "I'm looking for the men who held up a bank in Rushville, Nebraska six weeks or so, ago."

"Oh, yes, I read about that in the paper. But if you're a railroad detective, why are you looking for bank robbers?"

"Those same men also robbed a train."

"Do you think any of them are here in Laramie?"

"Not necessarily," Rand said. "This is just where I've wound up after wandering around for so long."

"Do you have any names?"

"There were four, and we have the names for three of them. The fourth man wore a hood. I'll give you names we have, just in case you've heard of any of them. That would be Perry Hoyt, Ely Slack, and Nate Campbell."

Charles shook his head. "I'm sorry. None of the names mean anything to me."

"Well, one of them, if you ever saw him, you would remember. He's bald, but it isn't like a normal bald head. He has no hair because of a botched scalping attempt, more than likely by the Oglala Sioux. Also, there's a long three-corner, purple lightning flash of a scar on his right cheek. That would be Perry Hoyt."

"Well, you're right about one thing, if I had ever seen anyone of that description, I would have remembered."

"I think I might come off the trail for a few days, just to sleep in a bed and eat food I haven't cooked," Rand said.

"And enjoy a few beers?" Charles asked, with a smile.

Rand lifted his nearly empty mug. "Well, maybe a

little more than a few," he replied matching Charles' smile.

OVER THE NEXT several days Rand and Charles became friends. Rand also
    met Edward Steele, Holliday's lawyer.

"How much do you know about Charley's business?" Steele asked Rand as the two men shared a lunch in the Holliday House Restaurant.

"Not too much. I know he has a saloon, a hotel, and this restaurant. And, though we haven't actually spoken of it, I've sort of gotten the idea that all these pretty girls do more than smile and serve drinks."

Steele chuckled. "You've met Winnie Callahan?"

"Uh, yes, I didn't know that was her last name. She's older, and not quite as pretty as the other girls."

"She's the madam."

"I see."

"The girls are all prostitutes, and Winnie's in charge of them. The Holliday House is also a brothel."

"I sort of got that idea," Rand said.

"Yes sir, Charley's found a way to make a lot of money by way of the oldest profession." Edward laughed. "Actually, I can take credit for getting him into that particular business. He didn't want anything to do with it at first."

RAND'S first meeting with Edward Steele left him with a bad taste in his mouth about the lawyer, and he spoke of it to Charles.

"How well do you know Edward Steele?"

"Oh, as well as anyone knows his lawyer, I suppose. I

wouldn't say that we're friends, exactly. But I see no reason to mistrust him. Why do you ask?"

"I don't know. There's just something about him that gives me an uneasy feeling."

"Well, he arranged a loan for me, and I'm thankful to him for that."

ABOUT A WEEK AFTER THAT CONVERSATION, Rand decided it was time for him to move on. He was standing at the bar telling both Charles and the bartender goodbye, when the peace of the saloon was shattered.

"Loomis, you are a card cheatin' son of a bitch!"

The shout came from a man at one of the tables, and it was loud enough to get the attention of everyone in the saloon.

"You accusin' me of cheatin', Dolan?"

"I ain't just accusin' you, I'm tellin' you, you're cheatin'. One of those four sevens you just laid down was my discard," Dolan said.

The loud exchange caused the piano player to turn away from the keyboard and the music halted with a few discordant notes.

"This could be trouble," Charles said, as he started toward the table where the card game was being played.

Loomis, the man accused of cheating stood up then, with his gun in his hand.

"Nobody calls me a cheater 'n gets away with it," he said with a snarl as he pulled the trigger.

Dolan, the man who had accused him, fell backward.

"Loomis, put that gun down!" Charles ordered.

"The hell I will," Loomis said, turning the gun toward Charles.

Rand had watched the dramatic scene play out from

his position at the bar. Then, seeing Loomis turn his pistol toward Charles, Rand drew his own gun.

"Drop it!" Rand ordered.

Loomis pulled the trigger, and with a loud gasp of pain, Charles put his hand over the bullet hole in his stomach. Rand followed Loomis' shot with one of his own, and Loomis fell with blood and brain matter erupting from the wound in his head.

"Charles!" Rand shouted, and holstering his pistol, he knelt beside his friend.

"Rand, stop him," Charles said in a strained voice. "Stop him before he can hurt anyone else."

"He won't hurt anyone else. Hal, get the doctor," he called to the bartender.

"We should get him in bed," Polly, one of the saloon girls said.

Rand nodded in agreement, and he took Charles by the shoulders while one of the other saloon patrons took him by his legs. They carried him upstairs to his apartment.

"I want to talk alone with Rand," Charles said.

"I'll bring the doctor up when he gets here," Polly said as she and the other man who had helped bring Charles up to his apartment left.

"I have a niece," Charles said.

"What?"

"I have a niece, named Carrie. Her parents died of swamp fever when she was a baby, and I'm her only relative. I didn't want the responsibility, so I took her to an orphanage. She doesn't know about me."

"Do you want me to get word to her? If I can find her, I'll get her here to see you."

"There won't be time," Charles said. "I'm dying."

"You don't know that."

Charles reached out to grab Rand's hand, and he squeezed it tightly. "Yes, I know. Believe me, when your time comes, you know."

"The doctor will be here soon," Rand said, not knowing what else to say.

"I want you to do something for me."

"I'll do what I can," Rand replied.

"I haven't seen her since she was a baby, and she knows nothing about me, but I have kept up with her. Edward Steele is holding a letter that I wrote to Carrie. She's in St. Louis. I'd be much obliged if you could get the letter to her."

"All right, I'll get it to the post office today if you want that."

"No. Don't mail it," Charles said as he started gasping for air. "I want you to take it to her."

"I . . ." Rand wanted to tell him that he was looking for bank robbers, and he didn't have time to go look for the niece of a man he hardly knew, but he could see the pleading in Charles' eyes. "All right," he said. "I'll take it to her."

Polly and Dr. Petrey arrived at that moment.

"He's hurt bad, Doc," Rand said as he stepped away from the bed.

Doctor Petrey began to examine Charles. Within a minute, he began putting his stethoscope away.

"Is he going to be all right?" Polly asked.

Doctor Petrey looked at both Polly and Rand. "He's dead."

3

RAND WAITED UNTIL AFTER CHARLEY'S FUNERAL BEFORE he went to see Edward Steele.

"Yes, I know what he's talking about," Steele said. He chuckled. "Better you than me."

"What?"

"He told me when he gave me this package that if anything happened to him, he wanted me to personally take it to his niece. I'm glad he's pushed that responsibility off on somebody else. I really don't have time to go to St. Louis."

"I don't either," Rand said. "I've got four bank robbers to chase down."

"Yes, the ones who robbed the bank in Hastings."

"Rushville," Rand corrected. He sighed. "But I told him I'll do it, and so I will."

"You don't have to do it, you know. The girl doesn't even know about Charles, so it won't make any difference to her whether you deliver the letter or not."

"What would happen to Charley's businesses if they don't go to her?"

"I imagine the saloon, the hotel—everything he owns would be put up for public auction, and whatever money the auction brings in would automatically go to the city of Laramie. It would be a good thing for all involved. Whoever makes the winning bid would get a thriving business at a bargain price, and the city of Laramie would have extra money in its coffers."

You have the letter?"

"Yes, I have it."

"Then give it to me. I'm going to honor my promise to Charley."

"All right, but I think you're making a big mistake."

Edward Steele lowered the door to one of the shelves of his barrister book case, then pulled out an envelope and handed it to Rand.

"Here it is," he said. "Oh, and you might want to take this." Reaching back into the case, he removed what appeared to be the front half of a locket. "Charley told me that when he dropped his niece off, he left the other half of this locket with the orphanage. The intention was should he ever need to prove he was the legitimate claimant, he could use this to prove it."

"Is the envelope sealed?" Rand asked.

"No, you can read the letter if you want to. I have."

"I'll wait until I'm on the train, on the way to St. Louis."

"One thousand dollars," Steele said.

"What?"

"If you find this woman, and to be honest with you, I'm not even sure she actually exists, but if you find her, tell her I, personally, will buy the Holliday House for one thousand dollars."

"The property is worth more than that, Steele, and you know it."

"If a young woman raised in an orphanage, is given the choice of owning a whore house or selling it for a thousand dollars, I think she might find the offer to her liking."

WHEN RAND RETURNED to the Holliday House that night, he was sitting alone at a table in the saloon, when one of the bargirls came over. He wasn't in any mood for conversation, but he knew that Polly was genuinely saddened by Charles Holliday's death.

"Hello, Polly," he said.

Instead of asking Rand to buy a drink for her company, she took a seat across the table from him.

"You're looking for the men who killed your girlfriend, aren't you?" Polly asked.

"Yes," Rand replied. He wouldn't have referred to Nora as his girlfriend, but it was close enough.

"Is one of them named Ely Slack?"

Rand took in a quick intake of breath at the question.

"Yes!" he said excitedly. "Polly, do you know something about Slack?"

"He 'n three other men have come in here a few times. I never said nothin' about it, 'cause he told me his name was Brown. I didn' find out 'till yesterday that his real name was Slack, 'n I didn't know he was one of the men you were lookin' for 'till Hal told me."

"Is he sort of a rat-faced fella with a hooked nose and beady eyes?"

Polly laughed. "Yes, that pretty much describes him."

"Where is he, do you know?"

"I don't know exactly," Polly said. "But I heard 'em talk about Buford a few times."

"Buford?"

"It's a real small town, 'bout twenty miles east of here."

"Is it on the railroad?"

"Yes, it is."

A broad smile spread across Rand's face. This was the best lead he had gotten since the robbery occurred.

"Did any of the other three men have a beard?"

Polly shook her head. "No none of 'em had a beard, but one of 'em had a moustache, 'n it's black. His name's Morris, or at least that's what the others called 'im. I don't know if that was his first name or his last."

"So we've got Slack and Morris. Do you know the names of the other two?"

"Well, I know what they're callin' themselves. There's one that's got two or three teeth missing in front. His name is Collins. And the other one's missin' an earlobe. One of 'em said that it got bit off in a fight. His name is Lewis."

"Thanks, Polly. Go buy yourself a drink. No, go buy yourself twenty drinks."

"Thank you, Rand!" Polly said, her smile as broad as Rand's.

IT TOOK a little over three hours for Rand to ride from Laramie to Buford. Buford was a town with no more than a dozen houses, a post office, a railroad depot, a saloon, a blacksmith shop and a grocery store with a livery attached.

Rand dismounted in front of the livery.

"Lookin' to board your horse, Mister?" The man who asked had gray hair, and a long gray beard. "The name's Hank Borgmeier, I own this place."

21

"Yes, thank you, Mr. Borgmeier. How much is it per night?

"A quarter a night, thirty-five cents if I feed 'em."

"Here's ten days for board and feed. I'll be taking a train to St. Louis, tomorrow. Would it be all right if I spend the night in the stall with him, tonight?"

"That'll be fine, and no extra cost. I'll take good care of 'im," Borgmeier said.

"Thanks."

Leaving the stable, Rand stepped into the saloon. It was considerably smaller and not as well appointed as the Holliday Saloon, but Rand wasn't there for the ambience. He was there for information.

Rand knew better than to just come right out and start asking about Slack or Brown, as Polly had said his name was. That would not only be an ineffective way of getting information, it could also cause Slack to be aware that someone was looking for him.

Two hours, two beers, and a supper of beans and bacon later, Rand left the saloon without any useable information. He walked back down to the livery, then let himself into Diablo's stall.

"I'm going to be leaving you here for several days old boy, but I'll be spending this last night with you before I go."

Diablo snorted and nodded his head, as if he understood what Rand had told him.

ONE OF THE perks of being a railroad detective was free passage, and when Rand boarded the train the next day, he took advantage of that.

"Well, we should certainly be safe," the conductor

joked. "You're the second railroad detective we'll have on this trip."

"Oh? Who's the other one?"

"Matthew McIvor. Do you know him?"

"Yes, I know Matt. Which car is he in?"

"He's in the first car after the dining car."

"Thanks," Rand said. "I'll look him up once we're underway."

Rand took a window seat, then waited until the train pulled away from the station before he removed the letter Charley had written to the niece he had not seen since she was an infant.

He had not looked at the letter before, because he considered it an invasion of privacy. But as he thought about it, he decided it might be a good idea to know what he was getting into, so he examined the envelope for a moment, then removed the letter and began to read.

My dear Carrie,

If you are reading this letter, it will be because I am already dead. It will come as neither a shock nor a loss to you, as you never knew me. That is my fault, and I have lived with the sin of that fact for my entire life. You see, I was the one who brought you to the orphanage in St. Louis. My name is Charles Holliday and I am your uncle.

After I left you in St. Louis, I made my way to California. I had been struck with gold fever, even as your father tried to dredge a farm out of the snake and mosquito-infested swamps of Southeast Missouri. He kept me there while he was alive, but when he and your mother contracted swamp fever and died, I vowed that nothing would keep me there any longer . . . not even the God-given obligation I had to you, my brother's only child. So, when I heard of an orphanage in St. Louis, I put you in a saddlebag and rode 150 miles up to St. Louis to put you in the New Life Orphanage. I promised the good folks there that I would be coming back for you in no more than a few months, but it was a promise I had no intention of keeping. I headed straight for the gold fields of California.

I nearly died during the trek to California. When I arrived, I discovered that what gold there was had all been mined or claimed, and I was forced to make a living the best way I could. I found work in a hotel . . .not very glamorous work, I'm afraid, but it was honest and it kept me going. Eventually, I managed to buy my own business in Laramie, Wyoming, and that brings me to the purpose of this letter. You are the only relation I have, and as your mother was without brother or sister, I am the only relation you have. Therefore, I am leaving my hotel to you. It is called the Holliday House and it will make a decent living for you if you care to come out here and run it. Even as you are reading this, I am facing Divine Providence, and I've a lot to ask His forgiveness for. But before I ask His forgiveness, I must plead for yours. I hope you can find it in your heart to do that.

With love,

Your Uncle Charles.

Rand folded the letter and returned it to the envelope. He sat there, thinking about its contents for awhile. Then he remembered that Matt McIvor was on the train.

It was easy to pick him out when he stepped into the car. Matt was a big, red-headed man with a beard and an easy laugh. He greeted Rand as he came up to his seat.

"Rand, m'boy," he said, "you're a sight for these tired old eyes now, or my name's not Matthew McIvor."

"Hello, Matt," Rand acknowledged, sticking his hand out to clasp Matt's.

"Have a seat," Matt invited. "Where are you headed?"

"St. Louis."

"Ah, I thought you might start there, seeing as he's a river-boat gambler on the Missouri."

"What?" Rand asked, confused by Matt's comment. "What are you talking about? Who's a river-boat gambler?"

"Perry Hoyt. Isn't that why you're going to St. Louis?"

"I . . . no, I haven't heard anything about that."

"Oh, well I know you're looking for him and the others, so I thought maybe you knew. But I just heard about it myself, so I can see how word might not have reached you yet. The last report we have on Hoyt is that he's been gambling on the river boats going up and down the Missouri River."

"Which one?"

"He doesn't stay on the same boat. So far, he's been on the *North Star*, the *Benjamin Gaye*, and the *Western Lady*. No telling which one he's on now."

"Thanks for telling me," Rand said. "Oh, listen, I wonder if you could check someone else out for me too."

"I'll do what I can. Who are you lookin' for?"

"I'm not looking for him, I know where he is. I guess I would just like to know who he is."

"All right, who is this mysterious character?"

"His name is Edward Steele?"

"What did this fella, Steele, do?" Matt asked.

"That's just it, he didn't do anything. But he's a lawyer and there's something about him that just doesn't seem right to me. He seems sort of sleazy."

Matt laughed. "M'boy, you tell me what lawyers aren't sleazy. But, I'll see what I can find out for you."

"Thanks."

Rand was glad that he had run into Matt. His information was the best lead he had gotten since he had learned the names of three of the robbers.

ST. LOUIS – NEW LIFE ORPHANAGE:

When Rand stepped down from the hired cab, for a moment, he wondered if the driver had brought him to the right place. What he saw on the other side of the waist-high stone fence, was a very large, two-story house with wings to either side, and Corinthian columns across the front. It looked more like a grand mansion, than an orphanage. There was also a very spacious lawn and when he saw several children playing, he was convinced that he had come to the right place. He also saw a beautiful young woman looking over the children, and he wondered if this might be the Carrie Holliday he was coming to see.

Rand was still standing just outside the gate, when he saw a man coming toward him. The man looked to be in his mid to late forties, well dressed, and rather dignified looking. The expression on his face reflected some concern about a strange man, standing at the gate, apparently studying the children.

"Is there something I can do for you, sir?" the man asked, the expression in his voice echoing his concern.

"I would like to speak to the head man."

"If you mean to speak to the director, that would be me. I'm Edward Talbot." Talbot extended his hand.

CARRIE WAS WATCHING the children at play, when a little girl came up behind her and pulled on her skirt to get her attention.

"Hello, Rosemary. What do you need?" Carrie asked with a smile.

"Who's that?" Rosemary asked, and Carrie looked in the direction the little girl was pointing.

Coming through the front gate of the orphanage, was a tall, fair-haired, blue-eyed man. He was walking toward the front of the house with Mr. Talbot. Talbot had been the director of the home for as long as Carrie had been here, and as a little girl, she had always thought Mr. Talbot was a very big man. Her perspective changed as she grew older, and now she saw that he was nearly dwarfed by the handsome man who was walking beside him.

Despite the innocent appearance of the meeting between Mr. Talbot and the stranger, there was something . . . perhaps a premonition or an intuitive awareness, which Carrie found frightening. No, frightened was not the correct definition of her reaction, she decided. Intrigued would better describe her feelings.

But why did she feel this way?

She watched as Talbot and the stranger went inside.

RAND FOLLOWED the director into his office, where Talbot indicated a chair with a wave of his hand.

"Please, Mr. Colby, have a seat," Talbot invited. "What can I do for you?"

"Mr. Talbot, I am looking for a young woman named Carrie Holliday."

"May I ask what your interest would be with Miss Holliday?"

"First, let me establish my credentials so to speak," Rand said. He removed the locket cover, and held it out toward Talbot. "This is half of a locket. Her uncle,

27

Charles Holliday, informed his attorney that he had left the other half of this locket here with his niece when he brought her to you. The locket, he felt, would prove to be a way of identifying himself."

Talbot took the locket cover examined it for a moment, then opened the safe and pulled out a small box. Removing a piece of jewelry from the box, he held the locket cover, to the locket half.

"Perfect match," he said. "I took this locket half from Charles Holliday twenty-two years ago. He swore that he would return but he never did. He didn't even try to stay in contact with Carrie. Nary a letter or telegram ever crossed this threshold."

"He told me that his biggest regret was that he never returned for his niece," Rand said.

"Then why isn't he here now instead of sending you in his stead?"

"He died this past month, Mr. Talbot."

"I see, but that begs the question. Why are you here?"

"He entrusted me with a letter for Miss Holliday. He owned a business establishment—a hotel, in Laramie, Wyoming, and as she is his only heir, he has left it to her. I'm here to take her to Wyoming if she wishes to claim the business."

"All right," Talbot said as he rose from his desk. "Wait here, sir. I'll send my wife to fetch Miss Holliday."

MRS. TALBOT STEPPED out the back door and called to Carrie.

"Carrie, dear, please come into the house. Mr. Talbot has a need to see you."

Puzzled, Carrie followed the grandmotherly old woman inside. Mr. Talbot was standing in the parlor ... a room no child from the orphanage was permitted to enter. Even though Carrie was no longer a child and was now a part of the staff, she still had reservations each time she went into the restricted room. If Mr. Talbot wanted to speak to her in the parlor, it must be important.

"Carrie, have a seat," Mr. Talbot invited. He cleared his throat. "You may have noticed the man standing at the gate."

"I saw him," Carrie answered.

"He is in my office, now. He's here because of you."

"Because of me? I don't understand," Carrie said. "How could he be here because of me? I've never seen that man before."

"I know," Mr. Talbot said. He sighed. "Many years ago, when you came to us, we were given one half of a locket. It belonged to your mother."

"My mother? You have a locket that belonged to my mother? Why have you never shown it to me?"

"We were instructed to hold the locket as a means of authenticating anyone who might come to inquire about you. Mr. Colby, the man in my office, is that person. He presented the other half of the locket, then gave me a letter for you."

Talbot handed an envelope to Carrie.

"For me?" Carrie said. "In my entire life, I have never received a letter." Carrie opened the envelope with eager fingers, then pulled the letter out and began to read.

4

AFTER CARRIE FINISHED READING THE LETTER, SHE looked up and blinked her eyes several times to fight the tears that had begun to form. "My uncle," she said. "I have a relative. At long last I have found a relative, only he's—"

"Dead," Mr. Talbot said quietly. "Yes, child, I'm sorry you had to learn about him this way."

Carrie wiped the tears from her eyes as she finished the letter. She had never known a more bittersweet moment in her life. At long last she had managed a glimpse into her past. Nobody knew of the nights she had lain awake, wondering, praying, dreaming about what her parents might have been like and what had happened to them. And now, here in this letter, there was a real link with that which the most ordinary person knows, but which she had been denied. Then, just as the window opened, it closed, finally and forever, because the never seen writer of this letter, her Uncle Charles, the one connection with her parents, was now dead. There had been one line in the letter, which was particularly telling. "You are the only relation I have, and as your mother was without sister or brother, I am the only relation you have." That meant she was all alone now. Of course, she had always been alone, but it had never seemed so lonely, as it did right now at this very moment.

"As you can see," Mr. Talbot said, "he has left a hotel to you. The gentleman who arrived today has brought a further message from your uncle's lawyer."

"What is the message?" Carrie asked.

"I will let him tell you," Mr. Talbot said. "I thought it was prudent to inform you about your uncle before you met with Mr. Colby."

"Mr. Colby?"

"Rand Colby," Mr. Talbot said. "He is the gentleman who brought this letter."

"I see," Carrie said. "Would you show him in, please, Mr. Talbot."

When Rand Colby stepped into the room a moment later, he looked at Carrie with a genuine expression of sympathy.

"Miss Holliday, I am sorry about your uncle," he said. "He was a fine man, and all who knew him spoke well of him."

"You knew him?" Carrie asked, her curiosity now more dominant than the sorrow of losing someone she had never known.

"Yes, I knew him. I confess that I hadn't known him for very long, but in that short time, we became friends."

"I ... I never knew him," Carrie said.

"No, I suppose not," Colby said. "Nor did any of Charley's friends know of you until he told me about you as he was dying. His last conscious thought was of you, and he asked me to deliver this letter to you. I was honored that I'm the one he chose."

Carrie thought it was nice that she would be her uncle's last conscious thought, but she would have preferred for him to have thought of her long before that.

"Mr. Talbot says that you bring a further message from my uncle's lawyer," she finally managed to say.

"Shyster," Rand said.

"I beg your pardon?"

"Edward Steele, the man who represented your uncle was a shyster. I'm convinced that in the final year of your uncle's life, he managed to steal a great deal of money from him."

"Then why didn't my uncle dismiss him?" Carrie asked, surprised by the remark.

"Because your uncle couldn't see it," Rand said. "He was a trusting man. Steele had fooled a lot of people with his Eastern manners," Rand said, "but he hasn't fooled me."

"Could it be, Mr. Colby, that you are letting personal prejudices color your judgment?" Mr. Talbot asked.

"I will admit that I don't find him trustworthy," Rand said.

"And yet you are here, performing an errand for him?"

"No," Rand said. "I'm here performing an errand for Charles Holliday, and I feel it's only right that I offer to escort his niece back to Laramie if she decides that's what she wants to do."

"And that is the message you bring from Steele as well?" Talbot asked.

"No, Steele wants to pay you a thousand dollars for

the business if you wish to sell. I have his bank draft for that amount."

"One thousand dollars?" Carrie asked. "You have one thousand dollars for me?"

"If you are willing to sign over the property deed to Edward Steele, I do," Rand said.

Carrie leaned back in the chair with her head spinning. She could scarcely even imagine so much money, and now it would be hers, just for the signing of a piece of paper.

"In addition," Rand went on, "I have two hundred dollars in cash, left to you by your uncle."

Rand pulled an envelope from his inside jacket pocket and handed it to her. She felt it fat with bills, and she looked inside and gasped. If she had never imagined one thousand dollars, she had never seen two hundred— at least, not all at one time.

"My," Carrie said. "Oh, my."

"Which will it be?" Rand said easily.

The thought of all that money made Carrie's head swirl, and yet at the back of her mind, was the exciting prospect of what it would be like to turn the money down and go to Laramie. She was a person with no past, but if she reached out and chose it now, she could certainly be a person with a future.

"What do you suggest?" Carrie asked.

"I suggest that you take the money," Talbot said quickly. "Why, child, you could put that money in the bank, and by living frugally, have security for some time to come."

"Or you could come to Laramie with me and reach for the brass ring," Rand suggested smiling easily. "What do I suggest? I suggest you keep the hotel. If Steele offered you a thousand dollars for it, you can believe it is worth at least five."

"Five thousand?" Now the figures were getting so high as to be out of hand, Carrie thought.

"Come with me," Rand said. "If you don't like it out there, you can always sell the hotel and come back to St. Louis."

"How would we get there?"

"By riverboat as far as Omaha," Rand said. "And then by train. It is not a hazardous journey, and in this day and age, it isn't even an arduous one. We could be in Laramie in a little more than a week."

"A riverboat?" How often, over the last twenty years, had Carrie watched the riverboats ply by, bound for romance and adventure. She looked at Rand Colby, and a trip to Laramie in the company of this man appealed to her. She smiled. Her mind was made up.

"When do we leave?" she asked.

5

THE *WESTERN LADY* WAS TIED UP AT LACLEDE'S LANDING, taking on passengers and cargo for its trip up the Missouri. Carrie was already one of the passengers, and she stood against the railing, watching the activity with a fluttering excitement, the likes of which she had never before experienced.

The boat's engine vented itself, and its loud rushing noise startled Carrie. As the white tendrils of escaped steam drifted across the deck, however, she smiled at her fears. It wouldn't do to get frightened over every little thing now, she thought. She had quite an adventure before her, and she would have to keep her courage, as well as her wits about her.

Rand Colby had brought her to the boat, secured passage and a stateroom for her, then telling her that he would return after taking care of some business in St. Louis, he had left her. She was disappointed that he had left, because she had hoped he would be there to share some of the excitement with her.

Though his presence may have added to the excitement, his absence certainly didn't take anything away, and she moved from one end of the boat to the other, seeing up close, and with curious eyes, those things she had only managed to dream about in the past.

One of the boat's officers walked by, smiled gallantly at Carrie, then saw several barrels out of place.

"Here, you deckhand," he called to one of the sweating laborers. "Move those barrels forward, man. They have no business being here."

"The cargo officer told me to put them here," the deckhand complained.

"Well, I'm the purser, and I've got to keep this deck cleared for the passengers' promenade. Now, move them forward!"

"Yes, sir."

Clang, clang! Clang, clang!

"Make way! Make way! Load comin' aboard!"

"Cap'n, this here drayman says he ain't leavin' the boat, less'n he gets a receipt signed by you personal!"

"What was on the wagon?" the captain called down.

"Ten penny nails, Cap'n."

"All right, you inventory the shipment and if the load agrees with the manifest, I'll sign the receipt."

"Yes, sir," the man on deck answered. "Let's get this stuff counted," he said to the drayman.

Carrie looked up toward the wheelhouse, where the captain was leaning against the window frame, watching the activity. The wheelhouse was a magnificent structure, all glass enclosed, nestled between the two towering smokestacks. Behind the captain, Carrie could see the great wheel by which the boat was steered. When the captain saw Carrie looking up at him, he saluted her, and Carrie returned an embarrassed smile, then looked away.

Carrie walked from the railing back to a bench in the middle of the deck and sat down for a while. She wasn't particularly tired, but her new shoes were hurting her feet. She pulled her skirt up slightly, and looked at her shoes. They were very narrow, with an open top and a raised heel. The salesclerk had assured her they were the latest in fashion, and he showed her a picture of them in *Harper's Bazaar*. He did not warn her, however, that they would be very uncomfortable. She wished she could take them off and walk about the boat barefoot, but she knew such a thing would really be scandalous.

Carrie had spent fifty dollars of the two hundred dollars, providing herself with a wardrobe she thought would be suitable for the trip. She had never bought a new dress of her own, before. All of her clothes had come from the clothing barrel, provided by the good people of the churches that supported the orphanage. It was a new and exciting experience to pick out her own dresses and accessories.

The dress Carrie was wearing now, was pale yellow, festooned in green faille. It was as bright and pretty as a spring flower.

"Cap'n, load is aboard!" someone shouted up from the deck.

"Very well," the captain called down. "Cast off the bow line."

"Cast off the bow line," the deck officer repeated. "Make way to get underway!"

"Oh, no, wait!" Carrie called, standing up quickly and shouting to the deck officer. "Wait, we can't leave now! Mr. Colby hasn't come aboard! You must wait for him!"

"Sorry, Miss," the deck officer said. "Only the captain can do that."

"Then how do I get up there?" Carrie asked. "I must talk to him."

"Beg your pardon, Miss, but it'd be best if you don't bother him right now. It's always a busy time when we're gettin' underway."

"But Mr. Colby—"

The officer smiled. He was a man in his late forties, though years of hard work kept his body lean, strong, and youthful looking.

"I don't expect Mr. Colby will have any trouble," the deck officer said gently. "There's many a boatman along the river that can bring him out, even if we are underway. It happens all the time. The river winds around so, that he'll have no problem catchin' up to us." He touched the bill of the cap he was wearing. "Now, if you'll excuse me, ma'am, I got lots of work to do."

Carrie wanted to go on, to pursue this matter further, but she had no idea where to go or what to do. Finally, reluctantly, she decided to put her hope in what the deck officer had said. If this did happen often, there was probably no cause for alarm.

But, what if Mr. Colby didn't show up? What would she do then?

Even as Carrie worried about it, she managed to calm her fears. There was really no problem at all, she decided. She was, after all, an adult, and that meant she was perfectly capable of handling things herself. She had been too long dependent upon the methodical ways of institutional living. Although she had been a rebellious young girl at the orphanage—she had finally succumbed. Her meals had been planned for her, her clothes provided for her, nothing had been left to chance, and no decision was left to her. Now it was all changing, and the best way to handle the change was just to jump right in.

If she could. Now, at last, she would take charge of her life, make decisions and charge forward.

The boat whistled, and the steam engine began puffing loudly. At the stern of the boat, the huge paddle wheel began turning, splashing up water that sparkled in the sun. There were several shouts of excitement from those on deck, and many ran to the railing to watch. Carrie saw the river bank slipping away, then she forgot about Mr. Colby in the excitement of the moment and moved back to join the others at the railing, to watch. She looked down at the muddy water and saw the distance widening between the boat and the bank as the boat began slipping away. Along the cobble-stoned levee, dozens of well-wishers had gathered to wave goodbye to those on the boat, and Carrie returned their waves happily, though she didn't know any of them.

None of the children from the orphanage were there. The orphanage was north of LaClede's Landing, so the boat would be passing right by on its way to the mouth of the Missouri. Carrie knew that all the children would be outside, standing along the wrought-iron fence, waving at her, and she had promised to wave back at each one of them.

The boat backed all the way out into the middle of the channel, then turned and started beating its way against the current. For a moment, it looked as if the current would prevail, for even though the paddlewheel was turning and boiling the water into a froth, the boat was sliding backward in the river, as evidenced by the shoreline. Finally the paddlewheel managed to arrest the backward motion, then, gradually, the boat started forward against the powerful current. They would have to do battle against the current for the entire trip.

By a series of telegrams, Rand had learned that Perry Hoyt was not on the *North Star*, or the *Benjamin Gaye*. That didn't mean for certain that he was on the *Western Lady*, but it was certainly worth further investigation.

He hurried down to the dock to board the boat, but it had already pulled away.

"Miss the boat, did you?" a man asked.

"Yes, and I'm responsible for a young woman who has already boarded." Rand sighed. "I can take a train to Jefferson City and get on the boat there, I guess."

"I can get you on board here, for ten dollars," the man offered.

"How?"

The man smiled, and held out his hand. "Ten dollars," he said.

Rand put a ten-dollar bill in his hand. "If you can't get me on board, I'll be taking the money back," he said.

On board the boat, Carrie watched the city of St. Louis, from the river, as they passed it by. She had read in the St. Louis Dispatch that the great gateway city was the fourth largest city in America, and now she could believe it. This was the first time she had ever seen it from this vantage point, and she saw that it spread for miles back from the river.

St. Louis was a great city of commerce, and there were half a dozen trains moving alongside the river, and as many as fifty boats tied up at the docks. The roads leading down to the river were clogged with wagon traffic. Eades Bridge, a monument to man's engineering ability, spanned the river, bringing commerce from the Illinois side, and the eastern seaboard. As the boat passed beneath the bridge, Carrie looked up in wonder at the high, elegant structure.

Finally, the commercial heart of the city was passed and they were in the northern hills residential area. There, on one of the bluffs overlooking the river, Carrie saw the orphanage. She took a handkerchief from her purse hoping those at the home would better be able to see her wave. When the boat grew close enough, she could see all the children and the Talbots standing at the fence, waving furiously.

Carrie waved back, and as she did, she heard, by some freak carriage of sound, a voice clearly across the flat expanse of water, a young voice say: "There she is! I see her! Ain't she pretty?"

"Goodbye!" Carrie called, and she waved at them. "Goodbye!"

At that moment, the children who were standing at the fence unrolled a large, hand-painted sign and held it up for Carrie to see.

Goodbye, Carrie, and Godspeed, the sign read.

Suddenly Carrie realized that she was probably seeing her young friends for the last time, and tears sprang to her eyes. Now the handkerchief, which was being used to attract the children's attention, was put to another use, and she dabbed at her eyes and fought back the lump in her throat that threatened to break out in open sobs.

Carrie had been so excited by the prospect of the adventure before her that she had not had time to be sad until this very moment. This was, after all, the only home she had ever known, and the Talbots were her only connection with her childhood.

The Talbots were not overly demonstrative, and they never had been. Mrs. Talbot explained the reason once.

"It doesn't pay to get too close to any of the children," Mrs. Talbot had told Carrie, when Carrie, as a little girl, had cried over the fact that one of her friends was leaving the home for good.

"Mr. Talbot and I just work for the church, and we don't have any say-so in what children are adopted and what children are left behind. If you get too close to the children, then every time one of them leaves, your heart will break. That's why we must be as we are. We have to be happy that Mary is getting a family, and you should be too."

The idea made sense to Carrie, and she kept it in mind for her entire life, that someday she might leave. Though she was an adult before she finally did leave, she saw now, more than ever, the validity of Mrs. Talbot's reasoning. Even so, it was a moment that tugged on her heartstrings.

By the time the boat was ready to make the swing into the mouth of the Missouri, most of the city had fallen behind, and now she was looking out over trees and farmland. Because there was nothing left to see, and because she suddenly realized that she was more than a little tired from all the excitement, she decided to go to her stateroom and take a rest.

Mr. Colby had made a point to secure an outside stateroom for her. Carrie had not understood the difference then, but now she realized why, because her stateroom had a window, which allowed a comforting breeze to pass in from the river. It also afforded her a private viewing of the scenery, and it would make the trip infinitely more pleasant than if she were in one of the inside rooms with no window at all.

The stateroom wasn't very large, but it certainly seemed adequate. There was a bed on one side of the room, a small vanity and wash-basin beside the bed, and a closet on the other side of the room. The room and all the furnishings were painted white, though the coverlet on the bed was red.

Carrie lay down on the bed, and now she could feel the pulsating thump of the engine beneath her, and hear the sounds of the river around her. The sounds and the motion were soothing, and she soon fell asleep.

"Miss Holliday? Miss Holliday? It's the last serving in the dining room," a man's voice called from outside her door.

Carrie opened her eyes, and for just an instant she wondered where she was. The room was dark and unfamiliar.

"Miss Holliday?" the voice called again. "Carrie?"

It was Rand Colby's voice, Carrie noticed with relief. Everything came back to her at once then, and she realized where she was and what she was doing. She knew also, that she had been slightly worried about Rand Colby, but now that she heard his voice, she knew he was on the boat with her and that worry dissipated quickly.

Carrie hopped out of bed and stepped quickly to the door. She opened it, and the golden glow of the hallway lanterns illuminated Rand Colby standing there smiling at her.

"Oh, where have you been?" she asked. "I was so worried!"

"I had some business in St. Louis," Rand said. He smiled broadly. "I must confess, your concern for my well-being touches me."

"I wasn't concerned for you, I was—" Carrie had started her retort, because she felt he would get the idea that she was interested in him. Then she realized that if she went on, it might seem that she was frightened at the prospect of making the trip alone. The dilemma thus imposed made her interrupt the statement in mid-sentence. "Anyway, you are here, now," she said.

"Yes," Rand said. "I hired someone to take me up river, then I found a man with a skiff who brought me out to meet the boat. I was about to take my dinner when the purser informed me that you haven't eaten either. Do you intend to?"

"Oh, yes, I am starving to death," Carrie said. She looked down at her new, yellow dress, and brushed at the wrinkles, which had come from sleeping in it. "Oh, the wrinkles."

Rand laughed. "There will be many, many wrinkles before we complete our journey," he said. "It will do you no good to start worrying about them now."

"I suppose not," Carrie said. "What are we having for dinner?"

Rand looked at her in surprise. "We are having whatever you want," he said. "Have you . . . have you never eaten in a restaurant before?"

"No," Carrie said, blushing at the confession. "I've never eaten anywhere, except at the home."

Rand laughed again. "What an innocent you are," he said.

"I'm glad you find my lack of experience amusing," Carrie said rather sharply. "I shall make an effort not to embarrass you."

"I'm sorry," Rand said easily. "I meant nothing by it, please don't take offense. I'm sure there is nothing you could do that would embarrass me . . . though I'm not as sure the reverse is true. At any rate, you shall dine in the boat dining room tonight, and it is just like a restaurant. Besides, which, you own one."

"I own a restaurant?" Carrie asked. "I thought my uncle left me a hotel."

"The Holliday House, in Laramie, yes," Rand said. "It also contains a restaurant, as well as a saloon."

"A ... a saloon? You mean a place where spirits are served?" Carrie asked in a shocked tone of voice.

"Yes," Rand said.

"A saloon," Carrie said. "You made no mention of a saloon, sir."

"I didn't think it was necessary," Rand said.

"The first thing I shall do is close the saloon," Carrie said.

"That wouldn't be a good idea," Rand replied. "The saloon makes more money than anything else."

"But surely, sir, you would not expect a woman to run a saloon?" Carrie said. "Why, such a thing would be absolutely scandalous!"

"I suggest you defer making any decision on that until you are in Laramie," Rand said. "Besides, you wouldn't have to run it yourself." Rand wondered when, or even if, he should tell her about the prostitutes who worked in the Holliday House.

"The decision is already made," Carrie said. "I will close the saloon."

They walked across the promenade deck of the boat, and Carrie saw a splash of red light from the mantled lantern. The river was black now, though it winked in reflected gold and red close to the boat, then, moon reflected silver in the distance. There were no lights ashore, though Carrie could clearly see the timbered hills beneath the moon and stars. Ahead of their path, a bright bar of gold light spilled onto the deck through a double doorway.

"The dining salon," Rand said. "Not to be confused with saloon," he added sarcastically.

"I am familiar with the word, sir, even though I may be an 'innocent,' as you put it."

"Ah, Mr. Colby, I see you found Miss Holliday," a well-dressed man said, greeting them as they stepped into the dining salon. "And will she be joining you?"

"Yes," Rand said.

"Good, good, I have prepared a very special table for you. If you'll come this way, please?"

Carrie glanced around the dining room. She had never seen anything as beautiful as this. Half a dozen chandeliers hung from overhead, glowing in soft golden light, with the hundreds of glass facets exploding in spectrums of rainbow color. The tables were covered with beautifully worked damask cloths, and they were all laid with a bone China service, which seemed to glow with some soft, inner light.

Rand held Carrie's chair out for her, then sat across from her. The wine steward approached, carrying a bottle of wine.

"I believe this is the wine you specified, sir," the wine steward said, showing Rand the bottle. Rand looked at the label.

"Yes," he said. He looked at Carrie. "You do like wine?" he asked.

"Wine? Uh, yes, of course," Carrie said, thinking how awkward her answer must have sounded.

"Have you had wine before?"

"Certainly," Carrie answered. Then as the wine steward poured a small amount of wine into a glass goblet and handed it to Rand, Carrie added, softly, "In Communion."

Rand chuckled. "My, my," he said. "In Communion? I do seem to be the devil's agent, don't I?"

Rand held the wine glass up and looked through its deep red body, toward the light. Carrie looked at the wine, and thought she had never seen a more beautiful color. Rand swirled it under his nose and sniffed its bouquet, then tasted it. Finally he nodded at the wine steward that the wine could be served.

"Very good, sir," the wine steward said. He poured Carrie's glass, then Rand's, and leaving the bottle in a silver bucket of ice, he withdrew quickly.

Carrie tasted the wine, and she could feel the controlled fire of its fruit on her tongue. It was delicious and heady, and it seemed that it made her head spin almost immediately, though she couldn't be certain if it was the wine or the atmosphere.

"Here is the menu," Rand said, handing a large ornately printed and beautifully decorated card to her. "It is broken down into soups, entrees, vegetables, cheeses, and desserts. Select anything you wish."

Carrie looked at the menu. Among the entrees, were such things as Halibut au Gratin, Saddle of Venison with Jelly Sauce, Partridge with Bread Sauce, and Leg of Mutton. She looked at it in dismay. She really had no idea how to make the selections.

"It is customary for the man to order," Rand suggested. "So if you don't mind I will order for both of us."

"Yes," Carrie said with relief. "I think that would be nice."

"Did you see anything in particular that you liked?"

"I'm sure I will be pleased with anything you select," Carrie said, grateful she didn't have to fumble making a wrong decision.

Rand ordered terrapin soup, duck with apple sauce, boiled potatoes and asparagus. From the soup through the Neapolitan ice cream they had for desert, Carrie experienced one new sensation after another. She had eaten both potatoes and ice-cream, though she had never seen three different flavors of ice-cream prepared as one. She had never eaten terrapin soup before, nor had she ever tasted roast duck. With it all, she drank the wine, never demurring, as Rand continued to keep her glass full. It was the most exciting evening Carrie had ever known, or imagined.

Rand pulled a long, thin cheroot from his inside pocket and lit it at the golden bubble of flame from one of the table candles.

"Would you like to take a turn about the deck?" Rand asked, leaning back in his chair as a wreath of blue aromatic smoke encircled his head. "Or, as it has been a full day for you, I suppose you would prefer to go right to bed."

"No, I'm not tired at all," Carrie said with a quick excitement. "I'd love to walk around the deck."

"Good," Rand said. He pulled a watch out and looked at it. "Ah, it is very nearly eleven o'clock. I should imagine we will have the deck to ourselves at this hour. That's good, it's much more pleasant when you aren't being jostled about so."

Carrie followed Rand out onto the deck. It was, as Rand had promised, totally deserted. Even the deck-hands seemed to be gone. Rand took another puff of his cheroot, and a spark from the glowing tip was whipped away by the breeze. They walked up to the bow of the boat, where several bales of empty cloth sacks were stacked, being shipped to the farmlands, where they would be filled with grain.

"Here," Rand said, patting his hand on one of the bales. "This will make us a soft place to sit."

Carrie sat beside him, looking out ahead into the night, at the river as it unfolded before them.

"I've often wanted to travel on a riverboat," she said. "And at last I am doing it." She hugged herself, partly from the chill breeze brushing her cheeks. "It's a dream come true!"

"These boats—and the trains—make the trip west much easier now," he said. "But it wasn't always this nice. When I was quite young, my family left Boston. We came as far as St. Louis by train, but from there we went by wagon train. For those of us who survived, it was a three-month journey."

"Were you attacked by Indians?"

"No," Rand said. "We suffered from sickness, bad weather, no water, sometimes no food, but we never had Indian trouble. In fact, the few times we did encounter Indians, we were able to trade something we would have had to abandon soon anyway, for a little food."

"Oh," Carrie said, still enjoying the heady effect of the wine. "Look at the stars. There are so many, and they're so bright, I feel as if I could reach out and grab one."

"Look," Rand said, pointing to a flash of light streaking through the sky. "One of them is falling."

"It isn't really a star falling, you know," Carrie said, in all seriousness. "I learned about that in school. They're called meteors. They're little pieces of rock falling into the earth's atmosphere from outer space."

"Rock? Why do they glow?"

"It's the friction," Carrie said. "They move through the air so fast that the friction heats them up and they glow like the iron in a blacksmith's forge."

"Well, what do you know about that?" Rand

exclaimed, and Carrie was secretly pleased that she had managed to tell Rand something for a change.

"Did you enjoy your first visit to a restaurant?" Rand asked.

"Yes," she said. "I enjoyed it very much. This has been a day of firsts for me. Almost everything I did today, I did for the first time."

6

"Bow watch, standing by to sound, Cap'n," a voice suddenly called, cutting through the velvet blanket of darkness.

At the sudden and unexpectedly close shout, Carrie was brought back to reality.

"Evenin', sir, ma'am," the deck officer said. Carrie noticed that it was the same person she had spoken to when she was afraid Rand was going to miss the boat. He was carrying a line, with a weight on the end, and he stepped up to the railing at the very bow.

"Good evening," Rand said.

"I see your gentleman friend made it aboard the boat after all," the deck officer said to Carrie. He smiled. "I told you there was no call to worry."

"On the bow!" a shout came from the bridge. The shout was augmented by a megaphone, and it sounded very close.

"By the bow!" the answer came.

"Sound the bow!"

The deck officer dropped the weighted line over

board, then he turned and shouted, "By the mark . . . ten!"

"I thought this part of the river was clear," Rand said. "Why are you sounding?"

"There was a big storm here last week," the deck hand replied. "The sandbars shifted. By the mark . . . seven!" he shouted, having sounded a second time.

"What's he doing?" Carrie asked.

"He's measuring the bottom," Rand said. "This boat will draw well with five feet of water. Any less and it gets dangerous."

"By the mark . . . five!"

Rand stood up and stepped up to the rail to watch the sounding more closely. Carrie, hearing the number five called, also moved to the rail.

"By the mark . . . four and a half!"

"Rand!" Carrie said in a frightened voice. "It's under five!"

From the stern of the boat, the slapping, splashing sound of the paddle wheel suddenly stopped but the boat still drifted forward, its momentum enough to carry it against the current.

"By the mark . . . four and a half!"

"Let's hope it gets no less," Rand said quietly.

"By the mark . . . twain!" the deck officer called happily. "Mark twain, Cap'n, we're clear of the bar!"

The paddlewheel started splashing again soon after that, and the boat resumed its normal speed. The deck-hand drew in his line and weight, touched the bill of his cap, then bid them both goodnight.

"I'd better go to bed," Carrie said, as soon as the deck-hand was gone.

"I thought you said you weren't tired," Rand said.

"I ... I guess I'm more tired than I thought," Carrie

replied. In truth she wasn't tired at all, and she doubted whether she would sleep a wink this night.

Rand smiled, again showing his even white teeth. "I'll walk you to your room."

"Where is your room?" Carrie asked.

"Right here," Rand said easily, pointing to the bales of empty cloth sacks.

"Here?" Carrie said, looking around. "Where? I don't see anything."

"When I booked passage, I'm afraid there was only one stateroom left," Rand said. "I got that for you. I took deck passage."

"Oh, but surely you won't have to be out here all the time?" Carrie asked, concerned now at the conditions under which Rand would have to travel.

Rand chuckled. "Believe me, I've traveled under much more difficult conditions. I'll be fine."

Rand escorted Carrie back to her room. "Have a pleasant night," he said. "I'll see you tomorrow."

HAVING RETURNED TO HER STATEROOM, Carrie lit the lantern, then saw her reflection in the mirror. In the soft golden light, she could see that some of the wrinkles had fallen out of her dress. Determined not to let the dress become any more mussed, she closed the shutters over her small window, then took the dress off and lay it out carefully.

RAND PUSHED the swinging doors open and stepped into the gaming salon. The salon was brightly lit and there were half a dozen card games in progress. The bar was open, and a piano player was playing a snappy rendition of "Buffalo Gals." Glasses clinked cheerfully and poker chips slid into bright red, white, and blue piles in the center of the tables, as the games went on.

Rand walked over to the bar and ordered a whiskey. After paying for the drink, he turned to look out over the room. He sipped his drink slowly as he studied the tables. It would have been much faster to make the entire trip by train, but upon learning that there was a chance that Perry Hoyt would be on this boat, he decided that this would be the way they would travel.

The bartender was wiping the bar with a damp cloth, and he leaned over to speak with Rand.

"If you're looking for a game, sir, I heard that gentleman over there say this would be his last hand. There'll be an empty seat then."

Rand saw Hoyt at that precise moment. A discerning observer would have noticed a slight narrowing of Rand's eyes, and a hardening of his jawline.

"Thank you," Rand said calmly. "But I would prefer to wait for an opening at that table."

"Sir, it's none of my business," the bartender said, "but I wouldn't recommend playing cards with that gentleman in the black coat."

"Oh? And why not?" Rand asked.

"He's a hard case, that one," the bartender said. "The captain was very upset when he learned this man was taking passage with us again. He's a card sharp, with a most amazing run of . . . luck, shall we say? And twice on the river, when his luck has been questioned, he's called the unfortunate fellow out and killed him."

"He's killed two people?" Rand asked.

"Two that we know of, sir," the bartender replied. "There may have been more."

"Why isn't he in jail?"

"In both cases it was adjudged to be a fair fight, though one could scarcely call any fight between an ordinary citizen and a professional killer fair."

"What's his name?" Rand asked.

"He says his name is Smith, but nobody knows for sure," the bartender replied. "He's a professional gambler, and they say he's goin' up 'n down river, first on one boat, then another'n. I just wish there was some way we could prevent him from ever ridin' on our boat."

"Bartender, a whiskey, please," a passenger asked from the far end of the bar, and the bartender excused himself and hurried to answer the request.

The gambler the bartender had pointed out was completely bald, but with puffs of scar-tissue on top of his head. There was a long three-corner, purple lightning flash of a scar on his right cheek. Rand had no doubt who this man was, and he wasn't named Smith.

So, Rand thought. At long last we meet, Perry Hoyt.

"I don't know how you do it, Mister, but you're too good for me," one of the players at the table said, pushing his chair back and standing. "I'd better quit now, while I've still got enough money to do business when I get to Omaha."

Rand finished his drink and set the empty glass on the bar, then walked over to the table. "Empty chair?" he asked.

Other than Hoyt, the players around the table looked up at Rand with curious, but superficial glances. Hoyt scrutinized the handsome young stranger, and as he studied Rand, Rand studied him.

Hoyt's eyes were pale blue, almost as indistinct as the eyes of an albino. Some might describe his eyes as ice, others might say he had dead man's eyes.

"We're playing for heavy stakes," Hoyt said. "This ain't no game for folks that don't have no guts."

"That's the way I like it," Rand said. He took out a sizable sum of money and bought chips from one of the game attendants.

"Five card stud," Hoyt said, as he started to shuffle the cards before him.

"Perhaps as the table has a new player, you wouldn't object to a new deck?" Rand suggested.

"There's nothin' wrong with these cards," Hoyt replied with an irritated growl.

"Let's let these gentlemen decide, shall we?" Rand suggested.

"That deck is cold, I'd like to see a new deck," one of the players suggested, then the others agreed.

"All right," Hoyt said, sweeping the cards to one side. "I can take your money with one deck as easy as with another."

The game attendant who sold Rand the chips, produced a new deck of cards, and Hoyt began shuffling them for the deal. Rand watched him carefully. He had heard that Hoyt was very adept at marking the cards, while he was shuffling, and his source of information was correct. Hoyt marked an ace, though he did it so easily and skillfully, that Rand couldn't be sure he saw it. That same ace turned up in Hoyt's winning hand.

Hoyt won the second hand as well, but he dropped out of the third and let the pot go somewhere else.

Rand was down almost a hundred dollars before he was satisfied that he understood Hoyt's system. Now he was ready to make his move. It was evident that Hoyt was about to make his move as well, because Rand drew one king down, and two kings up. Hoyt had one ace up, and as Rand could now read the marks, he knew that

Hoyt also had one ace down. Everyone but Hoyt had folded to Rand's kings.

"A trey for you and no help," Hoyt said, flipping the cardboard out. "A seven for me, and no help."

"Fifty dollars," Rand said, sliding the chips forward.

Hoyt smiled, though with the twisted scar on his face, the smile was almost imperceptible. He slid his money into the pot, then raised it fifty.

"I might draw me another ace," he said. "I'm sure not goin' to be spooked off by a couple of lousy kings."

"Then maybe this will frighten you off," Rand said. He raised Hoyt's bet by five hundred dollars. Those around the table gasped in surprise, and the word spread quickly so that soon, everyone had left their own games to come and watch this one.

"Are you sure you want to do that?" Hoyt asked.

"Yeah, I'm sure," Rand said.

"I don't know if I have that much," Hoyt hedged, looking at the chips in front of him.

"Sure you have that much, Hoyt," Rand said easily. "Why, your share alone had to come to around fifteen thousand dollars, didn't it? Unless you let the others cheat you out of it."

"What?" Hoyt asked, looking up from his cards quickly and narrowing his eyes as he stared across the table. "What'd you call me? My share? My share of what? What are you talkin' about?"

"Come now, Hoyt, I'm sure you know what I'm talking about," Rand said.

The purple scar on Hoyt's cheek deepened, and he began to rub his finger across it lightly. He leaned toward the table.

"Mister," he said in a low, hissing voice. "You ain't makin' no sense here. I thought we was playin' poker, 'n you up 'n start callin' me Perry Hoyt, 'n talkin' about a haul from a bank robbery."

"I didn't use your first name, and I didn't say anything about a bank robbery," Rand said.

"Yes, you did, you said—"

"I just mentioned your share," Rand said. "That could mean a share of anything." Rand looked at the others around the table, who were following the conversation with interest and a little, visible, anxiety. "Did any of you gents hear me say anything about a bank robbery?" he asked.

"No, sir, Mister, I didn't hear you say nothin' like that," one of the men said.

"Me neither," another nodded.

"Where'd you get the idea he was talkin' about a bank robbery, Hoyt?" one of the men in the crowd around the table asked.

"Well, I ... I thought you said somethin' about a bank robbery," Hoyt said, now visibly nervous.

"Now that you bring it up, there was a bank robbery about eighteen months ago, in the town of Rushville, Nebraska. It was the Cattleman's Bank and Trust. Maybe you are thinking of that bank," Rand suggested.

"Yeah," Hoyt replied. He rubbed his scar again. "Yeah, maybe that's it. I just heard about it, 'n when you started talkin' like that, I guess I thought you was accusin' me."

"I can see how you might have made that mistake," Rand said. "There were four men involved, and the take was sixty thousand dollars. That means one man's share would be about fifteen thousand dollars."

"So that's where you come up with that figure, huh?"

"Yes," Rand said. "They had a pretty good description of one of the men, too. He was said to be a real ugly cuss. A bald-headed man with scars on top of his head, and a purple scar on his cheek. That fits the description of Perry Hoyt." Rand paused for a moment before he added, "and you."

Hoyt was rubbing his scar as Rand was speaking, and he dropped his finger as quickly as if he had touched a hot stove. He looked at Rand through his narrow eyes, and the ice in his eyes seemed to grow much colder.

The other players at the table sensing an imminent confrontation between Rand and Hoyt, stood up quickly and moved back to give the two men room. Even those players who had gathered around the table, saw the necessity to step away. The circle around the table grew wider, and now only two men remained: Rand, sitting calmly on one side and Hoyt, growing more agitated, on the other side.

"Mister, who are you?" Hoyt asked. Again, his voice came out in a quiet, angry hiss, like the warning of a rattlesnake.

"Who I am isn't important," Rand said. "The important thing is, I know who you are. I also know about Ely Slack, and Nate Campbell, and I'll catch up with them just as I have with you. And, I figure that either you or Slack or Campbell will tell me the name of the fourth man."

"You'll eat breakfast in hell!" Hoyt suddenly shouted, jumping up from the table so quickly that his chair turned over. Almost as soon as he was up, there was a gun in his hand.

Rand flipped the table at that exact instant. The table hit Hoyt's gun hand, and that forced the gun barrel up, just as Hoyt fired. As a result, the bullet from Hoyt's gun went into his own neck. Dropping the gun, he grabbed at the wound with a choking, gasping sound, then fell.

Rand knelt quickly beside him.

"Who was the fourth man?" Rand asked.

"I'll . . . wait ... for ... you ... in hell," Hoyt said, dragging the last word out in a death rattle.

Rand looked at him for a moment, then sighed and stood up. He looked around the room at the others, who were just now beginning to come back to the center of the circle. One of them gingerly touched Hoyt's body with his foot.

"Is he dead?" another asked anxiously.

"Either that, or he's sleepin' powerful deep," the one who was standing over the body said, giggling at his own remarks.

With the announcement that Hoyt was dead, the others seemed to breathe a collective sigh of relief. They moved in to stare down at the lifeless form, as ugly in death as he had been in life.

"Mister, if you're a bounty hunter, then I'll certainly swear you was the one that got 'im," one of the onlookers said.

"I'm not a bounty hunter," Rand said.

"Maybe not, but there is paper out on this fella, isn't there? If not, there sure should be."

"I doubt if anyone who ever met him will weep any tears over this," another said.

"Here! What is this? What's going on here?" the Captain asked, coming into the gaming salon at that moment.

"It's the gambler, Smith, Cap'n," the bartender said.

"Him again," the captain said. "Who did he kill this time?"

The bartender smiled. "No, sir, you got it all wrong," he said. "He didn't kill anyone. This time, he was the one who got kilt."

"What's that? Smith got killed, you say?" The captain

smiled, broadly. "Well, now, that is good news. I'd like to meet the fella that did it. He must be pure greased lightning with a gun."

"I didn't use a gun," Rand said quietly. He opened his jacket. "As you can see, I'm not even carrying a gun. And his name isn't Smith, it's Hoyt, Perry Hoyt. He's wanted for bank robbery and murder."

"You should'a seen it, Cap'n," one of the other players around the table said. "Hoyt pulled a gun and this fella just flipped the table up, cool as you please. Well, sir, that table drove Hoyt's gun up just as he fired, 'n he blowed his own head off."

"Mister, I don't know who you are," the captain said. The stern expression on his face changed to a smile. "But I owe you a vote of thanks. The fact is, the entire river owes you a vote of thanks. This man, Smith, or Hoyt, as it turns out, was as undesirable a fella as a body might ever want to run into—on the river or off. I, for one, am glad to see that he won't be on the river anymore.

"Where's your stateroom?" the captain asked. "I'm going to send you a bottle, compliments of the boat."

"I don't have a stateroom," Rand said. "You were all booked up by the time I secured passage. I'm staying on the deck."

The captain looked down at Hoyt's lifeless body. "Not any more you aren't," he said. "As I recall, this river rat always had the best stateroom available. He managed to travel first class, at everyone else's expense. I'd hate to see that go to waste. Move into his room."

"Thanks," Rand said.

"Tell me," one of the men asked. "How is it that you knew his name? And how come you knew about him bein' a bank robber?"

"I was a witness," Rand said. "I saw them leaving the bank, and I saw their second murder."

"Their second murder? You mean they kilt someone after they left the bank?"

"Yes," Rand said. "They shot Hugh Atchison, a teller at the bank, and a girl who was across the street from the bank, after they left. She was in a dress shop, trying on a dress. The robbers fired several shots to discourage anyone from chasing them, and one of those shots hit the girl."

"An innocent girl," one of the others said, shaking his head slowly. He looked down at Hoyt. "Killin' men like this is too good for 'em."

Rand pointed to the pile of red, white, and blue chips that had fallen to the floor from the overturned table.

"Since Mr. Hoyt folded, I guess the pot's mine," he said. He pointed to the cards, spread out beside the chips. One of the cards was face down, and he pointed to it. "He didn't even get a chance to deal himself that ace of spades. It would have gone with the ace of clubs he had showing, and the ace of hearts he had face down. That would have beaten my three kings."

One of the men turned over the cards then gasped. "It is the ace of spades and ace of hearts. But how did you know that?"

"He had the aces and kings marked," Rand said. "He was marking them with his fingernail." Rand scooped up the chips that had been in the pot. "You fellas figure out what you lost to him, and make it up out of his holdings. He's been cheating all of you, all along."

Two, well-muscled, smoke-blackened men came into the room then—obviously firemen from the engine room.

"Get him out of here," the captain said, pointing to

Hoyt's body. "We'll be passin' through Jefferson City in about an hour. We'll turn his body over to the sheriff there, along with my deposition as to what happened."

"Yes, sir," one of the firemen said.

The captain smiled at Rand. "You'll be the hero of the boat by tomorrow."

"Captain," Rand said. "I'm escorting a young lady to Laramie. I'd just as soon there be no fuss made about this, if you don't mind. I don't know how she would react to it."

"I'll do what I can," the captain said. "But when an event this significant occurs, people are bound to want to talk about it."

7

IT WAS IMPOSSIBLE TO KEEP THE STORY QUIET, AND BY THE next day it was on everyone's lips. But, as there was no official version, half a dozen, and then a dozen variations developed, including one in which there had been a full-scale shoot-out, resulting in one man being killed and three being wounded.

The captain answered all such rumors by saying only that there was a "minor disturbance," which was settled happily. Because of that, Carrie didn't know what really happened, though she had heard Rand's name mentioned several times. When she asked Rand about it, he said only that it was nothing to worry about, and refused to elaborate. Carrie did notice, however, that the captain seemed to be on exceptionally good terms with Rand, so whatever it was, she figured that Rand was not guilty of any wrongdoing, and her confidence in him was not shaken.

The rest of the river stage of the trip passed without incident. Rand spent quite a bit of time in Carrie's company and he seemed genuinely solicitous for her well-being.

There was a permeating sense of excitement throughout the boat on the morning of the fifth day. They would be arriving in Omaha by ten o'clock that morning, and everyone was busy preparing for that. The deck-crew hustled around cleaning up loose ends on board the boat, while the passengers, who had met and become friends during the cruise, crowded in as much last-minute visiting as they could, before each turned to his or her own business of checking luggage and doing everything necessary before disembarking.

Carrie was ready. She had enjoyed the boat trip very much, but that was the first part of her journey, and now she was ready to go on. Thus it was that when she was standing on the deck, watching as the boat turned in toward the Omaha docks, she felt her excitement at a fever pitch. She was eagerly looking forward to her next portion of her adventure.

The boat docked with the heavy bleating of whistles, the shouting of orders, and the clanging of bells, then the boat was made secure. The docks were quite busy, and though they weren't as crowded as the St. Louis Riverfront docks, that didn't detract from the excitement of those who were there.

"Lower the gangplank," the captain shouted through his megaphone, and Carrie watched the gangplank being lowered with ropes and winches, then she and Rand were caught up with the press of the crowd as they left the boat.

They stepped from the gangplank to the cobble-stoned levee, then walked up the levee to the road. There were more than a dozen fine carriages, taxis, and wagons waiting there.

"Buckboard to the railroad station," a man was shouting, as he stood beside a one-horse shay. "Buckboard to the railroad station, right here."

"You," Rand called to him. "Get the lady's luggage and take us to the station."

"Yes, sir!" the buckboard driver answered with a broad smile, happy to have the business. "Which piece is it?"

"It's a brown trunk, with orange and green ribbon on the handle," Carrie said. "You can't miss it."

"Orange and green ribbon?" the buckboard driver said. "That's a good idea, lady. You must do lots of travelin'."

"No, not really," Carrie said, with a blushing smile. She was too embarrassed to tell him that this was the first trip she had ever taken. She had read a travelers' tip in the St. Louis Dispatch which recommended that a distinctive ribbon be put on one's luggage when traveling by train, so it could easily be picked out from all the other luggage. Now she realized the validity of that advice.

"Oh, Mr. Colby," the captain said, coming up to them at that moment. "We just received a wire from the Attorney General in Jefferson City. He has ruled Hoyt's death as accidentally self-inflicted, while in the act of attempting a homicide. I thought you might like to know."

"Yes, thank you," Rand said.

The captain noticed the expression on Carrie's face then, and he touched the bill of his cap in a half-salute. "Sorry," he said. "I guess I wasn't thinking."

"It's all right," Rand said. The captain excused himself and returned to his boat. Rand and Carrie stood beside the buck-board, waiting for the driver to return with

Carrie's luggage. Rand's own valise had already been put on the back of the buckboard.

"Rand, what was he talking about?" Carrie asked.

Rand leaned against the buckboard and smiled at Carrie.

"Oh, it's nothing you need to worry about," he told her.

"He was talking about the incident on the boat, wasn't he? There was someone killed, and somehow, you were involved."

Rand sighed. "A man with a rather nasty disposition tried to shoot me," he finally said. "I knocked his gun aside, and he wound up shooting himself instead. I didn't want to tell you about it. I didn't want you to get upset."

"Rand, I'm not a little girl anymore," Carrie said. "I'm a woman, full grown. You don't have to shelter me from life. I know that things like that sometimes happen. I'm just glad you weren't hurt, and I'm glad that the authorities have already ruled on it so such a thing doesn't have to haunt you for the rest of your living days."

Rand smiled. "Well, maybe I've underestimated you," he said, thinking she was wiser than her years.

"Maybe you have," Carrie agreed.

"Here's your trunk, Miss," the buckboard driver said, returning with the trunk on his shoulder. He set it down on the back of the buckboard, and heaved a sigh, as the buckboard dipped under the trunk's weight. "You sure packed it well," he said. "It weighs a ton."

"It is quite full," Carrie agreed. She looked at the trunk. What she didn't tell the buckboard driver, or Rand either, was that within the confines of that small trunk, was the sum total of her entire life. She had left St. Louis, with no intention of ever returning.

"The Pacific Flyer leaves at one," the driver said. "If

you'd like, you could come by the house and the missus will fix you a nice dinner. And you'd have time for a bath, besides."

"Oh, a bath?" Carrie said quickly. "A real tub bath?"

"With soap and a towel," the buckboard driver said. "It'd be only fifty cents extra . . . uh, that is for each of you," he added quickly. "And the dinner'd be fifty cents apiece."

"Oh, Rand, could we?" Carrie asked. "I'd love to have a bath before we get on the train."

"All right," Rand said, smiling at her enthusiasm. "If it means that much to you, I don't see any reason why not."

"Giddap," the driver said, flicking the reins happily against the back of the horse. "The house is right on the way," he said, "so there won't be no problem at all with makin' the train," the driver told them.

The meal consisted of steak and fried potatoes. It was cooked well enough, and there was plenty of it, but Carrie scarcely noticed it, because she could think of nothing but the bath. When she finished eating, she mentioned the bath to the driver's wife, and she smiled, then handed her a bar of soap and a towel.

"My husband said the two of you was awantin' baths," she said. "So while you was eatin' I had my youngun fillin' up the tub. Just go right on upstairs, first door on your right."

"Thank you," Carrie said, taking the soap happily.

She noticed that the soap was homemade, though the woman evidently took some pride in the craft, for the soap was pleasantly scented, and it had been formed in a mold, so that it looked like one of the fancy, commercial soaps she often saw advertised.

The water was warm, if not hot, and when Carrie settled down into the tub it was as delicious a feeling as wrapping her body in silk. She knew that she had a train to catch soon, and that Rand also intended to take a bath, so she didn't tarry as long in the bath as she would have liked. If she could have, she would have spent the rest of the afternoon there, just soaking in the water.

IF CARRIE HAD THOUGHT the riverfront was crowded, it was nothing compared to the Omaha railroad depot. There were scores of people inside and outside of the depot building. There were all sorts crushed together—farmers, rough-looking ranchers, merchants, tired women, unruly children, soldiers, Indians, and several others, including some who were of a somewhat unsavory appearance. There were also many strange people, dressed in unusual clothes and even costumes that were unfamiliar to her, and Carrie overheard many foreign languages. She also smelled many unusual smells.

The walls of the Omaha depot were festooned with antlers and stuffed animal heads, and from nearly every antler there hung a hat or a garment of some sort. A big sign over the lunch counter advertised "Lunch baskets filled: 25 cents," and another sign requested gentlemen to please use the spittoons.

Carrie found a place to stand near one wall, away from the press of the crowd, while Rand went to the ticket window to get tickets for them. He came back a few minutes later and assured her that everything was all right. "The Pacific Flyer!" someone called through a megaphone. "The Pacific Flyer! All passengers for the Pacific Flyer, move to the platform, please!"

"That's us," Rand said, and he put his hand on Carrie's arm to escort her through the pushing crowd.

Carrie heard the whistle of the approaching engine

then, and she moved forward, eagerly, to watch the train come into the station. She looked down the track and saw the engine growing larger and larger as the train came toward them. The huffing sound of the steam seemed like thunder now, and the train was wreathed in tendrils of steam and billowing clouds of boiling smoke.

As the train rushed by, Carrie could feel its power in her body. She saw the gigantic driver wheels, taller than she was, and the feathers of steam escaping from the pumping piston rods, as the train pounded into the station so fast she didn't think it would be able to stop. Glowing cinders spilled from the firebox, and there was a roar of steel on steel as the many wheels of the cars rolled by, so fast as to be almost a blur.

Finally, the cars began slowing and grinding to a halt, until at last, the great train was still. Even with the train at rest, the hissing of steam and the occasional blowing of the relief valves made it seem like something alive.

With the train at a halt, the doors of the cars started coming open, and the baggage cart was pushed up to the baggage car. With the commercial movement, the train seemed less alive and more the machine of transportation it was designed to be.

A man in a blue uniform stepped down from one of the cars. He pulled a big gold watch from his vest pocket, opened the cover, looked at it importantly, then snapped it shut and put the watch back in his pocket. He had an air of authority about him, and he looked at the people who were queuing up to get onto the train. "Board!" he called.

The waiting passengers started toward the train.

"Hurry up," he said. "Hurry up, ladies and gentlemen. Get on board quickly, please, we have a schedule to keep."

There were so many people, pushing and shoving, at that moment, rushing to get on the train, that Carrie felt a slight panic. What if she and Rand could not get on the train? Half the humanity in the world, it seemed, had been inside the depot, and now half of those people were trying to board this train. She put her hand anxiously on Rand's arm.

"Oh, come on, let's hurry," she said, pulling on him. "I fear we will have no place to sit."

Rand laughed, quietly. "Don't worry about it, little one," he said. "We shall be all right."

"But, there are so many people trying to get on the train, it seems," Carrie said.

"Those are the emigrant cars," Rand explained easily.

"Emigrant cars?" Carrie asked. She looked at the cars the passengers were boarding. "What are emigrant cars?"

"Those cars are the cheapest fare available for people who are going west," Rand said. "Do you see all these people?"

Near the middle of the boarding line of passengers, Carrie saw a simply dressed man, woman, and three children, with the youngest child in the woman's arms. In the man's face there was an expression of grim determination and hope, in the woman's face a quiet acceptance, and in the faces of the two children who were old enough, excitement over their upcoming adventure.

"They aren't just taking a trip to visit grandma," Rand said. "They are pulling up stakes and starting life all over again, somewhere out there in the great West."

"Like me," Carrie said.

Rand looked at her with quick surprise on his face, then he smiled.

"Yes," he said. "Like you." He pointed to the family that was just getting on the train, the same family Carrie had noticed. "It's quite an undertaking for people like that, but the West does offer them that chance. However, to have any chance at success, they must get there as cheaply as possible. Now the railroad, you see, has a vested interest in getting people to settle the West—and in their success. The more people who can make a living out west, the more business that will mean for the railroad, not only now, but in the future. Therefore, the railroad has come up with the emigrant car. It's not much more than a converted cattle car, really. It has wooden benches instead of seats, and it will hold as many people as they can crowd into it. When the benches are full, the passengers will start sitting on the floor."

"Oh, how terrible!" Carrie said. "Those poor people."

Rand chuckled. "It's not all that bad. Most of them will arrive at their destination in less than a week. Before the railroad, it took several months of arduous journey on the plains. These cattle car accommodations are pure luxury, compared with what people had to put up with in a covered wagon on the Overland Trail, just a few short years ago."

"Rand?" Carrie asked, as the last of the emigrants found room on the train.

"Yes?"

"Where will we ride?"

Rand chuckled again. "Come this way," he said.

Carrie could see the engine better now, as they moved toward the front of the train. It was green with gold filigree, and the fittings were of polished brass. The engineer was leaning on the window, looking back down the train at those who were boarding.

The conductor came toward Rand and Carrie.

"Parlor car?" he asked.

"Yes," Rand said.

The conductor smiled broadly, the look of stern authority replaced with an expression of servility. He tipped his hat. "Very good, sir. I hope you enjoy your trip. We'll do everything we can to make it pleasant for you."

"Thank you," Rand said.

The conductor hurried down to the car before them, then placed a step box on the ground to help them into the car. He held out his hand for Carrie, and Carrie climbed up the steps, then went through the door at the end of the car. She had not mentioned it to Rand, but this was the first time she had ever been in a train car in her life.

8

THE CAR WAS MORE BEAUTIFUL THAN ANY DRAWING ROOM
Carrie had ever seen. The walls were richly paneled, and
the floor was covered with a plush carpet, which had the
design of a beautiful rose garden in its weave. The seats
were large and overstuffed, and the lighting and fixtures
were embellished with cut crystal, so that, even now, in
the daytime, they sparkled and flashed in a prismatic
effect.

"Your bedrooms are just at the end of this car, sir.
Compartments one and two," the conductor said,
looking at their tickets.

"Thank you," Rand said.

"The dining car is one car ahead, and the first seating
will be at five."

"When is the last seating?"

"That will be at nine, sir."

"We'll take the last seating."

"Very good, sir."

Rand pointed to one of the seats, inviting Carrie to
sit down. The seat was more like a comfortable parlor

chair than anything else. It was next to a curtained window, and when Carrie sat in it, she thought she had never felt anything so comfortable.

Rand sat across from her. There was a highly polished, generous-sized brass spittoon on the floor between them. A small metal plate on the spittoon said, "Union Pacific . . . please do not empty contents through window."

Rand accidentally kicked the spittoon as he sat down, but fortunately, it was empty. He reached down for it.

"We won't be needing this," he said. "Unless you will?" he added with a smile.

"No, of course not!" Carrie replied in a shocked voice, before she realized that Rand was teasing. When she realized he was teasing, she laughed.

The train whistle blew, then there was the sound of vented steam. Carrie gripped the arms of the chair as she felt the train start. It jerked, then jerked again. Finally, the lurching smoothed out and the train was rolling easily. Carrie looked through the window excitedly as the train rolled through the streets of Omaha. The whistle blew several times, and as they passed across the main street, she saw a man standing in front of his horse, holding the animal to calm it as the roaring engine and cars passed by. In the surrey the horse was pulling, a woman sat stoically, and two children waved excitedly at the train. Carrie returned their waves, as she pressed her face to the window.

The long, dirt roads of Omaha were crowded with horses and wagons, and Carrie wondered if anyone in Omaha was watching the train leave with the same longing for a sense of adventure that she used to have as she watched the trains and boats departing St. Louis.

"Pull back on that small lever and you will discover

that the seat back will recline," Rand said pointing to a lever on the side of the seat.

Carrie did as Rand suggested, and, magically, the seat leaned back. She rested her head against the back and watched as first the city of Omaha, then the houses outside the city, and finally the countryside itself, began slipping by. She saw a field of oxeye daisies waving in the sun, and the train whipped by them so quickly that they were but one long, yellow, blur.

How fast they were going now. How marvelous to be a part of an age, which allowed such distances to be traversed so quickly!

"You hardly touched your dinner," Rand said later, as he sat across the table from Carrie who had only picked at her roast chicken. They were at the final seating in the dining car.

"I suppose I ate too heartily at lunch," Carrie said. She looked around the dining car. It, like the parlor car in which they were taking their passage, was the last word in luxury. And it, like the parlor car, was practically empty. In the meantime, Carrie knew that just a couple of cars back, there was teeming humanity.

"Rand, what about the emigrants?" Carrie asked.

"The emigrants?" Rand replied, spreading butter on a roll. "What about them?"

"Where do they eat? Better, what do they eat? They can't eat in here, can they?"

"Oh, yes, they can eat in here, if they have the money," Rand said. "But eating in here for one day would cost them almost as much as their entire fare."

"Then what do they do?"

Rand chuckled. "They eat very well, believe me," he said. "Often, they pool their lunches and have one big picnic, right there in the car. They meet each other and often become friends, and then the entire trip becomes a big party. Chances are there is more laughter in one day on their car, than there is in a whole week on a parlor car. Don't feel sorry for them, Carrie, they are having a wonderful time."

"You sound as if you've ridden in the emigrant cars."

"I have," Rand said easily.

"Then why are we riding like this, now?"

"Because I thought your trip out should be as comfortable as possible," Rand said. "And also, because I work for the railroad as a detective, I'm afforded certain privileges."

"I do appreciate your concern for my comfort," Carrie said, "but I want a taste of adventure as well. I wish you wouldn't try to shield me from everything."

Rand laughed. "You shall have your adventure," he said. "I promise you that." He stood up. "Shall we go back to the car? I think they're trying to close up in here."

"Yes," Carrie said. "It's been a delightful meal—even if I couldn't eat everything."

There was some sense of adventure just in the walk back to the parlor car. Carrie did not mention it to Rand, but the passage from car to car was actually frightening to her. In order to go from one car to another, one had to step across the couplers. Each car was equipped with an apron, which passed out over the coupling joints, but the aprons did not quite meet, and every time the car paused over a slight track depression or elevation, the result caused one of the aprons to jump up and the other to sag down. That would create a gap large enough to trap the foot of an unwary passenger.

The sun had just been dying in a brilliant burst of color as they had entered the dining car. But it was pitch black outside the windows now, and when Carrie

77

stepped out onto the platform, she hesitated for a moment.

Here, the sound of the train was much louder, and she could hear the clanging and banging of steel against steel as the cars bumped against each other. The wind whipped in through the open vestibule, carrying on its hot breath, the smell of smoke and steam.

Carrie looked at the coupling aprons with a degree of apprehension. She started to step across.

"Allow me," Rand said, and he put his hands under her arms and lifted her across as easily as if she were a feather. He simply set her down on the other side, then stepped across as if it were nothing.

"Thank you," Carrie said.

Rand walked her to her compartment, then opened the door for her.

"I'll see you in the morning," he said.

"Good night," Carrie replied.

"Good night," he said, and he turned to go into his own compartment, which was just next door.

Once inside the compartment, Carrie was even more puzzled. There was no bed! Where was she supposed to sleep? She stepped back out of the compartment and knocked on Rand's door.

"Mr. Colby?" She called. "Rand, are you in there?"

The door opened.

"Is something wrong?" Rand asked.

"I ... uh ... there's no bed in my compartment," Carrie said. "I don't know where I'm supposed to sleep."

Rand smiled at her. "The bed is folded up into the wall," he said.

"What?"

"I'll do it for you," he offered.

Rand followed Carrie back into her compartment,

then he pulled the bed down for her. He folded the covers back and she saw the sheets, crisp and white, and the pillow, fluffed and ready.

"I'm sorry," she said. "I should have had enough sense to do this for myself, but—"

"Nonsense," Rand interrupted. "If you've never seen it before, how could you be expected to know what to do?"

"Thank you."

"You're welcome. Good night."

"Good night," Carrie replied.

RAND WAS AWAKENED by a tap on the door and, looking outside he saw that it was still dark.

"Yes?" Rand called.

"Mr. Colby, you wanted to be notified when we were approaching Buford." It was the conductor's voice.

"Yes, thank you," Rand said.

RAND COLBY STOOD on the side of the track as the train left. He watched it until the red and green lantern lights of the rear car had merged into one, and until the puffing of the engine was but a distant whisper. Finally, the wind blowing through the sagebrush and whistling around the water tower was louder than the train. Rand looked down the tracks, picked up his valise, and started toward the livery. A horse snorted and stamped his hoof impatiently as Rand approached.

"Easy, boy," Rand said, as he came in through the gate. "It's just me. I told you I'd be coming back for you."

"Who's there?" a sleepy voice challenged from the shadows of one of the stalls.

"It's just me, Hank," Rand said. "I've come to get Diablo."

Hank stepped out of the stall. Pieces of straw were clinging to his clothes and hair, evidence of the fact that he had been sleeping in the hay.

"Oh, Rand, I was wonderin' when you'd get back," the man said. He yawned and stretched. "Didja come in on the train?"

"Yes."

"It must be after three then," he said. "I guess I'd better get the fire goin' under the forge. I got quite a bit of work to do today."

"Do I owe you anything for Diablo?" Rand asked. He took a saddle that had been slung over a sawhorse and carried it and a blanket over to his horse.

"Naw, in fact you got two more days comin' to you," Hank said. He scratched a sulfur match against his pant leg and lit a lantern. A bubble of golden light filled the inside of the stable. The light disclosed the fact that Rand, who had spent the last several days dressed in fine clothes, was now in denim trousers and a cotton shirt. He looked more comfortable now than he had at any time over the last several days. Rand opened a sack and pulled out a belt holster and pistol and strapped it around his lean waist, then tied the holster string around his thigh.

"I appreciate it," Rand said. "Keep the two days— maybe I'll need them sometime in the future." He tightened down the cinch, then patted the horse's nose gently, as he slipped the halter on.

"Want some breakfast?" Hank offered. "I got some salt meat and biscuits."

Rand started to decline, but decided that it would save time to have breakfast now. Also, he hadn't asked

Hank for information earlier, so he thought this would be a good time to do so.

"Yes, thank you, I'll be glad to pay you for it."

Hank chuckled. "Well, I ain't runnin' no café, but a quarter ought to cover my cost for the fixin's."

Rand poured himself a cup of coffee. "Hank, you ever heard of a man by the name of Ely Slack?"

"Slack? No, I can't say as I have."

"He might be calling himself Brown."

"Dan Brown?" Hank asked.

"I haven't heard his first name. He may be running with a couple more men."

Rand described Slack and the other men that he had seen in Nebraska.

"Oh, yes, I've seen 'em around. I have to tell you the truth, if they're friends of yours, you could do a better job of pickin' your friends."

Rand chuckled. "Oh, believe me, they are no friends of mine."

"What are you lookin' for them, for?"

"One of them murdered the woman I was going to marry."

"Oh, damn," Hank said. "I'm sorry."

"You say they come into town from time to time. Do you have any idea where they might be when they aren't in town?"

"Don't have no idea, I'm afraid," Hank said.

"I thank you," Rand said. He led the horse out of the stable, closed the gate behind him, then swung up into the saddle and headed north.

9

Carrie was awakened by an insistent knock on her door.

"Miss," the conductor's voice called. "Miss Holliday, we'll be arriving in Laramie in about thirty minutes."

"Thank you," Carrie replied sleepily. She lay there a few moments longer, enjoying the comfort of the bed, relaxed by the swaying motion of the train and the rhythmic clicking of the wheels. She felt as if she could easily drift back to sleep.

"Laramie!" she said aloud. They were almost there!

Carrie sat up quickly now, excited by the prospect of arriving so soon, and she lifted the shade at her window and looked out across the prairie. A short distance from the track, she saw a dozen or more buffalo running away from the train, frightened by the puffing engine's bulk and speed. Except for the buffalo, she saw nothing else, for the prairie seemed to stretch on in unbroken emptiness, until finally it reached a far-off mesa, which looked quiet and serene under the gray early morning light.

Carrie had been stunned by the vastness of the

country they had been passing through, ever since boarding the train. With no trees or farmlands to interrupt the vista, it seemed to stretch on forever. She had read accounts of the Great American West, but now she was seeing it for the first time.

Of course, Rand had seen this country many times, so Carrie was convinced that Rand had no idea how awe-inspiring it was through her eyes.

Carrie dressed quickly, then stepped out into the passageway. She caught the aroma of cheroot and smiled happily, because she was certain he was in the seating area, waiting for her.

"Oh, we are almost here," she said, stepping out of the passageway. A man looked up at her and smiled, then she saw that it wasn't Rand, but a Mr. Cogswell, who had shared the parlor car with them.

"Yes, we are," Cogswell said.

"Oh, excuse me," Carrie replied, flustered by the fact that she had mistaken Cogswell for Rand. "I thought you were Mr. Colby."

"No doubt you were fooled by the cheroot," Cogswell said, holding it up. "Mr. Colby and I had a few drinks last night, and he gave me this. It is quite aromatic, don't you think?"

"Yes," Carrie said.

Carrie moved back to the passageway and stopped outside Rand's compartment. She knocked on the door.

There was no answer, so she knocked again. It would be best not to start this day with any unpleasantness.

Carrie knocked a third time, then she called him. "Mr. Colby? Mr. Colby, hurry, we are almost in Laramie."

There was still no answer, so Carrie stood very quietly, to see if she could hear him. "Mr. Colby? Rand?"

she called again. "Are you in there? Hurry up, we are nearly there."

The conductor was passing through the car at that moment, and Carrie saw him and hailed him.

"Have you seen Mr. Colby?" she asked. "I've tried to get him up for our arrival in Laramie, but I can't get an answer."

The conductor looked surprised. "Oh, Miss Holliday, you mean he didn't tell you?"

"Tell me?" Carrie replied, puzzled by the strange remark. "Tell me what?"

"He isn't on the train, Miss," the conductor said.

"Mr. Colby isn't on the train? What do you mean? He's in here, isn't he?" Carrie asked, pointing to the compartment. "He has to be. We're going to Laramie, and he's—"

"I'm sorry, Miss Holliday," the conductor said, shaking his head slowly. "I thought you knew about it, ma'am. He got off the train."

"He got off the train?" Carrie asked in a small, disbelieving voice. She felt dizzy and put her hand on the side of the car to steady herself. She took a deep breath. "Why?" she finally managed to ask.

"I don't know, Miss," the conductor said. "All I know is, he got off at about three this morning. We made a water stop at a place called Buford. There's not much there, just a depot, a water tower, and a trading post. I'm sorry, Miss Holliday, I thought you already knew. I was that positive that he wouldn't get off the train without telling you."

"Oh, uh, yes," Carrie said weakly. "Yes, I remember now, he did tell me. I just forgot about it, that's all."

Rand had said nothing to her, but Carrie was much too embarrassed to admit that.

"Are you all right, Miss Holliday?" the conductor asked.

"Yes," Carrie said. She forced herself to smile, rather than let the conductor see how Rand Colby's unexpected absence had affected her. "Yes, I'm fine. I'm just excited, that's all."

"I agree," the conductor said. "Laramie is an excitin' place. But you'd better sit down now, because the engineer will be puttin' on his brakes soon, and it could be dangerous to be standin'."

"Thank you, I shall," Carrie said. She walked back into the seating area of the car. She didn't want to sit next to Mr. Cogswell, because she wanted to be alone right now. Finally she chose the bench seat at the very rear of the car because it was one that she had not used before.

Carrie heard the train whistle blowing, and as she looked out the window, she could see that they were approaching a town. Or, could this rag-tag collection of tents, wooden shacks, and combination canvas and wood structures actually be called a town?

The conductor passed by again, moving quickly, leaning in a way to brace himself against the braking action of the train.

"Conductor, what is this place?" Carrie asked, pointing out the window.

"Why, this is Laramie, Miss Holliday," the conductor replied, smiling at her. "This is where you are going."

This is Laramie? Carrie thought. But surely it can't be. Perhaps this is a small town on the outskirts of Laramie.

Then, even as Carrie was thinking there was some mistake, the station platform came into view, and then the depot itself. It was a low, unpainted, wooden building, with a crudely lettered sign on the end. The sign read, "Laramie, Wyoming."

Carrie wanted to cry. Never in her life had she seen anything more depressing than the sight that greeted her now. She sat there for a moment, looking out over the town. She hadn't expected it to be as bustling and alive as St. Louis, but she had thought it would at least be a town. This was no town. It wouldn't even make a good village. It was more like the temporary encampment of a band of wild Indians, she thought.

With a sigh, Carrie stood up and started to the end of the car to detrain.

But, no, she thought. That's not fair. Rand Colby didn't talk her into coming. She came because she wanted to, and because she wanted a taste of adventure. Well, if adventure is what she wanted, adventure was what she was going to get. She tried to put on as cheerful a face as she could. She would just have to make the best of the situation.

Carrie stepped down from the train and stood on the wooden platform, looking around. Behind her the over-heated wheel bearings and gearboxes popped and snapped as the train sat there with the metal cooling. On the platform all around her, there was a flurry of activity, as people were getting on and off the train.

It was still early morning, and though there was quite a bit of activity around the depot itself, Carrie could tell by looking through the gray dawn light that most of the town was still asleep. She heard a rooster crow and a dog bark. Somewhere, from one of the nearby houses, the cry of a baby escaped through a window open for the early morning breeze. She saw a man walking from the outhouse, back to his house, pulling his suspenders back over his shoulders as he moved quickly up the path.

The door to the baggage car was opened, and a couple of men started off-loading trunks and bags. Carrie walked up to the baggage car and, when she saw her trunk being taken down, pointed to it, asking if they would set it to one side for her.

"Yes, ma'am," the handler on the platform said. He put it to one side, then returned to help with the rest of the luggage.

The conductor looked at his watch importantly. "'Board!" he yelled and waved, as the door to the baggage car was closed.

The baggage handler began pulling the cart away from the car, waving at the conductor to let him know he was finished.

The conductor stepped up onto the step of the last car and signaled the engineer. The engineer answered him with a couple of blasts from the whistle, and the train began to pull out of the Laramie station.

Carrie sat on her trunk and watched the train as it left. The conductor waved at her as his car passed by, and Carrie returned the wave with a strange feeling of loneliness. As long as she had been on the train, she had felt a sense of belonging, not only because of Rand Colby, but because she was a passenger on the train. As such, her position was clearly defined. It was just as it had been when she was in the orphanage. Both as a child and as an administrator, she had a clearly defined position. But what was she now, she wondered? A lonely, frightened, woman in a strange, faraway town.

A boy of about thirteen approached Carrie. He was wearing bibbed overalls, a ragged shirt that might have been blue at one time but had long since faded to gray, and no shoes. He was blond and freckled, and he reminded Carrie of some of the boys back at the home. She smiled at him and he smiled back.

"Ma'am, I got me a mule 'n a wagon for hire, iffen you need it," he offered.

"I shall surely need it," Carrie said easily. "I must move this trunk."

Carrie had not really made any plans on what she would do, once she arrived. But, as Mr. Colby had seen fit to abandon her, she was going to have to act on her own. That meant the first thing she would have to do was get a place to stay. But where could she go? She didn't know anyone, nor did she know anything about this town. Wait a minute, she thought. Where did people go when they went to a strange town? They went to a hotel. And what better position to be in now, than to own a hotel? Carrie smiled. She wasn't actually that bad off, after all.

The boy had left as soon as Carrie told him she could use his services, and when he returned, he was driving a somewhat rickety wagon pulled by a slab-sided mule. He stopped in front of her.

"She don't look like much," he said. "But it's good enough for near 'bout any haulin' job that needs to be done around town. And someday, when I got me enough money, why, I'm gonna go into the freight business for sure. They's a future in wagon freight. The railroads don't go ever' where, you know."

"Oh, I'm sure there is a marvelous future in the freight business," Carrie said, smiling at the boy's ambition.

The boy had to struggle with the trunk, but when Carrie offered to help him, he waved her aside. "A man's gotta stand on his own," he said.

"You seem to be doing quite a good job of it," Carrie said. "What is your name?"

"My name's Morton Forsythe," the boy answered. He helped Carrie onto the wagon, then climbed up on the seat with her and took up the reins. "Only most folks call me Mort."

"Oh, but Morton is such a fine sounding, elegant name. Would you mind if I called you Morton?"

Morton smiled, and Carrie believed she could almost see him blush.

"I reckon I don't mind," he said. "It sounds kind'a nice when you say it. What's your name?"

"Carrie Holliday," Carrie said. "And you must call me Carrie, not Miss Holliday."

"All right, Miss . . . uh . . . Carrie," Morton said. "Where are you goin'?"

"I'm going to the Holliday House," Carrie said. "Do you know where it is?"

Morton looked at her quickly, and for just a second, Carrie thought she saw a shadow pass across his eyes. A shadow of what, she wondered. Surprise? Disappointment?

"Yes'm," Morton said. "I don't reckon there's anyone in town what don't know where the Holliday House is. I'll take you right there."

"Thanks," Carrie said, puzzled by the change in the tone of Morton's voice.

The wagon pulled away from the depot and began rolling down the main street of the town, which ran at a right angle to the track. Carrie looked over the town as she passed through. If this was to be her new home, she should learn as much as she could.

There was a feed and grain store, a livery stable, a

doctor's office, and a drugstore on the west side of the street. A saloon, a laundry, millinery, and a grocer were on the east side. A man was sweeping off the board walk in front of the saloon, and he looked up as the wagon rolled by.

"Got a new one for the Holliday House, have you, Mort?"

Morton ignored the man's shout, but Carrie was surprised by it and looked around at the man who had called out. A smile was on his face, but it wasn't a particularly friendly smile. It was an uneasy smile, and there was something deep and hidden in his eyes, which made the smile almost frightening. She had seen the same expression in the eyes of men who had sometimes stared at her on the streetcars in St. Louis. Such stares were mysterious and always discomforting. She turned away from him.

"Who was that man?" she asked Morton.

"That's Mr. Stone," Morton said. "He runs the saloon."

"How did he know I was going to the Holliday House?"

"I dunno," Morton said. "I reckon it's 'cause you're so pretty."

Carrie looked at Morton in confusion. "Because I am so pretty? Morton, I thank you for the compliment, but I really don't understand what being pretty has to do with that man knowing where I was going."

"You don't reckon a woman could do what you do without being pretty, do you?" Morton asked, as if explaining something basic to Carrie.

"What I do?"

"Yeah, you know," Morton said.

In fact, Carrie didn't know at all, but she felt that it would be best just to let the subject drop for the moment. She returned to her examination of the town.

When Morton reached the end of the street, he turned right and there, before her eyes, stood the biggest and most substantial building in all of Laramie. A large sign on the front identified it as the Holliday House.

"Oh, my!" Carrie said, looking at the building. The character of the other buildings in town had prepared her for the worst, so she was quite pleasantly surprised to see how grand this building was. "It is absolutely beautiful!" she exclaimed.

"Yes'm, I reckon it is," Morton said. "I'd give a heap to look around inside again. It's been so long I pure forgot, but I recollect as it was awful pretty inside, too."

"Why don't you come in with me and have a look at it?" Carrie offered.

"Oh, no, ma'am," Morton answered quickly. "My mom would wale the daylights outta me, iffen she found out I ever went in that place." Morton blushed. "Well, the truth is, I'm too old for her to actually whup me, but she'd be so almighty upset that it'd make things awful uncomfortable for a while."

"Really?" Carrie answered. "Why?"

Morton snickered. "You know why," he said. "She says I'm not old enough to be in a place like the Holliday House."

"Oh," Carrie said. "I understand." The boy's mother undoubtedly objected to the saloon. Well, she had told Rand Colby that she was going to close the saloon, and this just reinforced her decision. If decent people were put off coming to the hotel because of the saloon, then that was all the justification she needed. "Well, if your mother doesn't wish you to come in, then I don't want to go against her wishes."

"I'll set your trunk on the porch," Morton said. "One

of the men'll take it in for you, 'n like as not, they'll carry it right on up to your room."

"Thank you," Carrie said. The wagon stopped in front of the hotel, and Carrie reached into her bag. "What do I owe you?" she asked.

"Ten cents," Morton answered.

"You are a fine, enterprising young man," Carrie said, handing him a dime. "And I've no doubt that you will have your own freight line someday, with dozens of wagons clattering about, all of them bearing your name on the side. I've seen such wagons in St. Louis, you know."

"Yes!" Mort said excitedly. "Yes, you know just what I'm thinking of. I thought I'd put my name right here, in big black letters. That way—"

"No, no, not black," Carrie interrupted. "Red! Don't you see? Red would show up much better."

"Yeah," Morton said, smiling again. "Yeah, red. Carrie, it's been a real pleasure," he said. "I like talkin' to you, 'cause you understand. And listen, if there's ever anythin' I can do for you ... I mean, I've heard tell of girls 'n women that gets into Holliday House and then don't like it, but they can't leave. Well, iffen that was to happen to you, you can count on me, 'cause I'll help you, even iffen I have to sneak you out."

Carrie smiled at Morton's puzzling remark.

"I thank you, Morton," she said. "But why would anyone want to leave Holliday House? This is my new home, and I intend to stay here from now on."

"Yes'm," Morton said, and the same look—mysterious, disappointed, almost contemptuous—crossed his face again, as it had when she first told him where she wanted to go.

"Morton, is everything all right?" Carrie asked, puzzled by his strange reaction.

"Yes'm, I reckon ever'thin's all right iffen you want it like this," Morton said.

"If I want it like what?" Carrie asked. "I don't understand what is troubling you."

"No, ma'am, I reckon you don't," Morton said. "But it ain't really none of my concern. It's your life, I guess, and if that's how it's gonna be, then that's how it's gonna be. I'll be tellin' you goodbye now, ma'am."

Morton touched his hat, then slapped the reins against the back of his mule.

"Bye," Carrie replied, still confused by his strange remarks. She stood there and watched him drive away, then turned and, with a resolute setting of her shoulders, pushed through the front door of Holliday House and into her new life.

10

Rand felt guilty about abandoning Carrie without so much as a hint of his intention to do so. He told himself that he wasn't under any obligation to explain his leaving, hell he wasn't really under any obligation to her at all.

He had gone to St. Louis to get her because of a promise he had made to Charles Holliday. But he had fulfilled that promise, he delivered the letter, gave her the option to stay or come, and had gotten her onto the boat and onto the train. He had never in his life met anyone so naïve. He wasn't sure she would have been able to arrange passage on the boat or the train, if he hadn't done it for her.

And that thought made him feel even worse. He had not only left her on the train to fend for herself, he hadn't been entirely truthful with her about the Holliday House. She thought it was a hotel. How was she going to react when she discovered that it wasn't just a hotel—it was also a brothel.

Carrie had been raised in an orphanage, and even

though she had been an employee of the orphanage, she was still a resident. An innocent resident, surrounded by innocents. He thought about giving up his search for the men who had killed Nora. He should return to Laramie and apologize to Carrie.

No. The damage has been done, and she probably wouldn't accept his apology anyway. Besides, he had made a vow over Nora's grave and to Grant Stanfield to bring to justice the men who had killed her, and he intended to do just that.

He continued his search.

BACK IN LARAMIE, Carrie watched Morton drive away, then she walked into the lobby of the Holliday House and stood there, looking around. There were more than a dozen chairs and sofas scattered about the lobby, and nearly half a dozen Persian carpets on the floor. Smoking stands and brass spittoons were in abundance, as well as several potted plants. A huge chandelier hung from the ceiling, and she could see by the fixtures that it was a gas instrument, so she knew that it must be beautiful at night.

A large, grandfather's clock stood against the wall, and the hands gave the time as 5:45. That explained the quietness of the place, for she saw no one around.

Carrie heard a door close from upstairs, then she heard footsteps. She looked toward the great, curving staircase. A man was coming down the carpeted stairs, busily buttoning his shirt. He was carrying his jacket in his hand.

"I just arrived on the morning train," Carrie said, pointing back toward the track.

"Most of the girls don't arrive so early in the morning."

Most of the girls? The man was making no sense whatever to Carrie, but she was too embarrassed to pursue the conversation any further, for fear of showing her ignorance.

The man looked around the lobby. "I say, my dear, doesn't anyone know you're here?"

"No," Carrie answered. "You're the first person I've seen, since coming to the hotel."

"Well, you just wait right there," the man said. "I'll get you all taken care of."

"Thank you," Carrie said. "You are most kind."

"Hal," the man called. "Hal, wake up, there's a new girl here." The man stepped over to the registration desk and called to someone behind it.

"What is it?" a voice asked irritably. "What do you want?"

"I want you to take care of this new girl," the man said. He looked back at Carrie, who was still standing in the middle of the lobby. "All right, honey, Hal here'll take care of you. I've got to get back. I'll see you around."

"Thank you again," Carrie said. Carrie walked over to the registration desk. "Are you the manager?" she asked.

"I'm just the desk clerk," the man answered. "Anyway, you don't want to see the manager. The person you want to see is Winnie."

"Winnie?"

"Yeah," Hal said. "But she don't get up 'till about eleven or so on the good days. Sometimes she don't get up 'till 'bout one in the afternoon."

Carrie gasped. "Is it possible someone could stay in bed that long? Why, they would be sleeping their life away."

"Well, she's—" Hal started, then he stopped. "I mean, you know, that's her," Hal stopped again, and he looked at Carrie with an expression of bewilderment on his face. "You don't know, do you?" he said. "Look here, ain't you here to see Winnie?"

"I don't know anyone named Winnie," Carrie said. "In fact, I don't know anyone in Laramie, though I do have a letter of introduction to a Mister Edward Steele. He was my uncle's lawyer, I believe."

"Your uncle? You mean Charley Holliday? He was your uncle?"

"Yes," Carrie said.

Hal smiled and stuck out his hand. "Well, I'm truly proud to meet you, Miss . . . uh, is your name Holliday, too?"

"Yes," Carrie said. "Carrie Holliday."

"Miss Holliday, I worked for your uncle for five years, 'n believe me he was a good man. It was a sad day when he cashed in his chips."

"Thank you," Carrie said. "I must confess, I didn't know my uncle. In fact, until I received his letter, I didn't even know of his existence."

"Well, all I can say is, that was Charley's misfortune. Where is your luggage? Is it still down to the depot?"

"No," Carrie said. She smiled. "A nice young man named Morton brought me. He put my trunk on the porch."

"Morton? Oh, you mean Mort. Yeah, he's a good kid. He used to do odd jobs around here, 'till Charley died. Then, after Charley died, Winnie moved in, and now Mort's mama won't let him around the place."

"Yes, that's what he told me."

Hal looked down at his feet and cleared his throat nervously. "Look, I'm sorry about that," he said. "I mean, seeing a pretty girl like you, you can understand what he must have thought."

Pretty? Carrie thought. That was the second time someone had called her pretty in conjunction with the hotel. What on earth did they mean?

"I wonder if there's a place where I could take a bath."

Hal smiled broadly. "Why, that ain't gonna be no problem a'tall," he said. "We built this hotel real fancy for the politicians and the rich folks that come out here when the railroad was bein' built. So, right up there on the second floor we got a men's and a ladies' washroom, with runnin' water."

"Running water?" Carrie asked, surprised to hear of such modern conveniences, here in the wild west.

"Yes, ma'am. Ole' Charley, he prided hisself in havin' the finest railroad hotel on the U.P. system, 'n he put that water tank in hisself. You see, they's a spring head back of us, 'n that spring feeds right in to a tank we got on top o' the hotel buildin'. It bein' hot as it was yesterday, well I reckon the water that's in the tank now is warm enough. It couldn't of cooled too much durin' the night."

"Thanks," Carrie said. "Now, which room shall I use?"

"Uh, well, I would say you could stay where Charley lived, but Winnie is stayin' there now. I could put you in one of the rooms."

"Very well," Carrie said. "I'll take one of the rooms. Would you have someone bring my trunk up?"

"Yes, ma'am," Hal said. "I'd be right proud to do that my ownself."

Carrie waited as Hal got the trunk, then she followed him up the stairs and onto the second-floor landing. He unlocked one of the many brown doors along the corridor and pushed it open, then, with a great sigh of relief, put the trunk down. He stepped back into the hall and pointed.

"That's the washrooms, just down at the end of the hall," he said. "As you can see, the doors are clearly marked, one for ladies, and one for gents."

"Thank you," Carrie said.

After Hal left, Carrie looked around the room. It had one high-sprung, cast-iron bed, a chest, and a small table with a pitcher and basin. A gas lamp fixture was overhead. On the wall papered with a small rose pattern, a neatly lettered sign read: "Gentlemen, please remove spurs while in bed."

A slight, morning breeze filled the muslin curtains and lifted them out over the wide-beamed planking in the floor. Carrie moved to the window and looked out over the town, which was beginning to awaken now, and she saw some activity behind the buildings. Water was being heated behind the laundry, and boxes were being stacked behind the grocery store.

Carrie turned away from the window and opened her trunk and began removing her clothes. Seeing the laundry reminded her that she would have to attend her own laundry today. She had saved one clean dress, to have something fresh to wear the first day she arrived, so she took it with her and then walked quietly down the carpeted hallway toward the ladies' washroom.

When Carrie stepped inside the room, she saw a woman sitting at a vanity in front of a mirror, applying powder to one of her eyes. The eye was swollen and black, and as Carrie looked more closely, she could see that the woman had been crying. An even closer examination disclosed the fact that she was a very young woman who was scarcely more than a girl. Carrie believed she couldn't have been over seventeen or eighteen.

"Oh, my," Carrie said, hanging up her dress and taking a step toward the girl. She reached out, tentatively, to touch the young woman's eye. She could feel the heat still there, so she knew that the injury was recent. "What happened to your eye?"

"Nothing," the girl said. She turned her face away from Carrie's hand.

Carrie had not been a governess for nothing. She had a great deal of experience in dealing with young people who were moody and sullen, so she reacted calmly to the girl's rejection of her concern.

"The powder will cover the discoloration," Carrie said. "But if you want the swelling to go down, you had best take a wet cloth and hold it there for a while."

"Thanks," the girl said. She took a cloth, wet it, then got up to leave. Just before she opened the door, she turned to look back at Carrie. "You're new here, aren't you?" she asked, her expression toward Carrie softening.

"Yes," Carrie said, smiling brightly. "I just arrived this morning."

"Are you about to take a bath?"

"Yes," Carrie said. "Why, does the water not work properly?"

"Yeah, it works all right," the girl said. "It's just that, I'd advise you to lock the door after I leave. Elsewise, you're likely to get some company that you don't want, if you know what I mean."

"No," Carrie said, puzzled by the girl's remark. "I don't know what you mean. What kind of unwanted company?"

"The men in the hotel," the girl said. "When they hear

the water runnin', they'll figure they got 'em a free show comin', 'n they'll just come traipsin' in here as pretty as you please."

"Oh, but surely not," Carrie said. "The sign on the door clearly says ladies."

The girl laughed a short, bitter laugh. "That's a joke, ain't it?"

"A joke?"

"Ladies," the girl snorted. "We ain't ladies and we never will be. That's why the men figure they got the right to come in whenever they want. The thing is, Winnie don't do nothin' about it. She says it's good for business to let them get a peek now and again."

"I'm afraid I don't understand," Carrie said. "How is this good for business?"

The girl studied Carrie for a moment before she spoke again, looking at her very carefully. "You ain't comin' to work for Winnie, are you?"

"No," Carrie said.

"I'm sorry," the girl replied. "My mistake. But that's all the more reason you should lock the door after I leave."

"Yes," Carrie said. "Thank you, I shall take your advice."

Carrie did lock the door after the girl left. Then she drew water into the tub, undressed, stepped into it, and washed away the grime and dirt from train travel.

Once, during her bath, someone tried the doorknob. She sat very still in the tub and looked at the knob as it twisted, and the door shook, but whoever it was gave up and left, without saying a word. Carrie breathed a sigh of relief.

A short time later, wearing her last clean dress and feeling like a new woman, Carrie walked into the dining room of the hotel. Had she not had the experience of the dining room on the boat, and to a degree, the dining car on the train, she would have been intimidated by this experience. As it was, she thought she handled the entire situation with a great deal of aplomb.

"Miss Holliday?" a man called from a table in the center of the room. He stood and smiled toward her.

Carrie looked at him, and saw a tall, handsome man in his late thirties. He had dark wavy hair, pale blue eyes, and a somewhat world-weary look about him. In his own way, Carrie believed, he was every bit as handsome as Rand Colby, though where Rand had appeared out of place in his fine clothes, this man looked as if he were born to them. He had a look of refinement to him. Yet, Carrie seemed to sense something else about him. There was an understated, though evident sense of . . . of what? Mystery? Danger? Whatever it was, it intrigued her.

"My name is Edward Steele," the man said, as he walked over to introduce himself. "I am glad to see you arrived in good order. No trouble on the trip, I presume? Everything went as expected?"

"It was a fine trip," Carrie said. "I had no trouble at all."

"Fine, fine," Edward said. He held a chair out for Carrie, then, when she was seated, he sat across from her. "I take it that Rand Colby gave you all the options?" He looked around. "Where is Colby? I would have thought he would be here with you. He was charged with the responsibility of your safe passage, was he not?"

"Mr. Colby," Carrie said, speaking the name in a tone of voice, "saw fit to desert me in the middle of the trip. I was left to my own devices."

Edward smiled sadly.

"Ah, yes, well, Miss Holliday, I'm afraid you will find that is typical of Mr. Colby. But then, you mustn't be too hard on him. He is, after all, a simple man, the product of his surroundings. You will find that many men out here have a tendency to be callous, sometimes to the point of brutality, disrespectful to the point of insolence, and frustratingly untrustworthy. Just thank your lucky stars that he didn't choose the time he was with you to show his explosive temper. He is known to be a violent man, and some have fallen before his gun."

Carrie gasped at the comment, and Edward, understanding her reaction, went on, quickly.

"Oh, don't misunderstand, Miss Holliday," he said. "I'm not accusing Colby of murder. I would never have consented to allowing him to escort you here, if that were the case. His killings, when they have occurred, have all been justified, by way of self-defense, and of course by his position as a railroad detective. You see, men of Colby's ilk believe that manhood may be measured by one's skill with a gun. In that Mr. Colby is exceptionally skilled with a gun, he has an exceptionally high opinion of his manhood."

"There was a man killed," Carrie said.

"I beg your pardon?"

"There was a man killed," Carrie said. "Only, it was ruled an accident. He was trying to shoot Mr. Colby, but when Mr. Colby shoved his gun aside, the man shot himself."

Steele sighed. "Trouble does seem to follow Colby," he said. "I must confess now, that I regret sending him on this errand. Though in truth, I was certain you would accept the money, rather than subject yourself to the ordeal of the trip."

"I want to keep the hotel, Mr. Steele," Carrie said. "There is nothing for me back in St. Louis."

"Uh, yes," Edward said, and Carrie could tell that he was disappointed in her decision, because he very obviously wanted to buy it for himself. "Well, as the deed has already been drawn up in your name, I see no problems."

"I understand there is gambling allowed in this hotel," Carrie said.

"Yes, there is."

"I want it stopped, at once."

"As your lawyer, Miss Holliday, I feel it only fair to explain that gambling is the primary source of income for your establishment."

"Then I shall just work harder to make the hotel offset what is lost by gambling," Carrie said. "We will turn the gambling salon into something else. I also want no liquor sold on the premises, except, perhaps, wine in the dining room."

"What will you do with the room?" Edward asked.

"What room?"

"The saloon and gambling occupy a large room downstairs. It isn't practical to turn that area into guest rooms. What will you do with the space you aren't using?"

"I want to do something for the community," Carrie said. "Yes, we'll turn it into a community meeting room. Edward, will you help me make the arrangements for that?"

Edward Steele smiled. "Yes," he said. "I shall be most happy to."

What a wonderful man, Carrie thought, as she began eating her breakfast. Why did Rand Colby have such a low opinion of him? He was being extremely helpful, and he didn't seem at all upset by the fact that she was keeping the hotel, rather than selling it to him.

Rand Colby's impression of Edward Steele was as erroneous as her own impression was of Rand Colby. It was good that she could now see who her real friend was.

11

LARAMIE WAS WIDE AWAKE AND AS CARRIE TOOK HER FIRST stroll through town, it was very busy. Rand had described the town quite accurately, it seemed. During one of their conversations on the way out, Rand had told her that Laramie was one of the major stops along the Union Pacific Railroad and, as such, had become a crossroads, not only of America, but of the world.

"It is literally teeming," he had said. "There are railroad builders, buffalo hunters, Indian fighters, ranchers, pioneers, get-rich-quick businessmen, gold hunters, politicians, and all sorts of people."

Two ladies were walking down the board walk toward Carrie, and she smiled and prepared to greet them. Then, to her surprise, she saw them glance her way, gather up their skirts and walk across the street to the other side before she could reach them. That's funny, she thought. Why didn't they wait and cross at the corner, where planks were laid across the streets to keep pedestrians out of the dirt and mud?

The thought didn't linger, for in the next block she

saw a wagon train being made up in the middle of the street. Near one of the wagons, she saw the same family she had seen boarding the train in Omaha—the man, woman, and three children, one of which was still in the mother's arms. The expression on the man's face was still determined, the woman was still as accepting, and the children, who were running around the wagon, still as excited.

Carrie walked all the way up one side of the street, crossed on the boards at the corner, and returned down the other side of the street. Several men smiled and tipped their hats, but, oddly, she saw not one woman to speak to, until she started back up the front steps of the hotel. Then she heard a female voice calling to her.

"Miss Holliday?"

Carrie saw the girl she had seen earlier in the morning, who had been treating her black eye.

"Well, hello," Carrie said, smiling easily, happy to have a woman to talk to. "How is your eye?"

"It's fine," the girl said. "Miss Holliday, I'm awful sorry iffen I was rude to you this mornin'. I didn't have no right to be rude like that, but I wasn't in a very happy mood."

"Think nothing of it," Carrie said easily. "It's hard to be in a happy mood if your eye's hurting, and it looked like it was." Carrie looked at the girl more closely. "It looks as if the swelling has gone down, at least."

"Yes'm," the girl said, touching her eye lightly. "But like as not it'll be black for near on to a week. It always is."

"It always is? You mean you've had them before?"

"Yes'm, lots of times," the girl said. "Mr. Donohoe—he likes to get a little rough on occasion. I'd just as soon not have anythin' more to do with him, but Winnie, she says I gotta, 'cause I'm the one he always asks for."

"I don't understand," Carrie said, confused by the girl's strange remark. "What do you mean Winnie says you have to?"

"Well, Winnie, you see, she's the madam," the girl said. "I just work for her. Only, that's what I'd like to talk to you about. I hear tell that you own this hotel. Is that true?"

"Yes," Carrie said. "My uncle left it to me."

"Miss Holliday, I want to work for you," the girl said. "I'm a real good worker, you'll see. I can do most anythin'. I can cook and wash and sew, and I can keep the rooms clean and the beds made up. Please say I can work for you."

"Well, I suppose I could use someone," Carrie said. "I don't know what the arrangement is right now. But what about Winnie? Didn't you work for her?"

"I don't want to work for her anymore," the girl said. "You gotta believe me, Miss Holliday, when I went to work for her, I didn't really know what I was gettin' into. Winnie told me all I would have to do is smile at the men and look pretty, and I'd make lots of money. I believed her."

"What is your name?" Carrie asked.

"Polly," the girl answered.

"All right, Polly, if you would like to work for me, I'd be glad to have you."

Polly smiled broadly, then rushed over to take Carrie's hand. "You won't be sorry, Miss Holliday," she said. "I can promise you, you won't be sorry, none a'tall."

"I'm sure I won't be sorry," Carrie said. "I'm sure we will be great friends."

"Oh, I'll have to find another room," Polly said

COLD REVENGE

quickly. "Winnie won't let me stay where I am now. And she ain't gonna like it none that I quit, neither. She's gonna be real mad."

"You let me handle that," Carrie said. "A person doesn't have to work for another person unless he or she is satisfied with the work and the wages. They can't be kept on against their will, that would be slavery, and slavery is now against the law."

"Thank you, Miss Holliday," Polly said. She smiled brightly. "When can I start? Do you have anything for me to do now?"

"Yes," Carrie said. "Come up to my room for a few minutes, would you? I need to talk to someone. I have a lot of questions I want to ask."

"I'll answer every question I can," Polly agreed easily.

There were no chairs in Carrie's room, so the two young women sat on the edge of the bed as they talked. As they sat there, Carrie studied Polly. Though the girl still didn't look older than seventeen or eighteen, there was something about her that made her look older than her years. At first, Carrie couldn't understand what it was that made the girl seem older, there were no wrinkles, or anything like that. Then she realized that it was the young girl's eyes. Polly had seen a lot of life, and all of it was recorded in the ridges on her soul, visible through her eyes.

"Tell me about this hotel," Carrie said. "Is it a nice hotel?"

"Oh, yes, ma'am," Polly said. "Why, I reckon it's about the fanciest hotel you could ever hope to see. I've heard the gentlemen who pass through here say it is the finest along the U.P. line."

"Do you think it could make money without gambling and drinking?"

"I don't know," Polly said. "I do know that only the nicest men come in here for the gamblin' and the drinkin'. Them's that makes trouble, most generally winds up down to the Bloody Bucket."

"The Bloody Bucket?" Carrie asked, screwing her face into a scowl. "What's that?"

"That's the saloon down to the other end of the street," Polly said. "There's generally lots of shootin' goes on down there, 'n there's a fight near 'bout ever' night. They ain't hardly never no fights in here. The saloon part's not what keeps the ladies away."

"That's something else I don't understand," Carrie said. "When I took a walk this morning, I didn't see one lady to talk to. They always crossed the street before I reached them, and I'm almost sure it wasn't just a coincidence."

"No'm, it weren't no coincidence," Polly said.

"And you know the boy, Morton?"

"Yes'm," Polly said. "Ever'one knows Mort. He's a very nice boy and a hard worker, too. He's helped me out a couple of times' though, if his mama knew it, she'd be powerful upset."

"That's just it," Carrie said. "That's what I'm talking about. Morton told me this morning that his mother wouldn't allow him in the hotel. Hal said he used to do odd jobs around the place before Winnie arrived. So, why can't he come in now?"

"Why, it's Winnie 'n me 'n the other girls," Polly said in embarrassment. "Since Winnie moved in here, none of the town ladies will come around the hotel."

"Why is that?" Carrie asked.

"Because of what we are," Polly said. "You know, our trade."

"Hal said you were 'soiled doves'," Carrie said.

Polly looked down toward the floor in embarrassment. "Yes'm," she said. "I guess, that means you don't want me to work for you?"

"No, why would you say that?"

"I'd understand iffen you didn't want me around," Polly said. "Not many folks are willin' to give a prostitute a second chance."

"A prostitute? You are a prostitute?" Carrie asked in shock.

Polly looked up in surprise. "Why, yes'm. I thought you knew. Hal told you we were soiled doves."

"I ... I must confess, I've never heard that term before," Carrie said. "And I didn't want to show my ignorance to Hal."

"Now, you'll really want me to go, won't you?"

"No," Carrie said. "No, not at all. Polly?"

"Yes'm."

"Polly, I know this is going to sound strange to you. I know that being a prostitute is bad, it's against the law and it's a sin. But, what exactly is a prostitute? What does a prostitute do?"

"Beg your pardon, ma'am?" Polly asked, looking at Carrie in shock. "You mean you don't know what a prostitute is?"

"No," Carrie said. "You have to understand," she went on quickly. "I was raised in an orphanage. I have led an exceptionally sheltered life, shielded from things which Mr. and Mrs. Talbot thought I shouldn't hear. I recall asking her about it once when I read the word in the St. Louis Dispatch. She said it was not something I needed to know."

"I can understand you not knowin'," Polly said. "Like I told you, I didn't know what it was either, 'till I got into it. I come to Laramie to try 'n make some money, after

my pa died, 'n I heard that Winnie was lookin' for pretty girls. I was flattered when someone told me I was pretty enough. Winnie said I didn't have to do anythin', that the men would do it all. I didn't know then, what the men would do."

"What do they do?"

"Why, they . . . look here, Miss Holliday, do you know anythin' at all about what a man 'n woman do, together?"

"I know that . . ." Carrie felt her cheeks flaming in embarrassment. "I know that they kiss," she finally said.

"Kissin' is the easy part," Polly said. "That's the sweet part. It's the other part that causes all the problems." When she saw that Carrie still didn't understand, she sighed. "Look," she said. "I guess I'm just going to have to explain ever'thin' to you. I only wish I could'a had someone explain it to me before I found out the hard way."

Polly began explaining then, sometimes using terms and words Carrie didn't understand at all.

"Don't worry, Polly," Carrie said, putting her hand on the girl's shoulder. "You are out of it now. You are working for me."

"Thank you," Polly said. "Now, all I have to do is tell Winnie, and—"

"Don't worry about Winnie," Carrie said. "You aren't leaving, she is."

"You're askin' her to leave?"

"Yes," Carrie said. "It wouldn't make much sense to close down the gambling and drinking and then leave the prostitution, would it?"

"No, I guess not," Polly said. "But Hal told me he told you about it, and you didn't say anything. He thought you were goin' to let her stay."

"He told me about the soiled doves," Carrie said. "I

thought he was talking about birds in a cage, what did I know?"

Polly laughed. "I see what you mean," she said. Then she got a look of concern on her face. "How are you goin' to do it? Get rid of Winnie, I mean? She can be pretty rough, sometimes."

"Then I shall ask Mr. Steele to assist me," Carrie said.

"Do you think he will?"

"Of course. He is my lawyer," Carrie said. "Why? . . . Do you think there is some reason he won't?"

"Not really," Polly said. "It's just that—" she paused.

"What?"

"Me 'n some of the other girls was talkin' 'bout it one day, 'n we just 'bout had it figured out that Edward Steele was Winnie's silent partner."

"Oh, no, I'm certain you are mistaken," Carrie said. "Mr. Steele is such a nice man, and a respectable lawyer besides. He is going to help me close down the drinking and the gambling."

"Yes'm, if you say so," Polly said. "But someone is Winnie's partner. She had to have some money to get started, 'n there've been a couple of times when she had to have help that could come only from a man."

"Well, I'm quite certain it isn't Edward Steele," Carrie said.

"Of course, it could be—" Polly started, then she paused. "No, I don't think it would be him. He just don't strike me as that sort."

"Who?"

"Rand Colby," Polly said.

"Rand Colby?" Carrie asked. "Yes, it might be him at that."

"No, ma'am, I'm sure it's not him," Polly said. "He's so much nicer a man than Mr. Steele, it just wouldn't be possible. 'N besides, he ain't really been here long enough."

"Nicer? How can you say that? I had breakfast with Edward Steele this morning, and I've never met a gentleman with better manners."

"Them's just parlor manners," Polly said. "It's all outside, like the fancy clothes he wears. What I'm talkin' about is inside. Inside, Rand Colby is twice a better man than Edward Steele."

"I'm afraid that hasn't been my experience," Carrie said. "Polly?"

"Yes, ma'am?"

"Thank you for the education."

"Yes ma'am, I'm glad I could help, some."

"REALLY, MR. STEELE," Carrie said, a short time later. "If she isn't accustomed to getting up this early, we don't need to disturb her now. We could wait."

"Nonsense," Edward Steele replied. He banged on the door again. "She had no business being in this apartment in the first place. This apartment is, by rights, the apartment of the owner of the hotel. That's you. And you are quite right in claiming it. You are also quite right in moving out the liquor and gambling and Winnie and her girls, to clean up the hotel."

"I knew you would understand," Carrie said.

"I understand perfectly, and I concur wholeheartedly." Edward banged on the door again. "Winnie!" he called.

"What is it?" a muffled voice finally answered from the other side of the door. "Who's out there? Who the hell is knocking on my door?"

Carrie had never heard a woman swear, and she was

both surprised by it and curious to see what sort of woman would use such language.

"It's me, Edward Steele! You're going to have to get up!"

"What time is it?"

"Nine o'clock," Edward said.

"Nine?" There was a sound on the other side of the door, then the door opened and Carrie saw Winnie for the first time.

Carrie stared at the woman with unabashed curiosity. Winnie's hair was red, but it was unlike any red Carrie had ever seen, and she knew that it had to be dyed. A blood-red gash of lip paint outlined her mouth, though some of it had smeared onto her cheeks. Dark smears were around her eyes, and white powder and deep pink rouge competed for attention on her cheeks.

Carrie had no idea how old the woman was; she could have been as young as thirty or as old as fifty, because her face wore the marks of terrible dissipation, if not wrinkles. Carrie also saw in Winnie's eyes the same weariness she had seen in Polly's eyes, only even more so. Winnie was quite a bit larger than Carrie, and she had enormous breasts, which were shockingly exposed by the sleeping gown she was wearing.

"I had no idea it was nine o'clock," Winnie said. "Has someone asked for me? Tell him to wait a few minutes and I'll be ready."

"It's nine o'clock in the morning," Edward said.

Winnie looked at Edward in disbelief. "In the morning?" she asked. "You woke me at nine o'clock in the morning?" Her voice grew louder. "Are you out of your mind? What do you mean waking me at nine o'clock in the morning?"

"This is Carrie Holliday," Edward said, pointing to Carrie.

"I don't give a damn if she's the Virgin Mary," Winnie said angrily. "In the first place, I don't need any more girls, and in the second place, I wouldn't hire anyone who woke me at nine o'clock in the morning. Now get out!"

Winnie started to close her door, but Edward put his foot in it and held it open. "No," he said, smiling at her. "You get out."

"What? What are you talking about?" Winnie asked in complete surprise.

"You didn't let me finish my introduction a moment ago," Edward said. "As I said, this is Miss Holliday, and she owns the hotel."

"She owns the hotel?"

"She is Charley's niece," Edward said. "I drew up the deed for her, myself. She is the legal owner of Holliday House, and she wants you and your girls to find another place to practice your sordid profession."

"My sordid profession? You call this a sordid—"

"I said get out, and I mean it," Edward said, interrupting Winnie in mid-sentence.

"I see," Winnie said. She looked at Edward, then at Carrie, and Carrie had never seen such anger in one woman's eyes. "I see how things are, now. When a new hen arrives in the henhouse, the rooster does her bidding."

"I'm glad you do see," Edward said easily, though Carrie did not follow quite what Winnie meant by her analogy. "Now, may we expect you off the premises by noon?"

"Please, I don't want to cause any hardship," Carrie

put in. "There's no need to establish such a rigid time schedule."

"Oh, don't worry 'bout me 'n my girls none, missy," Winnie said. "Me 'n the girls got no wish to be where we ain't wanted. Edward . . . that is, Mr. Steele," Winnie said, "if you see Polly, would you please ask her to come give me a hand?"

"Oh," Carrie said, speaking before Edward could respond. "That's another thing. I'm afraid that Polly won't be going with you."

"She won't be going with me? What do you mean? If I go, she goes."

"No, that's not quite true," Carrie said. "You see, Polly has decided that she doesn't wish to work for you any longer. She is going to work for me."

Suddenly a strange look came across Winnie's face, then she smiled, and finally she laughed, though it was a laugh without humor.

"Oh, now I understand perfectly," she said. "I've got to hand it to you, missy. You really planned this one out, didn't you? Polly is my best girl. She makes more money than any three others combined. I should have realized that you would want to go into business for yourself. And by taking Polly, you've really jerked a cinch into me."

"You are out of line, Winnie," Edward said angrily.

"I'm afraid you don't understand at all," Carrie said. "I don't want any prostitution in this hotel.

"I am also closing the gambling and drinking," Carrie added. "And I am going to make the space available for community activity. If the people of the community need a place to hold church services, then I would have no objections."

Winnie looked at Carrie in disbelief as she spoke, then she looked over at Edward.

"Is she on the level?" Winnie asked. "She plans to hold church services in a whore house?"

"She is absolutely on the level," Edward replied easily.

Winnie looked back at Carrie. "Why are you doing such a foolish thing?" she asked.

"It is my intention to have a respectable hotel," Carrie said.

"Missy, you may wind up with the most respectable hotel in the state, but I'll tell you somethin' else. You're goin' to have the brokest, besides."

"That is a chance I shall just have to take," Carrie said.

12

IT HAD BEEN A WEEK SINCE RAND STARTED LOOKING FOR the other three men and knowing that anyone out in the wilds would need a source of water, he had confined his search to rivers, creeks and streams. He had searched Chugwater Creek, the Laramie River, Lodgepole Creek, and was about to turn away from Horse Creek, when he saw a wispy pall of wood smoke drifting up in a long, diaphanous haze.

Someone was down there cooking breakfast, and as he drew closer, the rich aroma of coffee and bacon permeated the area.

A rustle of wind through feathers caused him to look up just in time to see a golden eagle diving on its prey. The eagle swooped back into the air, carrying a tiny field mouse kicking fearfully in the eagle's claws.

"You got yours," Rand said quietly. "I just hope I get mine."

Rand took a drink of water, wiped the back of his hand across his mouth, then recapped his canteen and slipped it back onto the saddle horn. He loosened his pistol in his holster, then urging his horse forward, started toward the encampment on the creek.

Rand covered the three hundred yards quickly and pulled Diablo to a halt behind a rock very close to the encampment. As far as he knew it could be an innocent hunter or traveler, he had certainly encountered several of those since starting his search. He thought it best to take a closer look before making his presence known. As he moved closer, he could hear voices, so he knew that it was more than a solitary traveler. Then he got to a place where he had a clear view of the men, but they couldn't see him.

There were four of them, which was good. After taking out Perry Hoyt, he was looking for the remaining three men who had taken part in the bank robbery in Rushville. All these men were armed, but because they weren't expecting an intruder, they had not bothered to post a guard.

That was when he saw Ely Slack. As soon as he saw him, the vision of him riding away from the bank in Rushville came back to him. This was one of the men who had killed Nora.

"You know what I think?" one of the men said. "I think we ought to ride into town and get us some more whiskey. We ain't got enough left to wet your whistle."

"If we do that, we might as well go on into Laramie," another said. "Hell, Cox, we could not only get us some whiskey, we could get us a woman."

"A woman? You mean just one?" Cox asked. "Tell me, Barney, what's wrong with a woman apiece? We got enough money from that train robbery that we can afford to do near 'bout anythin' we want."

Train robbery? Rand thought. He hadn't heard

anything of a recent train robbery. It must have happened while he was back in St. Louis. He wondered that he hadn't heard about it when he boarded the train in Omaha.

"Oh no we can't," Slack said. We ain't gonna spend a penny of this money, not for one year. By that time ever'thin' will have died down, 'n we'll be safe."

"Hell's bells, Ely!" one of the other men said disgustedly. He tossed the grounds of his coffee onto the ground. "I say we divide up now 'n each of us go our separate ways."

"And I say we stick together," Slack said. "If one of us gets caught, we're all in danger. The only way we can be safe is to stick together."

"Yeah, well what if we get caught together?"

"That's not very likely."

Rand raised up from behind the rock then, and he had his pistol leveled toward the four men.

"You'd better listen to him, Slack," Rand said. "He has a point. You're all going to be caught together. In fact, I just did it."

"What the…." Slack shouted. He started toward a rifle lying on a saddle near the campfire.

Rand snapped off a shot. A piece of the saddle leather split right in front of the rifle as the bullet tore into it. Slack jerked back, then, hesitantly, put his arms up. The others, seeing their leader raise his hands, followed suit.

"I'll thank you gents to drop your holsters—real slow," Rand said, and he made a menacing move with the end of his pistol. All four of the men carefully unbuckled their gun belts and let them slip to the ground.

"Who the hell are you, Mister?" Slack growled.

"I know," another said. "He's a damned bounty

hunter. Is that what you are, Mister? Are you out for blood money?"

"No," Rand said. "I'm the man who was going to marry the woman that Slack killed in Rushville."

Rand pointed to some rope on one of the saddles. "You got a knife, Slack?"

"No, I ain't got no knife."

Rand pulled his own knife from the sheath on his belt, then threw it so that it stuck in the ground in front of Slack. "Cut that rope into pieces so you can tie up your men and do a good job of it."

Reluctantly, but without any choice to do otherwise, Slack tied his men securely. Then, suddenly, and unexpectedly, he produced a hold-out gun and shot at Rand. Rand, who saw him swing around with the gun, fired an instant after Slack did. Slack missed, Rand didn't.

"Damn, Mister, you just killed my brother," the man with the red beard said.

Rand hadn't realized until then, that one of the men was Ely Slack's brother.

"Better him than me," Rand said, expressionless, as he began saddling their horses.

"Yeah? Well, iffen you hadn't sneaked up on us, you wouldn't of got none of us, I can tell you that for sure."

"Perhaps," Rand said. "Since Ely Slack was your brother, would you also happen to know Perry Hoyt and Nate Campbell?"

"What?" Red Beard Slack replied. His eyes narrowed. "Wait a minute, what are you trying to do? You're tryin' to tie me in with my brother and Hoyt and Campbell ain't you? You think I robbed that bank with them?"

"I don't know. There was a fourth man, but he was wearing a hood, and I didn't get a good look at him. Were you the fourth man?"

"No, I didn't have nothin' to do with it, and you can ask Hoyt or Campbell about it."

"I did ask Hoyt," Rand said. "Just before he died."

Red Beard Slack's eyes opened wide. "What? You kilt Hoyt too?" A tiny line of perspiration beads broke out on his upper lip. "Who are you, Mister? Are you some vigilante gone crazy?"

"Are you the fourth man?" Rand asked again.

"No!" Red Beard Slack looked at the others. "Cox, Barney, you two bear witness to this, now, this crazy man is liable to try 'n kill me. You seen what he done to my brother. He shot 'im down in cold blood." He looked back toward Rand. "I didn't have nothin' to do with that bank robbery, do you hear me? Nothin' at all. And I'm willin' to let you take me in so's I can tell the sheriff that. You got no right to shoot me now."

"I'm not going to shoot you," Rand said. "Unless you try something funny."

"I ain't gonna try nothin' funny. Look, you said your woman was kilt durin' that bank robbery, so I can see why you might be some put out by it, but I'm tellin' you, I had nothin' to do with it. We robbed the Bamforth train, but—"

"Arnie, you snivelin' coward!" Webster said. "Shut your trap!"

"Yeah?" Arnold Slack said. "Well, better to spend a little time for robbery, than to hang for murder. Don't you fools understand? They was murder committed in that bank robbery, 'n when them what done it gets caught, they're gonna hang, even if this fella doesn't shoot 'em."

"Where is Nate Campbell?" Rand asked.

"I don't know," Arnie answered.

"You do want to cooperate, don't you, Slack?" Rand asked, with a dangerous inflection in his voice.

"I don't know!" Arnie Slack said again. "Honest, I don't know. But the last I heard, he was somewhere around Boise."

Rand had also heard that Campbell was in Boise, but when he checked, Campbell had already left. At least he felt that Arnie Slack wasn't lying, because it was the latest information he had been able to get, also.

"Slack, you'd trade your own mother," Cox said disgustedly.

"Hell yes he would, we just seen 'im trade in his own brother," Webster said.

Rand made the men walk in front of him, while he led their horses, until he returned to Diablo. Get mounted," he ordered.

"What are you going to do with my brother?"

"He's coming with us," Rand said and lifting Ely Slack, he lay him stomach down over the saddle. Then, but not until he was mounted, did he have the other three men mount, one at a time. Tying a long rope around the neck from one to the other, he held the end of the rope. With one jerk he could dismount all three of them. That was the way he started them back south toward Laramie.

"Arnie," he said, later in the morning when the sun was high and all of them were sweating under its beating rays. "Who was the fourth man?"

"I don't know," Slack said.

Rand pulled on the rope, just enough to let Slack know that he controlled him.

"Go ahead and jerk me off the horse if you feel you have to," Slack whined. "I tell you, I don't know. M' brother never told me who it was. Hell, I'm not all that sure he even know'd who it was."

"You might as well believe him, Mister," one of the others said. "You've seen what a cowardly bastard he's turned out to be. If he had know'd anythin' he'd be spillin' his guts right now. You can count on that."

Rand rode along behind the three men in silence for the rest of the trip back to Laramie.

13

IT WAS MID-MORNING WHEN RAND COLBY RODE INTO town leading three mounted men with their hands tied and connected to each other by a rope looped around their necks. The other end of the rope was held by Colby and the slightest jerk on the rope would unsaddle all three of them, with the added possibility of breaking their necks. In addition to the three bound men, there was a fourth man lying belly down over his saddle.

The bizarre parade caught the attention of the citizens of Laramie who were attending to their morning business.

"That's Rand Colby," someone said.

"Who are those men with him?"

"I don't know, but it looks like he's takin' 'em to the sheriff's office."

"ALL RIGHT," Rand said when he reached the sheriff's office. "Get down."

"We can't none of us get down, what with a rope around our necks," Slack said.

"I'll help you down," Rand offered.

"I'll help too," Sheriff Kelly said, stepping out of his office then.

Rand and the sheriff helped the men dismount.

"Who's the stiff?" Sheriff Kelly asked.

"That's Ely Slack," Rand said, pointing to the body draped over the horse.

"Slack? He's one of the men you've been looking for, isn't he? One of the Rushville bank robbers?"

"Yes."

"These the other bank robbers?"

"No, they are train robbers."

"The Bamford train," Sheriff Kelly said with a broad smile. "Damn, Colby, you railroad detectives do good work. That was only a week ago, and here you've already caught 'em.

"Was Slack one of the train robbers, too?" Sheriff Kelly asked, with a nod toward the body that was still draped over the saddle.

"Yeah, both Slacks were."

"Both?"

"The ugly son of a bitch with the red beard is Arnold Slack, Ely's brother. That one's Harry Cox, and the other one is Barney Webster," he said, pointing to the other two.

"Cox and Webster, yes, I've got paper on both of them," Sheriff Kelly said.

Sheriff Kelly and Rand led the three men into the jail house.

"In there," Kelly said, indicating one of the cells. "Lenny," he said to the deputy, who was looking on with curiosity. "There's a body hanging over a saddle outside. Get him down to the undertaker."

"Yes, sir," Deputy Milner replied.

"Sheriff, I'm going to leave these fellas with you. I've got someone I need to check on," Rand said.

"I suppose you mean the other three Rushville bank robbers. I understand."

"No, this is a young lady. And for your information, there are only two of the Rushville bank robbers left."

Sheriff Kelly smiled. "A young lady, huh? Well, you don't want to desert a young lady."

"Yeah," Rand said, flatly. "Except the bad thing is I already have."

"YOUR UNCLE CHARLEY paid fifty dollars for that picture," Hal said. "He set quite a store by it. You ain't really goin' ter destroy it, are you, Miss Holliday? That'd be a pure shame."

Carrie stepped back and looked at the picture. The object of Hal's discussion was a very large painting which had hung behind the bar of the Holliday House saloon. The painting was of a young woman, reclining on a sofa, reading a letter. The letter had been delivered by Cupid, who hovered just above her, with his bow drawn and an arrow pointed at the lady's heart.

It was not difficult for Cupid to see where to aim his bow for the lady in the painting was totally nude, and her ample charms had been painted in exceptionally realistic detail.

At the bottom of the painting, the title was etched on a brass plaque. The title was, *The Invitation*, and Hal said there had been many jokes and remarks as to what the letter was an invitation to.

"You say he paid fifty dollars for that painting?" Carrie asked.

"Yes, ma'am, 'n it's been worth ever' penny too. Why, they's folks that's ridden for miles 'n miles just to have a quiet drink 'n look at that there picture. It's a real work of art, Miss Holliday. They was a professor feller here once, 'n he told me that."

Carrie sighed. "Very well," she said. "I won't destroy it. But, we can't very well let it continue to hang there, now, can we? If we are going to turn this into a room that can be used by the community for meetings and lectures, to say nothing of some church that might want it, then such a picture would be absolutely uncalled for."

"I'll find someplace to keep it," Hal said, taking the picture down quickly, before Carrie had a chance to change her mind.

"As long as no one can see it," Carrie said.

There was a hammering, crashing sound from the front of the room, a shouted warning, then the smashing of several glasses as a large shelf turned over.

"Oh, my," Carrie said, moving quickly to the scene of the accident. "Is anyone injured?"

"No, ma'am," one of the workers said contritely. "They's just a lot of glass busted up all over the place, that's all."

"Well, please be careful," Carrie said. "I wouldn't want anyone to be hurt."

"Miss Holliday, are these the curtains you wanted?" someone asked, holding up a bolt of cloth.

"Yes," Carrie said. "Yes, I was assured that these curtains will hold in the sound, thus affording everyone, even those who are in the last seat of the last row, the opportunity to hear a lecture."

"You want to lay the carpeting before or after we put in the rows of seats?" another worker asked.

Carrie looked toward the roll of carpet lying against the wall. She put her hand on her chin and contemplated for a moment, before she answered, then she changed her answer.

"Before. No, after! That way, I think there is less chance of harming the carpet with the seats."

"I think that's a good idea," the worker agreed.

Carrie walked over to lean against what was left of the bar and watched as the workers went about their task of converting the saloon into a lecture hall. She had suggested it as a possibility to Edward Steele, and he had agreed, even arranging the financing for her.

"I know I have a long way to go before I can convince the good townspeople that Holliday House is a place they can come to without shame," Carrie said, "but I am determined to do it."

A great deal had been done since Carrie started her renovations. The bar mirrors, liquor shelves, and gambling tables had been taken out. Most of the bar itself was gone, and soon, all of it would be. The walls had been repainted, and the room had been converted into a lecture hall.

Edward Steele had arranged the bank loan, which made the expensive conversion possible, and he had hired the workers to do the actual construction. Then, when Carrie contracted M. Jerome Clark to come and present a lecture to the people of Laramie, Steele printed and distributed the handbills for her.

Carrie was exceptionally pleased with the way her relationship with Steele was going. Any worries she may have had about him harboring some resentment over her not selling the hotel to him, were certainly dispelled by his actions.

"Well, well, well," a familiar, almost mocking voice said from the front door of the room. The voice interrupted Carrie's musings, and she looked toward him. "What have we here?"

The speaker was standing in the sunlight streaming through the door, and Carrie had to shield her eyes to see him. Then, as the door closed behind him, she saw why the voice was familiar. It was Rand Colby.

"Rand," she said. "What are you doing here?"

Rand walked into the room to look around at the work that was going on. Carrie noticed then that there was something different about him. The silks and fine clothes he had worn the last time she saw him were discarded, replaced by denim trousers and a cotton shirt, like those worn by so many of the men out here. She saw also, that he was wearing a pistol, and she couldn't help but recall her conversation with Edward Steele, when he told her of Rand's explosive temper and his skill with a gun.

"I came to apologize," Rand said, coming across the room.

"Apologize? Whatever for?" Carrie's voice was almost mocking.

"You know what for? I left you on the train without telling you. I think I owe you an explanation."

"You owe me nothing," Carrie said, flatly.

Rand stared at her for a moment. It was obvious by the tone of her voice that she was put out with him. And he realized, she had every right to be. He put his hands on his hips and looked around. "So, you are making good on your promise to close the saloon, are you?"

"Yes," Carrie said. "What do you think of it now? It is going to be a lecture hall."

"A lecture hall?"

"Yes," Carrie said. She walked over to a table to pick up a broadside, then she brought it back and handed it to Rand. "The famous M. Jerome Clark is coming next week. He is going to speak to us of his amazing adventures in Africa."

"I see," Rand said, looking at the poster. He rubbed his chin. "Where did you get the money for all this?" he asked.

"Mr. Steele arranged a loan."

"Steele arranged it, did he?"

"Yes. Oh, you were so wrong about him, Mr. Colby. I think Edward Steele is a fine man. He has been a big help to me ever since I arrived, and it's a good thing, too. Imagine the difficulty I would have had without him, especially as you saw fit to disappear just before I got to Laramie. I was left to shift for myself."

"Yes, I did do that and I'm sorry," Rand said, "but I had some business to attend to attend to."

"It doesn't matter."

The front door opened, and a bar of sunlight slashed anew, into the room. When the door closed, Carrie and Rand saw Edward Steele standing there.

"Well, Mr. Colby, have you come to see if Miss Holliday made it safely?" Edward asked. "As you can see, she arrived without harm, and she has begun to establish herself in Laramie. All, I might add, without you."

"I had some business to attend to," Rand said. "Not that I have to explain anything to you."

"Yes, the whole town knows that you brought in the men who robbed the Bamford train, three of them anyway. You killed the fourth one."

"You . . . you killed someone?" Carrie asked.

"I had no choice."

"You did leave her to cope with all this alone, however," Edward said, holding his arm out to take in the construction work.

"When I left the train, there was only a short distance remaining, and I knew there would be no difficulty. Anyway, I see you were certainly quick enough to fill the void," Rand said.

"It has been my pleasure to provide whatever assistance I could, yes," Edward said.

"Arranging loans, no doubt?"

"Yes."

"And just who countersigned the loans?"

"I did."

"And who stands to gain by default?"

"The bank, of course."

"I am thinking there may be a provision whereby you could assume ownership if you make the loan good?" Rand asked.

"As that is standard business procedure, yes," Edward said angrily. "Why are you trying to make it sound like it's something underhanded? Miss Holliday read the notes thoroughly before she signed anything. She's perfectly aware of that provision."

"Yes, I am," Carrie said. "There's nothing wrong with what Mr. Steele did. I took a course in school which explained how business loans were negotiated, and I know that is common practice."

"And did he also caution you that you're proceeding down a trail of folly? The way you're going now, your hotel is going to go broke."

"I did tell her that the saloon would be her biggest money-making operation," Edward said. "In fact, there has been no shortage of advice along that line, but she is a determined young woman with a great deal of courage, and I, for one, intend to see that she has every chance to prove herself."

"And every chance to go broke, leaving you in position to move in and pick up the pieces," Rand said.

"Oh, Rand, I'm sure that isn't true," Carrie said.

"You won't be able to change his opinion," Edward said. "Oh, by the way, I spoke with the editor of the newspaper, and he has agreed to do a story on the upcoming lecture."

"Wonderful, wonderful!" Carrie said, enthusiastically. "With ample publicity, we should have good attendance, don't you think so?"

"Yes, I'm sure of it," Edward said. "The newspaper and the posters will bring everyone in—from the city and also the surrounding area."

"Who is this M. Jerome Clark, anyway?" Rand asked.

"Oh, he is a marvelous man," Carrie said. "One of the ladies of my church, back in St. Louis, once heard him speak. She told me that both his subject and his delivery were fascinating. It will be a sterling beginning to our new endeavor. Of that, I am certain."

"What, exactly, do you hope to accomplish by all this?" Rand asked.

"I hope to win back the respect of the townspeople," Carrie said. "The Holliday House deserves that respect, and I intend to see that it gets it."

"It will do you little good to gain the respect of the townspeople, if you are going to lose the hotel to this shyster."

"I wish you two could be friends," Carrie said. "I find myself in a most uncomfortable position to be in the middle of you two."

"You'll have to try and ignore Mr. Colby's lack of understanding," Edward said.

"Do you really think I won't make it with the hotel?" Carrie asked Rand.

"I'm afraid not."

"Maybe I could if I had a dependable business manager," Carrie suggested. "I confess, I know absolutely nothing about running a hotel, or any other business, for that matter."

"I can believe that!" Rand said. "You've practically guaranteed your failure by everything you've done so far."

"Would you manage the hotel for me?" Carrie asked.

"Me?" Rand replied, surprised by the sudden and unexpected request.

"Yes," Carrie said. "I think you would make a wonderful manager."

Rand held up his hand and smiled. "Uh, thank you, no," he said. "I've got a job. I'm a railroad detective. You're just going to have to get someone else."

"But ... I was counting on you," Carrie said.

"I'm sorry," Rand replied. "I didn't give you any cause to think that I wanted to get involved with your business. You came up with that on your own."

"Yes, I did," Carrie admitted. "But I never thought—that is, I didn't dream you would turn me down."

"Carrie, look," Rand said, and now his voice wasn't challenging, but rather it was apologetic. "I can't run your hotel for you. I've got other things to do . . . important things, and until I've finished with them, I can't take on any other responsibilities. None, do you understand?"

"No," Carrie said. "What is it you have to do?"

"I'm fulfilling a pledge," Rand said. He sighed. "I know you don't understand, and even if I tried to explain it to you now, you wouldn't understand. But it is something that I must do."

"Go ahead," Carrie said. "Whatever it is that you find so important, you just do. I should have known better than to ask you in the first place. My experience with you has not shown you to be very trustworthy, anyway."

"I'm sorry," Rand said again, and with a sad smile, he turned and left.

Carrie watched him step back into the sun.

"Not to worry, Carrie," Steele said, using her first name easily. "I'll provide you with all the help you will need, and you can run the hotel on your own. Lots of women are getting involved in businesses these days, and I know you are as capable as any of them."

"Thanks," Carrie said, still staring at the door through which Rand had passed. It was very clear to her now that Rand Colby would not be available to help her in any way.

14

The Holliday House is a hotel which, during the days of rail-road construction, played host to many of this nation's richest and most powerful men. When the railroad building boom ended and the financiers and promoters returned to their headquarters in New York and San Francisco, the Holliday House, as so many other fine hotels, ran into difficulty. The emigrants and other passengers on today's trains cannot afford the luxuries offered by the Holliday House. Therefore, the Holliday House, owned by the late Charles Holliday, turned to other means to make ends meet. Gambling and drinking became one of those means, and the traffic in debauchery still another.

It was into this wicked den of vice, that Miss Carrie Holliday, late of St. Louis, was thrust when, upon the demise of her uncle, she inherited the Holliday House. To the chagrin and everlasting shame of this poor woman she came to Laramie, not to a genteel hotel, but a full-fledged brothel. But, alas, the power of goodness over evil can never be slighted, and thus it is with the most noble of purposes, that the Holliday House has been cleansed of its sin of flesh and spirit, and revitalized with a new purpose. Miss Holliday has vowed by all that's holy, to thrust the Holliday House back into the fore as a hotel of repute. The wanton fleshpots have been driven from its confines, alcohol and gambling have been abolished, and on Friday next, the good citizens of this fair city will be privileged to take receipt of a speech delivered by the well-known Dr. M. Jerome Clark, explorer and scientist.

The lecture was scheduled to begin in just five more minutes, and the lecture room was crowded with people. Carrie stood in the corner of the room and watched them as they took their seats. She was exceptionally pleased that so many of them were women.

"Miss Holliday," someone called, and Carrie turned to see Morton Forsythe standing there, smiling at her. At first, she almost didn't recognize him, because he was scrubbed so clean that his skin was pink. He was wearing homespun, though very clean clothes.

"Morton!" Carrie said. "How wonderful to see you again. But I thought you were going to call me Carrie. Didn't we agree on that?"

Morton blushed and looked toward the floor. "Yes'm," he said, "but my mom says you are a fine lady, 'n I got no business callin' you by your Christian name." He put his hand out toward a lady who was standing just behind him. She was of an indeterminate age, with hair the color and texture of dried straw. She was wearing a shapeless, much-patched dress. "This is my mom," Morton said.

"I'm very pleased to meet you, Mrs. Forsythe," Carrie said graciously.

"Miss Holliday, I want you to know what a fine thing I think you are doin' here," Morton's mother said.

"Why, I thank you for that," Carrie said. "I really do."

"And if you ever have anythin' for Morton to do in your hotel, why, he has my blessin' to do it."

"Thanks again," Carrie said. Morton's mother turned to find her seat, and Carrie looked at Morton and smiled broadly, and she mouthed the word, "Morton?"

"Just you and my mom," Morton said in embarrassment. "You two are the onliest ones that call me that."

At the front of the room the mayor of the town stood up and cleared his throat, then held out his hands calling for attention. The excited buzz of the audience died down, and the mayor was able to speak.

"Ladies and gents," he said. "On behalf of Miss Holliday, I want to welcome all of you to the Holliday House meetin' hall."

There was a smattering of applause.

The mayor looked at Carrie. "And, Miss Holliday, on behalf of the town, I want to welcome you to Laramie, and thank you for this fine hall."

This time the applause was even more generous, and Carrie beamed with pride.

"Now tonight, the first speaker to grace our new hall is a dandy."

The audience laughed.

"I'm proud to introduce the famous Dr. M. Jerome Clark."

After the welcoming applause, Dr. Clark walked to the podium, looked over the audience, then began his lecture. Carrie moved around quietly, observing the audience's reaction to the speaker. She was so concerned that she didn't hear a word Dr. Clark had to say, but when it was over, and the audience applauded grandly, she joined in the applause. Carrie was not applauding so much for the speaker, as for the fact that the evening appeared to be an unqualified success.

Carrie stood in the doorway after the lecture was over and said goodbye to everyone as they were leaving. Nearly everyone congratulated her, not only on the fine program, but on the fine thing she was doing for the town. She received half a dozen invitations to attend teas, and one invitation to join a local garden club.

When the last guest had departed, Carrie left the hall and went, tired, but happy, up to her apartment where she intended to take a nice cooling bath.

The nicest thing about her apartment, Carrie thought as she opened the door, was that she had her own bathtub and didn't have to go to the public room at the end of the hall.

"It went very well tonight," a man's voice said as she stepped inside.

Carrie gasped when she saw Edward Steele sitting quietly, on a chair in her bedroom.

"Mr. Steele!" she said, startled. "What are you doing here? How did you get in?"

"I have a key," Edward said easily, smiling at her and displaying the key. "I have a key for every room in this building."

"You . . . you have no right to be in here," Carrie said.

"I'm sorry," Edward said. "I really didn't want to upset you. It's just that, I know you missed your dinner tonight, since you were so nervous about the lecture, and I thought you might wish to eat in here."

"In here?"

"Look," Edward said, pointing toward the sitting room of Carrie's apartment.

Carrie walked over to the door and saw a table, set

with silver-covered dishes. An ice-bucket was in the center of the table, and a bottle of champagne was chilling in the ice bucket.

"Oh, it's beautiful," Carrie said.

AS THE TRAIN rounded the long curve, Rand could look through the window and see it, all the way up to the engine. Beyond the great drive wheels, the feathers of steam and the boiling smoke, he could see the grandeur of the mountains, a placid lake, and a canopy of fir trees, which made the most ambitious Currier and Ives print pale by comparison.

"Oh," the young woman in the seat in front of him said. "Oh, Ollie, have you ever seen anything more beautiful?"

Carrie had been impressed with the scenery too. He had enjoyed showing it to her and seeing it through her eyes.

He had felt bad about abandoning her when he left her on the train, and now, he had abandoned her again. But he had no choice. Cox had given him a lead on Campbell. He said that he had heard Ely Slack say that Campbell was in Walcott, and that was where he was going.

"Mr. Colby?" The conductor leaned over and touched the shoulder of the man who was staring, intently at the passing countryside. "Mr. Colby?" he said again.

The conductor's summons brought Rand back to the present, and he turned away from the window. The crowded depot platform, the celebrating crowd, the laughter and the music fell away quickly, to be replaced by the swaying, clicking sound of the train.

"Are you Rand Colby, sir?" the conductor asked.

"Yes," Rand replied.

"I was asked to give you this note," the conductor said, handing a piece of paper to Rand.

"Thanks," Rand said. He opened the paper.

Rand,
    Meet me in the baggage car.
    Matt

Rand smiled, then got up and walked forward through the train until he reached the baggage car. The door was locked, but he knocked on it, and after a moment it opened.

The baggage car also served as the mail car. Two postal clerks were working industriously, up front sorting the packages and mail into the proper bags for pickup along the route. Suitcases and bundles were piled up along the sides, and, at the open door, a man sat on a chair, enjoying the breeze and the view. He greeted Rand as he stepped inside the car.

"Rand, m'boy," he said.

"Matt," Rand acknowledged, sticking his hand out to clasp Matt's. "I know, now, why you became a railroad detective. It's because you like to ride trains. Last time we met, you were on a train."

Matt held up his right hand as if pulling on a cord. "Woo, woo," he said, laughing. "You're still on the train, too. Seems to me like you like ridin' 'em as much as I do."

"Yeah, well, I got a lead on Campbell, and I'm going to check it out."

"Where is he?"

"He's in Walcott."

"Yeah, well, if you do run into him, you be damn

careful. From what we've learned, Nate Campbell isn't going to be that easy to bring in."

"Maybe he'll try something, and make it easy for me," Rand suggested with a smile. "Say, Matt, last time we met, I asked if you could find out something about Edward Steele."

"I don't know what you've got against him, but everything the agency has managed to find on him checks out," Matt said. "He went to Harvard University, graduated with honors, fought honorably in the Civil War, wrote a paper for the American Law Journal in sixty-nine on interstate contracts, and has been a model citizen ever since."

"I don't know," Rand said. "I just don't like the son-of-a-bitch."

Matt laughed. "Laddie, it's been my experience that a dislike for a person, with no apparent reason, is generally tied into a lassie. Is there a girl involved? The one you went to St. Louis to get? Would he be makin' time with your girl, now?"

"I—" Rand started, then he stopped. "It has to be more than that, Matt," he said. "It just has to be. I tell you, this guy is no good."

"Maybe so," Matt said. He smiled. "And maybe you're seein' a bit o' green, 'n I'm not talkin' about the holy shamrock."

"That's what I like about you, Matt," Rand said with a wry smile. "You are full of support."

WALCOTT WAS A FORMER HELL-ON-WHEELS, an End-of-Track community which had sprung up during the time the railroad was being built. It was an unusual town because it didn't die as so many other End-of-Track villages did, but neither did it take root and grow into a successful city. It looked today much as it looked during its heyday as a Hell-on-Wheels, and it served much the same function, in that it had little to offer other than saloons, gambling houses, bad cafes, and prostitutes.

Rand walked down the street from the depot toward the most substantial looking saloon in a row of saloons. A drunk was passed out on the steps in front and Rand had to step over him in order to go inside.

The inside was dingy. The only light there came either through the door or filtered in through the dirty windows. It smelled of whiskey and stale beer and sour tobacco. There was a long bar on the left, with dirty towels hanging on hooks about every five feet, along the front of the bar. A large mirror was behind it, but like everything else about the saloon, it was so dirty that one could scarcely see any images in it, and what could be seen was distorted by imperfections in the glass.

Eight or ten tables were scattered about, with more than half of them occupied. A few card games were in progress, but most of the patrons were just drinking and talking. Half a dozen bar girls flitted around from table to table; here, wangling a drink, there, making arrangements to sell more of their services.

The bartender was pouring the residue from whiskey glasses back into a bottle. He pulled a soggy cigar butt, from one glass, laid it aside, then poured the whiskey back into the bottle without qualms. Rand stepped up to the bar.

"Yeah?" the bartender said.

"Beer," Rand said.

The bartender picked up a mug from the bar and started for the barrel.

"A clean mug," Rand said.

The bartender took a mug from under the bar and let Rand examine it before he drew the beer.

"I'm looking for someone," Rand said.

"Does this look like a lost and found?" the bartender answered sarcastically.

"I thought perhaps, as a friendly gesture," Rand said, "that you might help two old friends get together."

"Who are you looking for?"

"Nate Campbell."

"Nate Campbell ain't got no friends," the bartender said.

Rand took note that the bartender had acknowledged the name.

"Then he is here?"

"I didn't say that," the bartender replied, but even as he spoke, his eyes darted nervously toward the head of the stairs.

"Thanks," Rand said. "What do I owe you for the beer?"

"One dollar."

"Expensive beer."

"Yeah," the bartender said. "Well, I don't sell information, you understand, so I gotta make it up some other way."

Rand put a silver dollar on the bar, then moved toward the stairs.

As Rand started up the stairs, the conversation behind him died. Everyone stopped their gambling, drinking, and flirting with the women, to watch the drama that was about to unfold.

It's funny, Rand thought. No one said a word about why he wanted to see Campbell. His exchange with the bartender had been so quiet that he was certain it couldn't have been overheard by anyone else, and yet, everyone knew. They knew, and they were ready, almost anxious it seemed, to watch a life and death drama be played out.

The saloon waited, and as Rand reached the top of the stairs, he heard sounds from inside the room. The squeaking of bedsprings, the quiet, urgent moans of a woman in passion, and the sharp, animal grunts of a man.

Rand stood outside the room for just a moment, then kicked the door open and rushed in.

The woman screamed and jumped up from the bed. She ran out onto the landing.

"What the hell?" Campbell shouted, and he reached toward the bed post where his pistol was hanging.

Rand kicked the holster off the bed and the pistol clattered to the floor. He kicked it again, and it sailed through the door, across the narrow landing, and down into the saloon below.

"Get up," Rand said.

"Who are you?" Campbell asked. "What do you want?"

"I'll ask the questions," Rand replied. He cocked his pistol and the metallic sound of the turning cylinder clicked loudly. "Get up and get some clothes on."

"What about me, Mister?" the woman asked from the landing.

"Come on in, I have no business with you," Rand said. He stepped aside to let the woman back in, and she moved quickly over to the other side of the room where her clothes were.

"I've heard of knocking before you come into a room," the woman said easily. "But this is ridiculous."

Rand smiled. "I'm glad to see you're keeping your

sense of humor," he said. "I want to apologize for that, but I figured it would save a killing."

"Yeah?" Whose killing?" Campbell grumbled, as he dressed.

"What difference does it make?" Rand asked. "I don't want either one of us dead. I want you healthy, for your hanging."

"My hang—are you the law?"

"Let's say I'm a concerned citizen."

"Yeah? Well I ain't never seen no concerned citizen takin' a chance like that," he said.

"It depends on how concerned he is," Rand said.

Campbell' eyes suddenly narrowed as he studied Rand's face. "I know you," he said. "Your name is Colby, ain't it?"

"Right you are," Rand said. "Now, I want another name from you."

"You ain't getting' nothin' from me, Mister," Campbell said in a growling tone.

"Very well," Rand replied. "Suit yourself. But you're going to be awfully lonesome up there on that scaffold, all by yourself."

"Yeah?" Well, you ain't got that rope aroun' my neck yet," Campbell said.

"Let's go," Rand said, making a waving motion with the barrel of his gun.

Campbell walked out the door with his hands up, then along the landing, and finally down the stairs. Everyone downstairs was on their feet watching the action. Now they felt as if they were being cheated by the fact that Campbell was apparently going without resistance—there would be no fight.

Just as Rand reached the top of the stairs, ready to

follow Campbell down, an angry voice called to him. "You ain't takin' him nowhere, Mister!"

Rand turned toward the sound and saw a man standing in the doorway of the room at the end of the hall. The man was brandishing a double-barrel shotgun, and Rand saw him thumb back the hammers.

Rand leaped over the railing without a second thought, just as the gun went off. He heard the roar and could even feel the shock wave, though the shot from the gun missed him, and tore away a section of the banister, where he had been standing.

Rand landed on a table, and when the table broke, he was tossed to the floor. He rolled over onto his back and looked up, just as his assailant ran to the railing to fire the second barrel. Rand's gun roared, and the man dropped the shotgun, and clutching his chest, tumbled forward, breaking through the railing and crashing to the floor, following his gun down.

Rand swung his gun back toward Campbell, who was still standing on the stairs. Campbell put his hands up high and backed against the wall.

"Bishop!" he shouted. "Jay Bishop."

Rand got up, and dusted himself off, walking toward Campbell.

"Don't shoot!" Campbell pleaded. "I gave you the name. It's Jay Bishop!"

"Who?" Rand asked. "This fella?" he pointed to the man he had just shot.

"No," Campbell said. "That was my partner. I don't even know his real name. We just teamed up a couple of weeks ago." Campbell looked over at the body. "He called himself Blackie. He would have made me pay for bustin' me loose, he didn't do it out of friendship."

"Yeah," Rand said. "I heard you didn't have any friends. Jay Bishop isn't a friend, either, I suppose."

"Naw," Campbell said. "Why should that son-of-a-bitch get off scot-free when you've already got the rest of us. He's the one you want. He's the one who shot the teller, 'n he's the one who did the shootin' outside the bank."

"Where is he?" Rand asked.

"I don't know," Campbell said. "We split up right after the bank job, and we never saw him again."

"He was the only one of you to wear a mask," Rand said. "None of the witnesses have a description of him. What does he look like?"

"I don't know that, either," Campbell said. "Honest," he put in quickly when he saw the expression of disbelief on Rand's face. "Bishop always wore a mask—even when he was around us. We used to tease him about it, but he never let us see his face."

"Let's go," Rand said. "You're going to keep the sheriff company for a while."

In a move that was totally unexpected, Campbell leaped over the bar, then came back up with the bartender's hide-away shotgun in his hands. He swung the gun toward Rand, but Rand shot him before Campbell could pull the trigger.

Rand hurried toward the bar.

"Ain't no need to be checkin' on 'im," the bartender said. "You hit 'im right twixt the eyes."

Now there was only one left, Rand realized. And he had a name. Jay Bishop.

15

The trees and hills around Laramie turned gold, then fire-red as the colors of fall dazzled the eyes. As the fall wore on, the days grew shorter and colder, and then the late fall rains stripped away the leaves, leaving them in sodden piles, and baring the tree limbs. By winter, the bare tree limbs were rattling drily in the cold north winds.

The town of Laramie lay under a constant haze of wood smoke as the stores, houses, and hotels kept fireplaces and woodstoves roaring against the cold. The smell of wood smoke was everywhere. At first it was rather pleasant, but eventually it began to wear, hanging as it did in clothes, curtains, furniture, and every nook and cranny of daily life.

It had been five months since Carrie's arrival in Laramie. During those five months she had seen the earnings of The Holliday House steadily decline. Every month, in order to meet the loan payments, she had found it necessary to mortgage more and more of the hotel.

"Things will pick up in the summer," Edward told her. "Then the westward migration begins anew, and of course, there will be the hunting trips and holidays of the wealthy. They enjoy coming west, and they always stay at the best hotels and pay the best prices."

"I fear that we may not have a hotel for them when that time arrives," Carrie said.

"Trust me," Edward said.

"I do trust you," Carrie replied.

Carrie had no other choice, but to trust Edward Steele. She had irrevocably placed herself in his hands when she allowed him to negotiate the first loan for her. As time went on, she found herself more and more dependent upon him for everything. It was not a situation she enjoyed, for indeed, she had come west in the first place, seeking to gain a measure of independence. Instead, she found that just the opposite was the case.

Carrie saw Rand Colby only once during that entire period, and then for a few brief moments when he came to take a meal in the Holliday House Restaurant. She had sat at the table with him, and attempted to engage him in conversation, but he seemed preoccupied. Later, she heard that he had killed a man in a gunfight that week, and she began to wonder if Edward's description of him as a man who attracted violence, couldn't be correct.

It was on the morning of the first snow of the new winter, that she saw him again. He came into the lobby and hung his hat and coat on the hall tree. There was a crust of snow on his boots, but he stamped them off on the rug placed there, just for that purpose.

"Hello," Rand said, smiling, as he walked over to the registration counter. He looked around the hotel. "I see you are still in business."

"Yes," Carrie replied. "I'm sorry to disappoint you."

"Disappoint me?"

"You predicted my immediate failure," Carrie said. "Now, it seems I am making a liar of you."

Rand smiled easily. "It's one time I don't mind being wrong," he said. "I don't know what ever gave you the idea that I would want you to fail."

"You certainly seemed to give that impression," Carrie said. "You weren't around when I needed you."

"Carrie, you didn't need me, and you certainly didn't need Edward Steele. You are a strong, intelligent woman, and you are perfectly capable of managing your own affairs. I just felt you should have that chance, that's all."

"Yes, well, I'm doing quite nicely, thank you," Carrie said.

"I'm glad to hear that," Rand said. "But I hope you aren't doing so well that you don't have a room available. I'd like one for a short while."

Carrie smiled as she turned the book toward him. "Would you sign the guest book, please?"

Rand looked at the book and at the date above. Then he started looking back through the book and discovered that the hotel had accommodated only four paying guests in the last three weeks.

"You're doing quite nicely, are you?" he said.

"That . . . that's private business records," Carrie said, and she quickly turned the book away from him.

"Carrie," he said quietly. "It isn't going well, is it? It isn't going well at all."

"No," Carrie admitted with a sigh. "Oh, Rand, I . . . nothing is going right. I had hoped that people would rent the community room for meetings, but no one has. I thought if I would hire entertainers, people would buy tickets to attend, but I haven't even made enough money to pay the people I hired. And the restaurant, so few people use it that I've had to let all my help go. Now there is just Polly and me. Hal quit and went to work at the Bloody Bucket, and I can't blame him. In fact, I'm grateful to him, because now, at least, I don't have to pay his salary."

"What about Edward Steele?" Rand asked. "Isn't he doing anything to help you?"

"Oh, yes," Carrie said. "In fact, he is the only bright spot. He's managed to come up with loans in order to keep me going."

"Loans?" Rand asked. "On the hotel?"

"Yes, of course," Carrie said. "That's all the collateral I have."

"Carrie, don't you see what he's doing? He's getting you deeper and deeper in debt, then he can move in and take the hotel over, anytime he wants."

"Why would he want it?" Carrie asked. "If it isn't making money for me, it won't make money for him."

"It was making money when Charley ran it," Rand said. "The saloon and the gambling were making plenty of money."

"That's no good either, anymore," Carrie said. "I confess, Rand, I may have been wrong about the saloon. I mentioned it to Edward, though, and he said that we would probably not get the business back. He advised me to stick by my guns."

"And you listened to him?"

"Of course," Carrie said. "After all, he is my lawyer."

"Of course," Rand said. "I just hope you see through him before it's too late. Anyway, it's your decision to make, and anything I say would be prejudiced because I admit that I don't like him."

Carrie smiled. "I did get that impression," she said. "Here's your key."

"Would it be possible to take a bath?" Rand asked. "Have you any warm water?"

"I can have Polly heat some for you," Carrie said.

"Thanks," Rand said. He took the key, then started for the stairs. He stopped and looked back toward Carrie. "Will you be here for dinner?"

"I have to be," Carrie said. "I cook it."

"Then I shall see you for dinner," Rand said.

Rand checked into his room, then walked over to the window and looked out over the town. It was covered with a blanket of snow, and though there were hoof and footprints along the streets of the town, the area on the outskirts was an undisturbed pristine white.

Rand had spent the last six weeks on a wild goose chase. He had heard that a man named Jay Bishop was arrested in Phoenix. But when he went to Phoenix to meet him, it turned out that the man was only using the name, Bishop, and it was one of a half-dozen aliases he had used in his life. He had also been in the Arizona territorial prison during the time of the bank robbery in Rushville, so he couldn't have been the Bishop, Rand was looking for.

By the time Rand returned to Laramie, summer and even fall had gone, and winter had already set its mark on the town.

Rand had made no effort to contact Carrie during the time he was gone. He had thought of her, quite often in fact. But every time he thought of her, he tried, with a conscious effort, to put her out of his mind.

There was a quiet knock at his door, and Rand walked over to open it. Polly was standing there, holding a towel and a bar of soap.

"Miss Holliday said you wanted a bath?"

"Oh, yes," Rand said, smiling happily.

"I've heated your water."

"Thank you," Rand said. He took the soap and towel from her. "Tell me, Polly, are you enjoying working for Carrie?"

"Oh, yes," Polly said. "Very much. I just wish—" she let the sentence hang.

"You just wish what?"

"I wish she didn't let Edward Steele make all the decisions. I don't trust him."

"You and me both," Rand said.

"Of course, when you're as close as the two of them are, then there's no way of seeing the forest for the trees, I reckon."

"Close? What do you mean, close?"

"Close. . ." Polly said. "You know what I mean."

They had been walking toward the bathroom, and Rand stopped in his tracks.

"How close?"

Polly looked at Rand with an expression of anguish on her face.

"Oh, Mr. Colby, I'm sorry," she said. "I. . . I thought you knew. It's common knowledge around town. Everyone knows about it."

"No," Rand said. "I didn't know." He handed the soap and towel to Polly. "I don't suppose I'll be needing this, after all."

"Mr. Colby, where are you going?" Polly asked. "What are you going to do?"

Polly's question remained unanswered, as Rand hurried down the stairs. He grabbed his hat and coat from the hall tree, and rushed out into the snow, slamming the door behind him.

Carrie didn't see him leave nor did she hear the door close, because she was, at that moment, in the kitchen. In the oven, a small ham turned golden brown under its glaze of cherries and brown sugar, while at a work table, Carrie hummed a happy little tune and rolled out pie dough for the crust of an apple pie.

THE BUCKET OF BLOOD saloon had two potbelly stoves roaring and crackling and glowing red. Most of those who were gathered in the saloon were congregated around one of the two stoves, so that there were two distinct groups. Winnie's girls were working one of the groups, so Rand chose the other, until he saw that Edward Steele was there, drinking a beer and talking with a group of men.

"Well, Rand Colby," Edward said, as he saw Rand approaching. "News of your exploits has preceded you. Join us and regale us with stories of your prowess with the gun."

Rand stopped short. As he looked at Edward Steele, Polly's words came back to him, and he could see Edward and Carrie together. The thought made him so angry that a blood vein in his temple stood out and began to pulse. Without a word, Rand turned, and walked over to the other stove, to join those who were there.

"Well, well, well," Winnie said, smiling at Rand as he came over to sit with them. "Mr. Colby, how nice to see you."

Rand signaled to Hal, and when Hal brought a bottle and a glass, Rand had him leave the bottle.

Edward Steele left his stove and came over to speak to Rand.

"Are you really being unsociable, Mr. Colby?" Edward asked. "Is it my imagination that you spurned my invitation to join us? Or do you really dislike me that much?"

"I really dislike you that much," Rand said, taking a drink of whiskey.

"Yes, very well, I was afraid that was the case. I really do not see why Carrie has such a blind spot, where you're concerned. I've tried to tell her, time and again, that you're no good. But, for some reason, she rather likes you, and as our own relationship has progressed as far as it has, then I felt a duty of sorts to try and find some way you and I could get along."

"Don't waste your time," Rand said in a low, menacing voice. "Because such a way does not exist."

"Oh? But don't we owe it to Carrie to at least try? I'll tell you what," Edward said, with the superior cheerfulness of one who knew that he was enjoying the favored position in this discussion. "Suppose I take it on myself to invite you to have dinner with us tonight. I had not planned on eating at the hotel myself, but I'm positive that Carrie would love to have you join us, so I'll make a point to be there."

"No, thank you," Rand said icily. He took another long, Adam's-apple bobbing swallow of the whiskey, feeling the fire of it as it went down, wrapping himself around it, and hoping that its numbing effect would soon take hold.

"No? Well, 'tis a pity," Edward said. He turned to leave, then stopped and looked back at Rand. "Do enjoy your drink, old man, won't you?"

Edward laughed cruelly, then, with a farewell wave to those at the other stove, he left the saloon, and stepped out into the blinding white snow. Rand watched him leave with a fury inside, which was as cold as the blanket of snow outside. He took another long drink of whiskey and felt, with gratitude, its heat beginning to push away the coldness around his heart.

This was one moment when Carrie appreciated the fact that she had no business. The restaurant was completely empty—there were no guests in the hotel other than Rand Colby, and of course, Edward Steele, who maintained a permanent apartment there. That meant that the dinner she had planned for Rand would be private, especially as Edward had indicated that he would not be eating in tonight.

Carrie had taken great pains to set the table just so, with the finest China, silver, and crystal she could find. After the dinner was prepared and the table laid, she hurried up for a quick bath and change of clothes, so that now, as she waited, she knew that she and the table would have to make as pretty a picture as Rand had seen lately.

Carrie lit the two slender tapers, then as the tiny golden points of flame glowed over the table, she stepped back to enjoy the view. Yes, she thought. Rand Colby would be pleased.

"Oh, my dear, how nice," a voice suddenly said, and startled by the sudden intrusion into her thoughts, Carrie looked around.

"Edward? What are you doing here?"

"I changed my mind," Edward said. "I thought I would take my dinner in the restaurant, after all. But, I see that you were expecting me. How lovely the table looks. How lovely you look."

"But, I—" Carrie started, weakly.

"Or, am I mistaken?" Edward asked his voice still as soft as silk, but now with a keen razor's edge to it. "Have you prepared this fine dinner for someone else?"

"We do have a guest tonight," Carrie said.

"Yes, of course we do," Edward said. "I had nearly forgotten. We must be especially nice to our paying guests, mustn't we? But, I spoke with Mr. Colby a moment ago, and I invited him to dine with us. I regret to say, my dear that he declined."

"He declined? You mean he won't be eating here?"

"No, I'm afraid not," Edward said. "He's tied up with Winnie's girls, I believe. But then, now that you are no longer the innocent, I'm certain you can understand that a man who has been on the trail for a while has certain needs when he returns." Edward gave a ribald chuckle. "Those needs are not necessarily for food."

16

POLLY HAD STARTED DOWN TO THE KITCHEN, SHORTLY after she let it slip to Rand about Carrie and Edward Steele. She wanted to apologize to Carrie and tell her that Rand now knew. When she got downstairs, however, she saw that Carrie was having dinner with Edward Steele. She didn't want to talk with them, or even be seen by them, so she left the hotel and walked down to the Bucket of Blood where Hal now worked.

"Hello, Polly," Hal said. "Is anything wrong?"

"Anything wrong? Why do you ask?"

"What I mean is are you still working at the Holliday House? It's no secret that Carrie is having a hard time with it."

"Yes, she is, but I'm still working there."

"What are you doing here?"

Polly smiled. "I thought we were old friends, Hal. Can't I come visit an old friend?"

Hal returned the smile. "Sure you can, and I'll even give you a drink on me."

"Thanks, Hal. We miss you down at the Holliday House."

"I'll be back when the business picks up again," Hal said.

Polly took her drink, then looking around saw Rand. She had hoped he would be here.

Hal saw where she was looking. "He's been here for nearly an hour," Hal said. "He hasn't spoken a word to anyone, he's just sat there, drinking."

Taking her drink with her, Polly walked over to the table.

"May I join you," she asked, even as she was sitting down.

"It looks like you just did," Rand replied in a voice that was equally devoid of rejection or invitation.

"You shouldn't have left. Carrie had fixed a dinner just for you, but you left, and now she's sharing it with Edward Steele."

"Carrie doesn't understand," Rand said. "I thought she would, but she just doesn't understand."

"Understand what?" Polly asked.

"Understand," Rand repeated, without explanation.

"Would you like to come back to the Holliday House with me?" Polly invited. "We can talk."

"I don't want to see Carrie just now."

"You won't have to. We'll go to my room."

Rand stood. "Let's go," he said.

ONCE THEY REACHED POLLY'S room, Rand began to talk. As he spoke, it was obvious to Polly that this was something he needed to talk about. Though she didn't understand the term catharsis, she understood the principle, so she was quiet as he spoke the words that needed to be spoken.

"She died on the very day she arrived in town. All she wanted was the opportunity to live a normal life, to marry and have kids. It wasn't too much to ask for, was it? But it was taken from her by four animals whose greed and lust for blood ran unchecked. I vowed, that very day, that I would see all of them brought to justice."

"And have you?" Polly knew that Rand was talking about the bank robbery in Rushville.

"I've found three of them," Rand said. "Two of them are dead and one of them is behind bars."

"So, you've caught all of them but one?" Polly said.

"Yes, all but one."

Rand walked over to the window to look outside. The moon was shining brightly, and he could see quite clearly. He saw the sheriff's deputy making his rounds, checking windows and doors. In town, there were patches of gold on the snow, reflecting from the windows of the houses and buildings.

"The man I am looking for now, is named Jay Bishop." Rand turned away from the window and looked at Polly, who was sitting on her bed behind him. "Have you ever heard of him?"

"No," Polly said. "I'm afraid I haven't. I'm sorry."

"Until I find him," Rand said, "I can never be free of the vow."

"What vow?"

"The vow that I can never love another woman until I have found justice for Nora."

"And you won't find justice until you find this Bishop person?" Polly asked.

"No, not until I find him."

"What if you never find him?"

"Then I shall be bound by my vow until freed by death," Rand said.

"Rand, if that's the way you feel, you can't blame Carrie if, in her confusion, she takes comfort from another."

"I know that," Rand said miserably. He walked back to Polly's bed and sat on it, holding his head in his hands. "It's just that the thought of Carrie and Edward Steele is almost more than I can stand." He lay back on Polly's bed, his head was beginning to spin. "Whew," he said. "I think the liquor is finally taking hold. I'm feeling dizzy."

"Just rest," Polly said. She leaned over him then and began to massage his temples and forehead with long, cool fingers.

"Uhmm," Rand said. "That feels good."

WHEN THE DOOR popped open in Rand's room, it was like an explosion going off in his head. He opened his eyes wondering what was happening, only to see Sheriff Kelly and both of his deputies standing at the foot of his bed, all with drawn pistols pointed right at him. He started to sit up.

"Make one move without me tellin' you, 'n you're a dead man!" the sheriff said. He cocked his pistol, and Rand could see the cylinder rotate.

"What is this?" Rand asked. "Sheriff Kelly, what's going on? Why are you in my room?"

"I never thought you would do something like this," Sheriff Kelly said.

"Something like what? Sheriff Kelly, what is it you think I did?"

"I'll ask the questions around here," Sheriff Kelly said. "Why did you kill Polly?"

"What?" Rand asked, the word exploding from his lips. "What are you talking about?"

"You were seen with her last night," Sheriff Kelly said. "You were seen in her room."

"Yeah, I was makin' my rounds," Deputy Milner said. "And I seen you peekin' through her window."

"And this mornin', she was found dead," Sheriff Kelly added. "Murdered."

"Murdered! And you think I had something to do with it? This is crazy," Rand said. He started to get out of bed.

"I said stay there!" the sheriff said, and he punctuated his statement by bringing his gun barrel down sharply over Rand's head.

The next time Rand awakened, he was in a cell. His head was aching, both from the blow from the sheriff's gun, and from the prodigious amount of whiskey he had drunk the night before.

He groaned and tried to sit up, but his head ached so that he had to lie back down. It was several moments before he was able to sit up, then he sat on the edge of the bed until the pounding in his head had subsided to a dull throb.

"Well, you 'bout ready to talk now?" Sheriff Kelly asked.

"Could I have some water?" Rand asked.

"Don't know as you deserve any," the sheriff said. "Anyone that'd do what you done to that poor girl, ain't got no right to be treated like a human." Despite his remarks, he handed a tin cup of water through the bars to Rand.

"What happened to Polly?" Rand asked, as he took the water.

"You tell me," the sheriff replied.

Rand drank the water thirstily, then handed the cup back to the sheriff. "I saw her last night," he said. "But when I left her, she was alive and safe in her room."

"In her room?"

"Yes," Rand said. "Why?"

"It's interestin' that you would make the distinction about her bein' in her room," the sheriff said.

"Why should I try to hide the fact that I was in her room?" Rand asked. "I was there. Besides, Milner said he saw me there."

"Yeah," the sheriff said. "But you see, she wasn't found in her room. She was found in the stable, nekkid 'n strangled. Besides that, her body had bruises all over it, liken as if she had been beat."

Rand winced. "My God," he said, "what a terrible thing to happen to her."

"Yeah," the sheriff, said. "So, you can see why the town is so hot about it. I tell you the truth, Mister, I got all I can do to keep a lynch mob away from you." Sheriff Kelly turned away in disgust, and Rand lay back down and thought of the young girl who was so alive last night, and he felt more sorrow than he had felt at any time since Nora had been killed.

17

"MISS HOLLIDAY?" MORTON CALLED THROUGH THE DOOR, which led into the kitchen. Carrie was in the kitchen, making a pot of coffee. She turned at Morton's voice, and smiled at him, though Morton could see that she had been crying.

"You been cryin' ain't ya?" he asked.

"Yes," Carrie answered.

"Was Polly your friend?"

"She was very much my friend," Carrie said. She took a cup down. "Do you drink coffee, Morton?"

"Yes'm," Morton said. He watched as Carrie poured the steaming black liquid into the cup, then handed it to him.

"Miss Holliday?"

"Yes?"

"Rand Colby didn't kill her."

"Oh, Morton," Carrie said. She put her hand on his and squeezed it. "I wish I could believe that. You don't know how much I wish I could believe that."

"You can believe it," Morton said. He took a drink of

his coffee. "I know who killed her."

"You know? How do you know?"

"I seen it," he said. "That is, I seen it after it had already happened. I seen the man that killed her drag her body to the livery stable."

"Morton, are you certain?"

"Yes'm," Morton said. "You see, I had a job cleanin' out the livery, 'n I got tired and lay down in the straw to take a little nap. I slept longer'n I intended, and when I woke up, I seen someone draggin' somethin'. It was dark 'n I couldn't see too good, until he moved by the open door, then the moon 'n the snow made it bright enough I could see who it was. It was Gilbert Donohoe and he was draggin' poor Polly's body."

"Morton, why didn't you go to the sheriff with this?" Carrie asked.

"I was afraid the sheriff wouldn't believe me," Morton said. "Besides, I figured it would be best to come to you, seein' as you're such good friends with Edward Steele. Him bein' a lawyer 'n all, I thought he would know what to do."

Carrie smiled, then impulsively, she reached out and hugged Morton.

"Don't worry, she said. "You did the right thing. I'll inform Mr. Steele about it at once, and he'll take care of everything."

Armed with her new information, Carrie walked through the snow to Edward's office to ask him to intercede on behalf of Rand Colby.

"I don't know," Edward said. "In the first place, it's a known fact that Morton likes Rand Colby, almost to the point of hero worship. It wouldn't be hard for him to concoct such a story, if he thought it would help Colby."

"You mean you don't believe him?" Carrie asked,

surprised by Edward's reaction.

"I didn't say that," Edward said. "I was just telling you what some might believe. After all, he was seen in her room that night, and I believe the sheriff told me today, that Colby has confirmed that he was in her room."

"He has admitted that he was in her room?" Carrie asked.

"That's what I understand," Edward said. "Of course, he had no choice but to admit it, since the one who saw him was Lenny Milner, and because he is a deputy, I'm afraid the court would consider him an unimpeachable source. Of course, the question is, just what was Colby doing in Polly's room?"

"I ... I don't know," Carrie said.

Edward chuckled. "Perhaps Polly didn't give up her former profession, shall we say, entirely."

"Well," Carrie said resolutely. "Whatever the reason, I don't think Rand Colby killed her."

"I don't either," Edward said.

"You don't?" Carrie said excitedly. "You mean you'll get him off?"

"I have no authority for such a thing," Edward said. "I can represent him as his lawyer, if he will allow me. Given his feelings about me, he may not even want me as counsel."

"He will," Carrie said. "I promise you, he will. I'll talk to him."

"Very well," Edward said. "Talk to him, and if he agrees, I will represent him. But, Carrie, you are absolutely positive you want to do this?"

"Yes, of course," Carrie answered. "Why not?"

"He has abandoned you at every turn," Edward said. "If the situation were reversed, don't you think he would abandon you now?"

"No," Carrie said. "I'm certain he wouldn't."

"Then are you willing to pay a price for having me represent him?"

"A price?" Carrie asked, puzzled by the statement. "You mean a fee? Of course, I suppose so. What sort of fee?"

"Half of Holliday House."

"Half of Holliday House?" Carrie asked in a gasp. "You want half of the hotel?"

"Yes," Edward said. He smiled a silken, easy smile. "But in truth, half of the hotel would be mine for the asking, anyway. I already hold mortgages on notes, which come due and payable by the end of this week. If I foreclosed, I would have fifty percent of the hotel."

"You hold mortgages? I thought the bank held them," Carrie said.

"My dear, banks frequently attempt to protect their loans by selling mortgages. I merely purchased the mortgages back, as soon as the loans were made."

"But, how could you?" Carrie asked. "I thought you were representing me. Isn't that taking unfair advantage of me?"

"Not at all," Edward said. "After all, I'm asking you now, to turn over half the hotel to me voluntarily. Let me run it and make it into a profitable organization. We both stand to benefit by such an arrangement. And in return, I will do everything in my power to get your Mr. Colby off from the murder charge which has been sworn against him."

"All right," Carrie said with a sigh. "If that is the price for getting Rand free, than I shall pay it, willingly."

Edward chuckled. "The ironic note, my dear, is that Mr. Colby will not appreciate your efforts on his behalf. In fact, he may even hold it against you for even trying."

"I don't care," Carrie said. "I believe Morton. I believe Rand Colby is innocent. I don't believe he could do such a thing. And I want to see the person who is responsible for Polly's death brought to justice. That can't happen until the law realizes that they have the wrong man and correct their mistake."

"I'll do what I can," Edward said. "In the meantime, I shall turn my efforts toward saving our hotel."

Carrie signed one-half of the hotel over to Edward Steele, then she left his office and went to the sheriff's office to see Rand Colby.

"I don't know why you want to see him," the sheriff said. "A man like that certainly deserves no one's sympathy." The sheriff escorted Carrie back to Rand's cell, then he turned to go back to the front office. He looked back at her, just as he went through the door. "Don't stand too close to the bars," he warned. "He could reach through and grab you, 'n you'd be dead before I could get back here to help."

"I'm in no danger, sheriff," Carrie said easily.

"Yes'm. Well, I reckon that's what Polly thought, too."

Rand said nothing until the sheriff left, then he looked at Carrie.

"Do you think I did it?" he asked.

"No," Carrie said.

Rand sighed. "Thank God for that."

"Morton saw the man who did it," Carrie said. "His name is Donohoe."

"What? Then why am I in here?"

"Edward doesn't think the sheriff will believe Morton. After all, it's well known that he likes you. And the deputy said he saw your face in Polly's window."

"I see," Rand said.

"Were you there?"

"In Polly's room?"

"Yes. Were you there?"

Rand paused for a moment before he answered. "Yes, I was there, but it isn't what you think. I . . . we were just talking, and that's all."

"Rand, I have hired Edward to represent you."

"You have what?"

"I have hired Edward to represent you. I think he can get you off."

"I can hire my own lawyer," Rand said.

"I've already hired him," Carrie said. "Besides, you wouldn't be able to get anyone who could represent you as well as Edward Steele."

"You think he's that good a lawyer, do you?"

"People here have confidence in him," Carrie said. "And, as this is where your trial will be held, I think it is important that you be represented by a local lawyer."

"Even if he is a good lawyer, what makes you think he'll represent my best interests?" Rand asked.

"Because I have paid him dearly," Carrie said.

"Paid him in what way?" Rand asked testily.

"I've signed over half the hotel to him," she said.

"You signed over half the hotel so he would defend me?" Rand asked, visibly moved by her sacrifice. "I . . . I thought."

"I know what you thought," Carrie said.

THE TRIAL WAS CONDUCTED three weeks later, ironically in the Community Meeting room of the Holliday House. The circuit judge and the prosecuting attorney arrived in Laramie by train from Cheyenne. The jury was composed of twelve men, good and true.

The *Boston Evening Transcript* had another reason for

covering the trial. They knew what no one else in the courtroom knew. They knew who Rand Colby's grandfather was. For the time being, they decided to guard their information. It would provide an extra degree of interest when they wrote their story.

A fresh snow had whitened the surrounding countryside by the day of the trial, and though the storm which brought the snow had gone, the cold had persisted. The temperature was hovering near the zero mark, and both stoves in the meeting room were roaring when the judge entered.

"All rise."

There was the sound of moving chairs and feet as the courtroom rose for the judge's entrance. The judge, in robes, took his place behind the bench which was fashioned from a piece of left-over bar. He rapped his gavel once and they sat down.

"Wyoming versus Rand Colby, who is charged with . . ." the judge leaned over and squirted a stream of tobacco into a spittoon, then straightened up again. "Murder," he concluded. "How do you plead?"

Edward Steele stood. "My client pleads innocent, Your Honor."

"Very well," the judge said. "The state will now present its case."

The prosecuting attorney was a small, baldheaded man, with penetrating gray eyes and a mouth that never smiled. He began constructing his case, and he did it so brilliantly, that Rand began to wonder if Steele would be able to get him off, even with Morton's testimony.

"Defense calls Morton Forsythe," Steele said.

After Morton was sworn in, he testified that he had been in the livery stable when he saw Gilbert Donohoe dragging Polly into the livery. Donohoe left her there, and when Morton had gone over to check on her, he saw that she was dead.

"Did you report Polly Castlebury's death to Sheriff Kelly?" the prosecutor asked on his cross examination.

"No, sir."

"Why not?"

"I was a'feared," Morton replied.

Steele's next witness was Winnie Callahan.

"Without getting into details as to exactly what it is that you do, did Polly ever work for you?" Steele asked.

"Yes."

"Do you know Gilbert Donohoe?" Steele asked.

"I know him."

"What do you know of the relationship between Donohoe and Miss Castlebury?"

"He used to beat her," Winnie said.

Steele's next witness was Rand Colby himself.

"Mr. Colby, did you kill Polly Castlebury?"

"No," Rand said in a clear voice. "I did not kill her."

"Your witness," Steele said.

The prosecuting attorney, a man named David Byrd stood up and walked over to face Rand.

"Were you in her room on the night of the murder?" Byrd asked.

"Yes," Rand answered.

"Speak up, please, I'm not sure the jury can hear you," the prosecuting attorney said, though Rand had spoken loudly enough. Rand knew that it was just a means of scoring on what the prosecutor thought was a telling point.

"I was in her room," Rand said more loudly than before.

"What were you doing there?"

"We had gone there to talk," Rand said.

There was a ripple of ribald laughter from the men in the room, and the judge banged his gavel a couple of times until they silenced.

"Talk?"

"Yes."

"What about?"

"About my relationship with . . ." Rand paused, then looked toward Carrie, who was sitting in the front row. "About my relationship with a mutual friend."

"Mr. Colby, have you killed men?"

"Yes," Rand replied, without amplification. During the summation, Edward Steele reminded the jury again of Morton's testimony. He also told them of the testimony of the others who had seen Donohoe accost Polly, and he alluded to the fact that the girls who worked with Winnie had all given statements to the effect that Donohoe had a history of abusing women in general, and Polly in particular.

The prosecutor's testimony suggested that Morton's testimony was suspect because of his hero worship of Rand Colby. He pointed out that Rand Colby was a man with a reputation for violence and gave a quick history of the men Rand was known to have killed. And he reminded them that he, by his own admission, had been in her room, and he recommended murder in the first degree, as the verdict.

The jury required twenty-three minutes to return their findings. The headlines of the *Boston Evening Transcript* told the story, in its next edition, transmitted by wire from Laramie.

GRANDSON OF RAILROAD TYCOON FOUND INNOCENT!

18

THERE WAS LAUGHTER AND MUSIC AND THE SOUND OF tinkling glasses, as people gathered in the Holliday House meeting room to celebrate. Officially, Edward Steele was celebrating his court victory and Rand Colby's acquittal, and thus, Rand should have been there as well. But Rand wasn't there.

Unofficially, Edward was celebrating his new partnership in the Holliday House, and the announcement that the noble experiment of converting the saloon into a meeting room, was being ended, and the saloon was to return.

As a full partner in the operation, Edward Steele had the right to have a voice in the establishment of Holliday House policy. It was his idea that the saloon be returned.

The first night of operation the house was crowded to beyond capacity. That was because all the drinks were free. It was an exceptionally expensive night, but as Edward said, "One that is necessary if we are to let people know of our change in policy."

Not only drinking returned. There were several

tables of poker games as well, and Carrie even saw Winnie and her girls circulating freely among the party goers.

"Edward," Carrie said when she first noticed them. Edward was talking quietly with three men Carrie had never seen before. "Edward, Winnie and her girls are here. You know what that means don't you?"

Edward looked up at her and smiled patronizingly. "Now, Carrie, it doesn't mean anything," he said. "This is a party, after all, and the whole town has been invited. We can't very well stand at the door and be selective about who comes in here, can we?"

"I will not have Winnie doing business here again," Carrie said.

"Now you just wander around and have a good time," Edward said. "Smile at the people and tell them how glad you are that they're here. We need good relations, if we're going to make it."

"Very well," Carrie agreed, and with a smile she did not feel, she began to wander through the room, greeting people, telling them how glad she was they had come and inviting them back after the saloon was in full operation once again.

It did not go down well with Carrie. On the one hand she felt like a failure, on the other a hypocrite. She had so sanctimoniously cleaned up Holliday House, and now she was trying her best to reestablish those very things she had thrown out.

As Carrie moved through the crowd, she was subjected to many indignities. Her breasts, legs, and derriere attracted pats, touches, squeezes, and pinches, which were awkward and annoying, and what was worse, the bestower made no attempt to mask the incidents as seeming accidental encounters.

"Hey, darlin', now that the drinkin' is beginnin' again, how 'bout the other things?" one of the partygoers called. He smelled of whiskey and he reached for her as he spoke, but Carrie adroitly managed to avoid his grasp.

"What other things?" she asked in a tone of voice, which clearly indicated her aggravation.

"You know what other things," the man replied. "The man and woman things, like Winnie was runnin'. Are you gonna take Winnie's place? If you do, put me down for the first visit."

Those around him laughed heartily at his bold comment, and Carrie, her face flaming mightily under the verbal, as well as fondling abuse, turned and walked back to the table where Edward Steele was still engaged in serious conversation with the three strangers.

"Edward, these . . . these people," Carrie said desperately, indicating those in the room. "They are impossible!"

"Impossible? What do you mean?"

"The things they are saying," Carrie said. "Edward, they are making the most rude suggestions, and their hands . . . they're putting their hands all over me."

Edward laughed at her outrage. "This is a party, Carrie, and they are just celebrating. Besides, you are a grown woman. You should be able to take such things in stride."

"There is no reason I should ever have to take boorish behavior in stride," Carrie said angrily. "And I won't accept this."

"Then my advice to you is to leave the party," Edward said easily.

"You mean you aren't going to do anything about it?"

"Be reasonable, Carrie," Edward said. "What can I do?

They haven't broken any law. And these people are going to be our customers."

"I see," Carrie said so angered by Edward's refusal to do anything that the words were barely forced from a throat, which was tight with fury. She spun around and started for the stairs.

"Carrie, where are you going?" Edward asked.

"You are the one who gave me the advice," Carrie said. "You told me to leave the party, and that is just what I am doing."

"But I'm tied up here with these gentlemen," Edward said. "One of us should circulate through the party and see to the needs of our guests."

"I know what their needs are," Carrie said, "and I have no intention of seeing to them."

By the time Carrie reached the top of the stairs, the sounds of the party were jumbled together into one dull roar, so that the words were no longer distinguishable. Despite that, her ears were still burning as Carrie hurried down the hall toward her own room.

There was one door which was open, and as Carrie approached it, she realized that it was the room Rand had taken when he had been released from jail. Carrie wondered why the door was open, and she looked in— just to make certain that nothing was wrong. She saw Rand lying on his bed with his hands folded behind his head, staring morosely at the ceiling. He saw Carrie standing in his door.

"Aren't you in the wrong place?" he asked. "The party is downstairs."

"I have no desire to remain at the party," she said.

"I'm sure it's not the same without you."

"May I come in?" Carrie asked.

"It's your hotel," Rand said. "Oh, I forgot. It's only half your hotel, isn't it?"

Carrie stepped into Rand's room and leaned back against the wall. "Why are you always so full of anger?" she asked.

"Am I?"

"Yes," Carrie said. "You are a man of anger and mystery. Does it have something to do with your grandfather?"

Rand looked at Carrie in surprise. "My grandfather? What do you know about my grandfather?"

"A reporter was here from the *Boston Evening Transcript*. He said you were the grandson of Emmet Leland. Is that right?"

"Yes," Rand said.

"He owns the railroad doesn't he?"

"He owns the Boston and Mississippi railroad," Rand said. "He holds stock in the U.P., but he doesn't own it."

"Why have you kept that a secret?"

"What is there to talk about?" Rand answered. "The B and M belongs to my grandfather, not to me."

"But it does have something to do with what drives you, doesn't it?" Carrie said. Now she moved all the way to his bed and sat down on it.

Rand sighed.

"Before my grandfather built the Boston and Mississippi railroad, he owned a shipping line. My father was the captain of one of his ships. My father and mother fell in love, but my grandfather didn't approve. So, my father and mother were married without his permission, and when my grandfather found out about it, he fixed it so that my father could never get another berth at sea. Not only that, he refused to speak to my mother again. My parents stayed in Boston for six more years, but my grandfather never came around to accepting them. Eventually, my father gave up, and we came west. My father tried a little of everything: panning for gold, ranching, farming, he even tried to run a store. But he was a seaman, born to command, and he never adjusted . . . never got his 'land-legs' he used to say. He started drinking . . . then one winter he got sick and died. I don't think he wanted to get well. He went in less than a week. My mother died the next year—dropsy, the doctor said. I think it was a broken heart. Just before she died, she told me that she had money put away, money that my father was too proud to touch. After she died, I used the money to buy a small farm."

"Oh, Rand, I'm so sorry," Carrie said.

Rand looked at Carrie, then he smiled and reached for her hand and took it gently in his.

"Listen to me," he said. "I'm telling you a story full of woe and self-pity, and here you never even knew your parents."

"Perhaps that is easier," Carrie said. "At least I couldn't miss what I never had. Have you ever heard from your grandfather?"

"Oh, I heard from him," Rand said. "After my mother and father left Boston, he vowed never to trust a sea captain again, so he sold his shipping line, and invested in a railroad. After a while he mellowed, then he decided he would like to see my mother. By then it was too late. He begged me to return to Boston, but I wouldn't do it. After several years and several letters from him, I decided I would at least go see him. I was going to tell him just what I thought of him."

"And did you?"

"No," Rand said. "By the time I got there I found an old broken man who was begging for forgiveness.

Nothing I could have said or done would have added to his misery, for he was already the most miserable person I had ever seen. In fact, I soon began to feel sympathy for him, and now, perhaps, even a sense of love. And it was while I was there that something happened."

"What happened?"

"I met someone there," Rand said. "She was the daughter of one of my grandfather's associates. We became engaged."

"Oh," Carrie said quietly. She pulled her hand away from Rand's. "I see."

"No," Rand said, reaching out to pull her hand back to his. "No, you don't see. She's dead."

"She's dead?"

"Her name was Nora Stanfield. She came west to marry me, against her own father's wishes, I might add, though, upon the urging of my grandfather, he at least grudgingly accepted it. She was killed on her first day in Rushville, gunned down by four bank robbers: Nate Campbell, Perry Hoyt, Ely Slack, and Jay Bishop."

"Perry Hoyt? Isn't he the—"

"The man on the boat," Rand said.

"Then ... his death wasn't an accident?"

"Not exactly," Rand said. "When I confronted him, he drew on me. I managed to knock the gun aside and he wound up shooting himself."

"But you did goad him into it?"

"Yes."

"Rand, it wasn't a mere accident that he was on that boat, was it?"

"No," Rand said. "I took that boat, because I knew he would be there."

"You were looking for him?"

"Yes."

"And the others? Are you looking for them as well?"

"Slack is dead, Campbell is in jail," Rand explained.

"Did you kill Slack?"

"I offered him the opportunity to turn himself over to the sheriff. He pulled a gun on me instead. I had no choice."

"You should leave such a job to the authorities. Let the law find these men."

"Have you forgotten? I am the law," Rand said. "I'm a railroad detective, remember."

"Yes, I do remember. How convenient for you to have official sanction for your personal vendetta," Carrie said. "Now only one is left. What will you do with him? Be the judge, jury, and hangman?"

"No," Rand said. "When I find him, I will turn him over to the proper authorities, just as I did Campbell."

"When you find him? You mean if you find him, don't you?"

"Not if, when," Rand said. "*I will* find him."

"What about Donohoe?" Carrie asked.

"What about him?"

"Donohoe killed Polly, or so Morton said. Will you be looking for him as well?"

"If I run across Donohoe, I will deal with him. But he isn't the focus of my search. The focus of my search is Jay Bishop."

CARRIE LAY IN HER BED, but she couldn't sleep. At first, she attributed her inability to sleep to the noises coming from the party below, but the party broke up around midnight, and still she couldn't sleep. She heard the big clock downstairs strike two in the morning, and she was still staring at the ceiling. Finally, with a sigh, she got up and walked over to look through the window.

The sky was black velvet with a million sprinkled stars, seemingly coming all the way down to the hills, white with snow. The moon was just behind a mountain peak, and the peak caught the moonbeams and scattered a burst of silver through the night.

In the corner of the room the woodstove popped and snapped as a trapped pocket of gas in a log exploded. The room was warm and cozy, so there was no reason why she couldn't sleep. So why was she standing here, looking through the window?

She knew why she couldn't sleep. She was thinking about the abrupt changes there had been in her life. A short while ago she had been a sheltered young woman, still living in the orphanage where she was raised.

Now, she was living a life she never could have imagined, owner of a hotel and a saloon, and exposed to the kind of violence she had only read about.

What was to become of her?

19

CARRIE WAS SITTING BEHIND THE DESK IN THE HOTEL office, working on the books. She heard laughter—first, the low rumbling of a man, then the high, shrill cackle of a woman. Glasses clinked and voices rose and fell in conversation, evidence of the business the Holliday House was doing under the new policies implemented by Edward Steele.

Carrie pushed the chair back, then stood and walked over to look through the window. The office was at the rear of the hotel, and she could see beyond the edge of the town to the rolling plains and mountains. It was spring, and most of the snow had melted in the lower elevations, though it still clung to the mountain peaks.

The valley was dotted with red, yellow, and purple hues as Indian paintbrushes, oxeye daisies, and lupines bloomed everywhere in colorful profusion.

Carrie sighed and turned away from the window. She realized that she had not actually been looking at the scenery despite its wild and rugged beauty. She had been looking at the railroad track—a thin, black line, which with the marching telegraph poles, stretched off, unbroken into infinity. She wished she had the courage to get on a train and follow that track to wherever it might lead her.

Suddenly there was a crashing sound, a woman's scream, followed by a roar of laughter, and Carrie, her curiosity aroused by it all, walked to the door to look out into the Community Room.

Community Room, she thought. That was an ironic footnote to this whole affair. Edward Steele had insisted upon calling the newly reopened saloon, the Community Room.

"After all," Edward said, "it is a place in which the entire community is welcome. And perhaps we shall have gained some good publicity by its brief history as a meeting place for Laramie's good citizens."

"But that seems so improper," Carrie had protested.

"My dear, it is about time you learn that the only propriety of business is to make a profit," Edward replied.

As a result of their discussion, and Edward's actions, the Community Room was no longer a meeting place for the good citizens of Laramie. Instead, it was given over to the service of hard liquor, the playing of poker, dice, faro, and other gambling games, and was now constantly peopled by the most unsavory group of characters Carrie had ever seen.

As Carrie looked out into the room at this moment to determine the source of the crashing sound she had just heard, she saw that the Community Room was full. The bar was restored, and there were a dozen or more men there, drinking, and talking boisterously. The tables were equally as full, and, above everyone's head, there floated a cloud of noxious blue smoke from the pipes and cigars of the patrons. The room was a mélange of unpleasant smells; bodies too long without a bath, wool clothes damp with the spring rains, cheap, oppressive perfumes, tobacco smoke, and stale whiskey.

The sound that had arrested Carrie's attention had been the crashing of one of the light fixtures. A young woman, emboldened by too much drink and encouraged by many of the men, had attempted to swing from the fixture nearest the door. It had not supported her weight, and when it crashed to the floor, several of the glass facets were broken. The laughter came from the fact that the young woman had cut her derriere and was now examining herself, by standing on the bar with her dress hiked and her undergarments pulled down exposing her wound to all who cared to see. The wound was not at all serious, and the young woman was merely using it as a pretense to show off her charms to the many men.

Carrie's face flamed pink, not only from embarrassment, but from anger. She wished she could order the woman and everyone else out of the place, but she knew they would only laugh at her if she tried to do so.

Carrie heard a sound behind her and looked down the hall to see Edward Steele standing at the side door. A man, whom Carrie had seen arrive by that route earlier in the evening, was just leaving, and Edward was bidding him goodbye.

Carrie wanted to go to Edward to ask him to intervene in the goings on of the saloon, but she knew it would be a wasted effort on her part. He was, seemingly, totally uninterested in what went on in the hotel now. Often, over the past few months, Carrie had gone to him to ask if there might be some way to police the activities at the saloon and gambling room, in order to preserve some dignity for the place. Edward had merely pointed out the increased profits, and then he let the matter slide.

It was not just his interest in maintaining the profit level that kept him from interfering with the hotel patrons. Edward had, of late, been involved in several other projects of mysterious origin. Carrie frequently saw him in deep and secretive conversations with strange men, some of whom were frightening to her, in their brooding ways. The person who had arrived earlier this evening and who was now slipping through the side door, was just such a person.

"Edward?" Carrie called.

Edward looked up toward Carrie, then smiled.

"Ah, Carrie my dear, there you are. I'm sorry, I'm afraid I got tied up in some business discussion, and I completely neglected to see you. We were going to work on the books, weren't we?"

"I've finished them," Carrie said.

"Oh, have you? Wonderful," Edward said. "How lucky I am to have a partner who is not only beautiful, but skilled as well." Edward rubbed his hands together. "How do the books look?"

"We have now made back all the money I lost during the summer and winter."

"Ah, wonderful, wonderful," Edward beamed. "See? Did I not tell you that our partnership would be mutually beneficial?"

"Yes, you told me," Carrie said, though judging by the tone of her voice, it was not a reply that shared Edward's enthusiasm over everything.

"Well, what is it?" Edward asked, puzzled by her strange behavior. "Why aren't you happy with the money we're making?"

"You know why I'm not happy," Carrie said. "Edward,

when I walked downtown yesterday, no one would speak to me. I think the people are more resentful of me now, than they were when I first arrived. Everyone believes I am a hypocrite, and I must confess to sharing that belief."

"Ah, don't worry about what the people in this town think," Edward said, dismissing her comment with an impatient wave of his hand. "They are all jealous of you, that's all."

"Jealous?"

"Of course," Edward said. "You are beautiful, you are going to be rich, and . . ." he smiled broadly and put his arm around her shoulder. "You are my girl."

Very pointedly, Carrie put her hand on Edward's hand and peeled his arm away.

"No," she said. "I am not your girl."

"But of course you're my girl," Edward said, laughing easily and self-confidently. "Everyone knows that."

"Perhaps you have noticed that I don't share that opinion."

"Of course I've noticed, my dear, and I understand . . . believe me, I do," Edward said. "You've been over-working and you're tired. Perhaps I should take more of the burden off your shoulders." Edward put his hand on Carrie's neck to massage it gently as he spoke, but she twisted away.

"No," she said. "I'm not overly tired. It isn't that at all."

There was another loud round of laughter from the saloon, then a woman's scream, and someone shouted that a fight was in progress. That disturbance inter-rupted the conversation before Edward could provide Carrie with an answer, and both of them moved back to the end of the hall, which overlooked the Community Room. There, rolling around on the floor, were two girls.

One was the girl who had been swinging on the light fixture and cut herself, and the other was a girl who evidently was angered by the fact that the first girl had shown her derriere, perhaps to the amusement of her own man friend.

"Got any bets, gentlemen?" one of the patrons was saying. "Got any bets on this action?"

"Go at it, ladies!" another said.

Edward found it amusing and began laughing at the scene.

"Edward, stop them," Carrie said. "Stop them, please! This is disgusting!"

"Where's your sense of humor?" Edward asked, still laughing. He pointed to the front door. "Look, three more men just came in. Perhaps we should arrange something like this on a nightly basis. It would be good for business."

Carrie, too angry even to respond to Edward's comments, turned and walked away from the scene. Then, she got an idea and hurried to the kitchen. There, she grabbed a bucket, filled it with water, and returned to the combatants, who were still rolling on the floor, pulling each other's hair and screaming. Carrie flung the water at them.

The water immediately cooled off the women and broke up the fight, just as Carrie had hoped it would. The two women got up, dripping wet and no longer anxious to continue the battle, preferring instead to attend to their own needs.

"Oh now, damnit, why'd you go 'n stop the fight?" someone asked.

"Yeah, we was enjoyin' it," another said.

Without so much as a word, Carrie left the Community Room.

. . .

THE TRAIN WAS forty miles west of Laramie, just starting up the long grade known as Stinkwater Pass. The fireman, anticipating the grade, had been stoking the fire for several minutes now, and the fire was roaring and the steam pressure was near the limit.

"There's the first marker," the fireman called, leaning out his cab window.

"Here we go," the engineer replied, lashing the throttle to full open. The engineer looked out his own cab window, then suddenly, let out an oath. "What the hell?"

"What is it?"

"Look ... up the track. Isn't that a lantern being waved back and forth?"

"Yes," the fireman said. "What do you think it is?"

"I don't know, but I can't stop now. If I do, we'll never make it up the pass."

The engineer pulled on the whistle, and its long, sad sound wailed out into the darkness.

"He ain't movin'," the fireman said. "Give 'im another blast."

The engineer sounded the whistle a second time, but the swinging lantern became, if anything, even more urgent.

"What does that fool think he's doing?" the engineer asked.

"Isaac, you don't reckon the trestle is out?" the fireman suddenly asked.

"Oh, my God," the engineer said. "The trestle over Freeman's Gulch. If it's out—"

"It's three hundred feet to the bottom," the fireman finished.

The engineer reached for the braking handle then, and air was vented through the entire length of the train, causing all the wheels to lock and making the train slide along the steel of the track. The inside of the cab was bathed in a shower of sparks thrown up by the wheels, and the engineer and fireman had to brace themselves to keep from being thrown into the rear of the boiler. Finally, and aided by the fact that they were already on an incline, the train came to a halt, sitting there with all the metal popping in protest.

The engineer had to vent some of the steam, because the pressure had been built up to allow the long climb, and without being used, it was in danger of blowing through the boiler plates. There was a gushing roar as it rolled away from the engine.

"All I can say is, this had better be important," the engineer said. "We're going to have to back more'n five miles to get up this head of steam again."

"I'll climb down and see what's what," the fireman volunteered.

"If this is some fool stunt, you tell 'em they put me more'n an hour behind my schedule, and I'm not used to runnin' behind schedule," the engineer said, pulling his watch from his pocket and looking at it.

"I'll let 'em know your feelin's," the fireman said. "'Cause if it's some fool stunt, why, it'll be my feelin's too."

The fireman had just stepped on the ladder to climb down, when a shot rang out. Startled, the engineer looked around and saw the fireman, with a pained expression on his face, fall. Quickly, he opened the throttle, trying to force the train to move forward. If he had reversed the throttle, the train would have had the incline to work to its advantage, and it would have begun moving. As it was with all the steam vented and fighting against the incline, the train moved only a few feet before someone jumped onto the boarding ladder and climbed to the top. He pointed a pistol toward the engineer.

"Stop the train," he said in a gruff voice.

"Stop it now, or you are a dead man!"

The engineer closed the throttle quickly, then stood there with his hands up, looking at the man who had a gun on him. The man was wearing a bandanna tied across his nose and mouth and a hat with the brim pulled low. That mask, coupled with the darkness of the night, made it impossible for the engineer to get a look at his features, though he tried.

"What are you going to do?" the engineer asked, tentatively.

"We're already a'doin' it," the man answered with a snorting laugh. "We're a'holdin' up your train."

"Please don't hurt any of my passengers."

"If you do like we tell you, they won't nobody get hurt."

"What about my fireman? You shot him."

"That was just to show you that we mean business," the robber said. "It was just his tough luck that we had to use him for an example."

The engineer and the robber stood in the wavering orange light of the firebox for several minutes, while the robber's cohorts went about their task of taking the money from the train. There were several shouts and a few incongruous laughs, but mercifully, there was no more shooting. Finally, one of the robbers rode up beside the cab of the train, leading a riderless horse.

"Come on," he called out. "We've got to get this stuff to Bishop."

The robber in the cab backed over to the ladder, then started lowering himself.

"See, it's just like I tol' you," he said. "Behave yourself, and nobody gets hurt."

The robber climbed down the ladder, straddled the horse, then with a kick of his legs against the animal's sides, rode away with the others. The engineer counted three of them, as they disappeared into the darkness.

20

As THE SUN DIED IN A FIERY BURST OF RED AND GOLD, Rand stood in a small aspen grove on a hill, watching nature's display. Beneath the trees there were lengthening shadows, while in the distance, the mountains donned a veil of purple.

By twilight the stars were out, sparkling cold and white in the dark velvet overhead. Trees whispered softly in the night breeze, while from a nearby glen a coyote rent the air with its plaintive call. Owls hooted, first one and then the other, as mates called, reassuringly, back and forth.

Rand listened to them, and their soft calls of companionship made him feel all the more lonely and heartsick for the way things were. If he could have, he would've ignored the vow he had made in his sorrow.

Rand spread his blanket and lay on the ground with his hands folded behind his head. He peered up at the dark blue vault of the sky and the thousands of winking stars. How beautiful they were and how perfectly ordered their structure.

The night deepened, and soon all nature slept. The coyotes, the owls, the insects, even the wind stilled. He closed his eyes and rested, and he may have even slept, but always, he was aware of the passage of time, and always he was cognizant of his terrible loneliness.

A gray dawn finally began to move in from the eastern slopes, pushing back the blackness of the night, until the small aspen grove that had shielded Rand for the night was illuminated by an ethereal light. Rand was up with that light, eating jerky and taking a drink of water for his breakfast, before putting his saddle on his horse and continuing his lonely, almost hopeless quest. He would find the man named Jay Bishop, for now he was doubly inspired to do so. There would be no peace on earth or in heaven until Rand had accomplished this task.

The town of Creston lay before him, shimmering in the late afternoon sun. To the east and west leading in and out of Creston, ran the railroad tracks that linked this tiny settlement with the rest of the world. It was a mere handful of souls abandoned from all civilization, except for the tracks. In less than one week in either direction, a determined traveler would be able to behold the wonders of San Francisco or Boston. What an amazing development the railroad had brought about in men's lives, Rand thought.

Rand took his horse to the livery stable, where he ordered the animal to be rubbed down with cool water, then given oats and rest. After taking care of his horse, he started toward the saloon, where he intended to have a bath, a beer, and a steak, in that order.

An out-of-tune piano was being played by a musician who had more determination than talent, but the patrons of the saloon didn't seem to mind. Rand stopped just inside the swinging doors and looked over the house, analyzing everyone with eyes that were equally at home on the hunter and on the hunted.

Four men sat at a table near the back of the room— obviously they were ranch hands in town on an errand or for a quiet drink. At the end of the bar a young man stood, drinking a beer. He was wearing a brightly colored shirt and jeans, and a pistol with a pearl handle. One glance told Rand he was a boy just approaching manhood, and the kid had probably worn the pistol for a photo session in the photography shop he had seen across the street. Two old men were playing checkers at one table, observed by half a dozen kibitzers, all as old as the players themselves. A bartender with a white shirt and gartered sleeves, stood behind the bar, wiping glasses. The bartender had a handlebar moustache, which he kept well waxed and twisted into fine points.

"What can I do for you?" the bartender asked, as Rand approached the bar, convinced that there was no one in the saloon of particular interest to him.

"I'd like to scrape off about six inches of trail dust," Rand said. "Then I'd like a beer and a steak if you can manage it."

"I can handle it," the bartender said with a smile. He pointed to Rand's clothes. "Fac' is, I can get your clothes cleaned, too, iffen you got a change."

"Much obliged," Rand said. "I've got a change in my tack, but I left it down at the livery stable."

"What's your name?" the bartender said. "I'll send someone down for it. It'll cost you an extra drink."

"Colby," Rand said. "And it'll be worth the extra drink to get into some clean duds."

"The tub's back there," the bartender said. "It'll cost

you a quarter if you draw and heat your own water, fifty cents if I gotta find someone to do it for you."

"I can handle it," Rand said easily.

For the next several minutes Rand pumped water, then heated it over a small wood stove, and finally poured it into the tub. He took off his clothes, then settled down into the hot water.

"Well, well, well. Tell me, lad. S'posin' I took a notion not to give you these clothes, then what would you do?" a thick Irish voice asked.

Rand looked up and smiled when he recognized his friend Matt.

"It's for certain, I won't spend the rest of my life in this tub," Rand said. "And when I come out, I'd be lookin' for you. What are you doing here?"

"I'm lookin' for you," Matt said. He put the clean clothes on a shelf, then sat on a chair near the tub. "You owe me a drink," he said, pointing to the clothes.

Rand laughed. "Don't tell me you're hustling drinks now. Have things gotten that bad?"

"I left word for you at the bank, the depot, and the livery. I told them that if you showed up to let me know. The liveryman was just telling me about you, when some old geezer come in lookin' for your clothes. When I told him I would take them to you, he got plumb hostile. It seemed I was takin' a drink away from 'im, so, I had to buy him one."

"A likely story," Rand said, smiling. He stood up and reached for a towel. "Why were you looking for me?"

"There's been another train robbery," Matt said.

"Yeah, I heard about it last week. They flagged a train down near Stinkwater Pass, didn't they?"

"Yes," Matt said. "There were three of them. We've got

a pretty good lead on them. These bills were marked, and some of the money has turned up in Wamsutter."

"Wamsutter? That's just west of here, isn't it?"

"Yeah," Matt said. "We're pretty sure we know where they are."

"So, why have you left word for me?" Rand asked. He was dry now, and he began slipping into his clothes. "It seems to me like you have this case solved."

"There was one interesting thing about this robbery I thought you might want to know."

"Oh?"

"As they were riding off, the engineer heard one of the men call to the others that they had to get the stuff to Bishop."

"What?" Rand asked his interest piqued now, by the revelation.

"I thought you might be interested," Matt said. "Didn't you say the name of the fella you're lookin' for is Bishop?"

"Yes," Rand said. "Jay Bishop. Do you think they meant him?"

"I don't know, but it has to be someone's name," Matt said. "I checked all the railroad maps, 'n the nearest town I can find called Bishop is way the hell back in Missouri."

"I'm going to Wamsutter," Rand said.

Matt smiled. "Aye, lad, I was that sure of you that I got you a pass on the nine o'clock train. You'll have time to eat your supper 'n dally a bit with the ladies if you've a mind to."

THE STEAK WAS tough and the potatoes were greasy, but it was the first sustenance Rand had eaten in three weeks that was neither dried nor wild. Because of that, he ate with relish. The beer was cool and smooth, and it aided in the digestion, as did the conversation with Matt. Rand enjoyed Matt's company, because he had been out of hearing distance of another human voice for over a month now.

"What were you doin' out there?" Matt asked. He laughed. "Prospectin' for gold?"

"No," Rand said. "I've already found something more precious than gold."

"Pard, the tender way you said that, it has to be a woman," Matt said. He smiled and stuck out his hand. "Congratulations."

"I wish I could take your congratulations," Rand said sadly. "But the truth is I haven't earned them."

Matt chuckled. "Oh, I see," he said. "You've found her, but she's not ready to come around to your way of thinkin' yet, is that it?"

"It's not that simple. It's just that I've made a vow, and I must keep it. It's a matter of honor, now."

"No," Matt said. "You can put all the high-sounding words to it you wish—-justice, vow, honor— but the truth is, it's a matter of vengeance, pure and simple. It's rotting your gut and burning your mind and leaving its brand on you so that you can't think of anything else. I'm sorry to see it come to that. You're too good a man to be wasted like that."

It was already dark by the time Rand stepped down from the train in Wamsutter. His first stop was the sheriff's office, where he learned that two of the three men who had been passing the marked money were already dead.

"Dead?" Rand asked, surprised at the news.

"Deader'n a doornail," the sheriff said. "They got into

a fight over the money and shot each other down in the Longhorn Saloon."

"When did this happen?" Rand asked. He poured himself a cup of coffee from a pot steaming over a small wood cooking stove.

"It happened day before yesterday," the sheriff replied. "You see, the truth is, that marked money started circulatin' more'n a week ago. Well, by the time we got the circular from the railroad, tellin' us about the money, it had already changed hands so many times, no one could be sure where it come from, first. Then these two galoots got into an argument, shot each other dead, 'n after they was already dead, we discovered that each one of 'em was carryin' a couple hundred dollars. By that time, their partner, the third man who rode in with 'em, had plumb disappeared."

The sheriff opened a drawer, pulled out two pictures and handed them to Rand. The pictures were photographs of the two dead men propped up on boards with open sightless eyes and small black holes in their forehead and bare chests. Their faces were frozen in the snarls of anger they had exhibited just before they died.

"Ugly critters, aren't they?" Rand commented.

"Ever see either one of 'em before?" the sheriff asked.

"Can't say as I have," Rand said, handing the photographs back.

"Well, I had their picture taken before we buried 'em, hopin' we could identify 'em."

"You don't have any names?"

The sheriff pointed to one of the pictures. "This one went by Snake and that one by Digger. I don't have any idea what their real names were."

"What about the third one?"

"Nope. No luck there, either," the sheriff said. He put

the pictures back in a drawer. "I'm sorry, I'd like to help you railroad fellas out, but I don't have anything for you."

Rand finished his coffee and put the cup down. "Well, I thank you, sheriff, for the help you've given me already. Now, if you don't mind, I think I'll go on down to the Longhorn and ask a few questions. If these fellas were hanging around down there, there's a chance someone might have heard them say something useful."

"No, I don't mind," the sheriff said. "Be my guest, ask all the questions you want."

Rand left the sheriff's office and walked along the board sidewalk toward the Longhorn Saloon. Even without the sign hanging out front, it would have been easy to find. It was brightly lighted casting a pool of golden reflections into the dirt street in front, and the sound of loud conversation and louder laughter spilled through the open windows and doors. Rand went inside, stepped up to the bar, and ordered a beer.

"Would you like someone to talk to?" a woman's voice asked.

Rand looked at the speaker, a young woman in her early twenties. She was gently rounded and wearing a dress designed to show her curves to the best advantage. Her hazel eyes sparkled with practiced gaiety, but there was a carefully constructed wall just beyond their light.

Rand smiled at her.

"Sure," he said, "a lonely man can always use some company."

"Buy me a drink, and I'll join you at a table."

"What's your name?" Rand asked after the two were seated.

"Lizzie," the girl said.

"Well, Lizzie, here's to you," Rand said, holding the beer glass toward her before taking a drink.

"Do you have a woman?" Lizzie asked after a few minutes of conversation.

"Why do you ask?"

Lizzie smiled sadly. "I believe you do have a woman," she said.

"I'm in no position to have a woman," Rand replied.

"That's a shame," Lizzie said. "You're a fine man, and any woman who would know your love is a lucky woman indeed."

Rand chuckled. "You can tell that from just from a few minutes of conversation?"

"I can tell goodness in a man . . . and I can tell evil," she said, and the last statement slid out in a voice, which had an edge of fear in its timbre. "Donohoe is such a man."

Rand sat up quickly. "Who?" he asked. "Who did you say?"

"Donohoe," Lizzie said, surprised by Rand's sudden interest. "Do you know him?"

"Yeah," Rand said. "I know him."

"I don't like your friend," Lizzie said. She turned her arm over, and Rand saw a small blue mark. "He did this with a cigar," she said. "I don't know why he did it, he just did it."

"Where is he now?" Rand asked.

"I don't know," Lizzie said. "He was with those other two men—you know, the ones who killed each other in a gunfight? After their fight, he just disappeared. Good riddance, I say, even if he is your friend."

"I said I knew him," Rand said. "I didn't say he was a friend. Where did he go?"

"I don't know. If he isn't your friend, why are you so anxious to find him?"

"He may have the answer to an important question," Rand said.

Lizzie shuddered. "There's no question in the world that I would ever want answered badly enough to ask it of him," she said. She leaned toward him and kissed him lightly on the cheek. "But if it's important, I hope you find him. Ask Jasper."

"Who?"

"Jasper, the bartender," Lizzie said. She smiled. "He has big ears. If anyone in Wamsutter knows anything, it's Jasper."

"Thanks," Rand said. "I'll do that."

21

"It is most generous of you to receive me, Miss Holliday," the man said. "You have a very nice place here," he added, looking around the room. He was in the office of the hotel, delicately balancing a cup of tea on his knee. He was a gentleman in his mid to late sixties, and he had dropped in quite unexpectedly, a few minutes earlier.

"Thank you," Carrie said.

"I must confess to a degree of surprise at finding a place this nice out here in the wilds of this rugged country."

"You will forgive me, Mr. . . . ."

"Professor," the man corrected gently. He smiled self-consciously. "Oh, I realize that it is a vain affectation to insist upon being called that, but it is my one accomplishment in life, and I find that the fewer one's accomplishments, the more urgently one clings to them. I am Professor Louis Heimrod, late of Harvard University, and now retired."

"Yes, I'm sorry," Carrie apologized.

"Not at all," the professor said smiling easily. "I am, after all, a man who does little to cause one to remember him. I daresay many of my students have found it easy to forget me, though I have managed to follow them closely all these years. That is why I am so happy to be here now, to once again, establish contact with William Edward. I haven't heard from him since we collaborated on his brilliant paper, which was published in the American Law Journal back in sixty-nine. That has been over five years now."

"By William Edward you mean Edward Steele?"

"Edward?" the professor said. He chuckled. "My, coming west must have done something to him. In the past, he preferred to be called William Edward. In fact, he rather insisted upon it. I think he wished to model himself after William the Conqueror. He always had plans of grandeur you know, even before he became a war hero. We thought he would come back and enter politics. I must confess we were all surprised by his decision to come west to seek fame and fortune."

"His decision was well founded," Carrie said. "Edward has become quite successful."

"I'm pleased to hear that. And tell me, my dear, is there any romance between the two of you?" the professor asked, with twinkling eyes.

"No!" Carrie answered sharply. She blushed at the thought of her past indiscretions with Edward Steele.

"I'm sorry dear, I shouldn't have asked a question that was none of my business. Given William Edward's feeling about women, I should have known better. He has never thought it worthwhile to give a woman the time of day. He never would have anything to do with a woman."

"Professor Heimrod, are you certain we are speaking

of the same man?" Carrie asked, surprised by the comment.

"I should think so," the professor said. He took an envelope from his inside jacket pocket and pulled out a letter. "We recently received an inquiry from the Union Pacific Railroad, asking for verification of William Edward's credentials. William Edward Steele, a graduate of our school, and practicing law here in Laramie. Is there more than one William Edward Steele practicing law here?"

"No," Carrie said. "There's only one."

"There you go, then," Professor Heimrod said. "We must be speaking of the same man." The professor put the envelope away, then pulled out his watch and looked at it. "Oh, dear me, if William Edward doesn't arrive soon, I fear I will miss him entirely. I'm bound on through for San Francisco, you know."

"I'm sorry, I don't know where he is," Carrie said. "He rode out on some errand this morning, and he didn't say when he would return. I expected him back by now, but he could be delayed."

"Yes, well it will be a shame if I miss him, but if so, perhaps I can see him on the way back through Laramie when I return. I'm fulfilling a life-long ambition, you know," he added with a smile. "I've always wanted to see the Great American West, and at last I am doing so. I shall have one week in San Francisco, before I return to Boston."

"Do you live in Boston?" Carrie asked.

"Yes. I taught there for forty years, never leaving the city except vicariously, through my students."

"Is Boston a beautiful city?"

"Oh, yes, it's lovely," Professor Heimrod said. "Why, have you a desire to visit there?"

"I should like to visit it someday, yes," Carrie said. "A ... a friend of mine has relatives there," she added, thinking of Rand Colby's grandfather.

Professor Heimrod chuckled. "You're speaking of William Edward of course."

"Of course," Carrie said, thinking it would be easier to let him believe that, than to try and explain anything to him.

"I suppose I shall have to call upon his sister when I return. She has been frantic with worry over him. William Edward was such a faithful correspondent, until just a few years ago. Then he broke all contact with everyone. No one knew where he was, until the Union Pacific inquiry. It was only by a fortuitous set of circumstances that I happened across the inquiry amongst the school records, or I should never have known of his whereabouts. I didn't even tell his sister I had made the discovery, because I thought it would mean much more to her, if she would suddenly get a letter from William Edward. I was going to talk to him about that." Professor Heimrod looked at his watch one more time, then snapped the case shut and put it away. He set the cup to one side and stood. "I fear I shall have to take that up with him on the way back through, next week," he said. "If I don't leave now, I'll miss the train, and as I've confirmed reservations in San Francisco, I must be on time. You will tell William Edward that I stopped by to see him, won't you?"

"Yes, of course I will," Carrie said standing with the professor. "I just wish you could stay long enough to see him. I'm sure he'll be sorry that he missed you."

"What is a few more days?" the professor asked, philosophically. "It has now been a matter of years. Just tell him that 'Old Roundtop' stopped by for a visit." The professor chuckled, as if privy to a private joke, and he rubbed his bald head.

"Old Roundtop?"

"Yes, William Edward will understand. It is the name he once gave me when he was one of my students. The name stuck, and class after class began calling me that, until I must confess, it is a way I frequently refer to myself, even in my own thoughts."

The whistle of an approaching train drifted in through the open window then and the professor looked around in alarm.

"You'll have time," Carrie assured him. "The train spends thirty minutes in the station."

"Thank you for the tea," the professor said, "and for your charming company. William Edward is indeed lucky to have found a business partner as lovely as you."

"You are too kind," Carrie said. "I'm sure Edward shall be looking forward to your visit when you come back through. I know I shall."

Carrie walked to the front door of the Holliday House with the professor, then watched as he hurried down the street toward the depot. She had spent an interesting, though strange, hour with him. The time was strange because if the facts had not told her otherwise, she would have sworn that the William Edward Steele the professor remembered and the Edward Steele she knew, could not be the same person.

Carrie returned to the office of the hotel to wait for Edward. There was a game going on in the Community Room but the large, somewhat boisterous evening crowd had not yet gathered. For that, Carrie was thankful.

As it turned out, it was a good thing Professor Heimrod didn't wait, because Edward didn't come back for four days. When he did return, it was in the company of another of the strange and frightening looking men with whom he had found so many opportunities to conduct business over the past few months. Carrie waited until the stranger had left before she approached Edward.

"Well," Edward said, smiling at Carrie as she joined him at his table in the restaurant. "To what do I owe this pleasure? Have you decided to allow things to return to the way they were?"

"No," Carrie said quickly. "Things will never be the same."

"Ah, yes, so you said," Edward said, as he buttered a roll and took a bite. "Umm, I must confess, I have missed the food of Holliday House during my business trip. Have you eaten?"

"Yes."

"What a shame. It would have been good to at least share a meal with you."

"I'll sit with you while you eat," Carrie said.

"Really?" Edward said. He smiled. "How nice. That makes my return all the more delightful."

"A friend of yours stopped by to see you while you were gone," Carrie said.

"A friend?"

"Yes," Carrie said. "One of your professors from law school."

"Oh? Which one?"

Carrie chuckled. "He said to tell you that 'Old Round-top' stopped by. You called him that, I believe."

Edward chuckled easily. "Yes," he said. "Tell me, how is Old Roundtop?"

"He seemed quite hale and hearty," Carrie said. "He's retired from his position and is taking a trip to the West.

He discovered you were here in Laramie and stopped by for a visit."

"How unfortunate that I missed him," Edward said.

"Edward, why did you quit writing your sister?"

"My sister?" Edward asked, looking at Carrie with a puzzled expression on his face.

"Professor Heimrod said that you used to be a faithful letter writer. Then, a few years ago, you just dropped out of sight. Neither he nor your sister, nor anyone else heard another thing from you."

"Nonsense," Edward said. "I've been right here, all along. You can check with anyone."

"Yes, but your sister didn't know that. And neither did Professor Heimrod. They thought you had dropped off the edge of the earth."

Edward forced a chuckle. "I think you'll find that both Professor Heimrod and my sister are prone to exaggeration. I don't write as regularly as I once did. I guess I just got out of the habit."

"You should write," Carrie insisted. "What is her name?"

"What?"

"Your sister," Carrie said. "What is her name?"

"Didn't Professor Heimrod tell you?" Edward asked.

"No."

"Oh. Well, it's, uh, Mary," Edward said. "Mary Steele."

"She never married?"

"No," Edward said. "At least, she wasn't married when I was last in touch with her."

"Then that's all the more reason you should write," Carrie said. "Perhaps it's because I have no family that I know how important it is for family members to keep up with each other. Promise me that you'll write to her?"

"I promise," Edward said.

. . .

RAND SLIPPED the saddle off the horse, patted him on the flank, and let the animal get his wind back. It had been a long, hard climb to Snowy Range Pass, and now he stood there, nearly 11,000 feet high, looking down over the other side at the Wyoming rangeland far below.

Rand walked over to a springhead, and knelt down to scoop the cold, clear water up to drink. He drank his fill, then splashed some of the water in his face. Behind him his horse blew and stamped his foot.

"I know," Rand said to the animal. "It was hard work climbing this pass. But it's all downhill after this. Besides, if Donohoe's horse could make it, then you don't have any excuse. You don't want folks going around saying Donohoe's horse is better than you, do you?"

Rand walked over and nuzzled his animal affectionately as he spoke. He saw the remains of a campfire nearby and walked over to feel the coals.

"Well, animal, we are making progress," he said, as he sifted the coals through his fingers. "This fire's no more than a couple of hours old."

Rand walked back over to look down the other side. Then, far below him, he saw a tiny plume of dust and he smiled.

"There he is," he said. "He's headed for Laramie, and he doesn't even know I'm after him." Rand looked at his watch. "Rest for about an hour," he said. "Then we'll go."

Rand pondered the situation as he waited for his horse to recover from the climb. Donohoe was leaving an easy trail to follow, because he didn't realize that anyone was after him. Even if he had known, Rand believed he could have trailed him.

From Wamsutter, Rand had followed him through a

string of settlements, trading posts, and saloons, leading toward the Medicine Bow mountain range. At every settlement, Donohoe had left his mark. He had a prodigious sexual appetite, and at each settlement where there was a prostitute available, he made use of her services. In each case, he had behaved in such a way as to be memorable, and at every stop there was a bitter tale of his mistreatment.

At the last settlement, Rand learned that Donohoe had to have a shoe adjusted on his horse. That adjustment left a crosspiece on the hoof print, making Donohoe's trail even easier to follow. Now, Rand nearly had him.

Is Donohoe Bishop? Or would Donohoe lead Rand to Bishop? It was the latter possibility, which caused Rand to follow with caution. He could have caught up with Donohoe at any time, but he preferred to wait, and see what would happen.

"Miss Carrie?"

Carrie looked up toward the sound of the voice, then smiled broadly, as she recognized Morton. "Morton!" she said excitedly. "Oh, Morton, it's so good to see you. I haven't seen you in such a long while."

"I know," Morton said. He was standing in the hall just outside Carrie's office, looking around nervously. "Ma doesn't like me to come in here anymore."

"I know," Carrie said sadly. "And I can't say as I blame her, Morton. This place—" she shrugged. "Well, it isn't what I wanted it to be. It isn't what I wanted at all."

"I know it ain't none your fault, Miss Carrie," Morton said. "It's Mr. Steele what's made it like it is."

Carrie sighed. "Yes, well, I'm sure Mr. Steele means

well. After all, until he began running things, I was facing bankruptcy. He's only trying to help me." Carrie smiled. "But all that aside, you are here paying me a visit, and I couldn't be happier. You're my best friend in Laramie, you know. Even if we don't see each other as often as I would like."

"Am I really your best friend?" Morton asked, beaming proudly.

"Absolutely," Carrie said. "I hope you aren't embarrassed to have a woman as a friend."

"Embarrassed! Why, heck no, I'm not embarrassed," Morton said. "Truth to tell, I'm proud of it, and I'll tell the world that, too."

Carrie laughed, then she spontaneously put her arms around Morton and gave him a big hug. She felt him stiffen self-consciously. She laughed again, as she saw him look at the floor in embarrassment.

"Oh," Morton said, coughing to cover his embarrassment. "I nearly forgot. A man down at the depot told me to give you this."

"A man at the depot?"

"He was a little bald-headed man," Morton said. "And he was real elegant talkin'."

"Elegant?"

"Yeah, you know, like he was real educated or something."

"Professor Heimrod," Carrie said. "He's come back through like he said he would. Where is he?"

"He left on the train, headin' back East," Morton said.

"He did?" Carrie asked in surprise. "But I thought he was going to stay and visit for a while." Carrie opened the envelope Morton handed her.

My dear Miss Holliday,

Forgive me, please, for not coming to see you during my trip back to Boston but pressing personal business has come up and I must go straight through. I attempted to use the thirty-minute layover to visit with William, but as before, I was unable to see him. Unfortunately, I used so much time looking for him that I had no time left to renew our own acquaintance. This letter will, I know, be a poor substitute for the visit I had so looked forward to.

In view of the fact that I was unable to see William this time as well, I thought it would be wise to leave you with the address of his sister. Perhaps you can prevail upon William to write to her and assure her of his well-being. If you cannot, then perhaps you would be good enough to contact her yourself. She misses him terribly, as does Ollie, her son. That is why it is most difficult for me to understand why William has so neglected his duty, as he set a great store by his nephew. Why, William wouldn't even recognize Ollie now, he has grown so. Here is his sister's address: Mrs. Ellen Frazier, 1304 Adams Street, Boston, Mass.

Sincerely, Louis Heimrod Professor at Law

"Oh, dear," Carrie said, as she finished the letter.

"What is it?"

"There's something wrong," she said. "This letter—"

"What's wrong with it?"

"I'm afraid Professor Heimrod has made a terrible mistake," she said. "He has come all this distance to see Edward and Edward is not the man he thinks he is. Edward's sister is named Mary, and the man Professor Heimrod is looking for has a sister named Ellen."

"Well, since the professor didn't stay, I guess he won't be too disappointed," Morton said.

Carrie folded the letter and put it back in the envelope, then suddenly, she got a very puzzled expression on her face.

"That's odd," she said.

"What?"

"When I spoke to Edward about the professor, he seemed to know him. Now how could that be?"

22

The sheriff looked up from his desk when the door opened, and when he saw Rand, he got a look of surprise on his face.

"Well, well, well," he said. "I never thought I'd see you in Laramie again."

"Why not?" Rand said. "I was acquitted, wasn't I?"

"Yeah, you were acquitted, all right," the sheriff said. "But some folks have prob'ly still got it in their mind that you was the one that done that poor little ol' girl in. What was her name, now?"

"Polly," Rand answered.

"Yeah, that's it, Polly," the sheriff said. "Truth is, all them whores is just alike," the sheriff added. "After a while it gets to where a fella can't tell one from the other. But the law still says that if one of 'em gets kilt, why we got to treat it just like any other murder. I hope you understand I was only doin' my duty when I arrested you."

"I understand," Rand said. "What about you, sheriff? Do you still believe I'm guilty?"

"I believe in the law," the sheriff said. "If the law says you're guilty, then you're guilty. If the law says you're innocent, then you're innocent. The law said you were innocent, so I don't have any problems with that. Right now, I've got paper out on Gilbert Donohoe."

"That's why I'm here," Rand said. "Donohoe is in Laramie."

The sheriff smiled. "No, he ain't," he said. "If he was, he'd be in my jail."

"He's in town," Rand said. "I trailed him here."

"When?"

"Today."

The sheriff stood up and removed his hat from a peg on the wall just behind him.

"In that case, I'll alert my deputies and we'll go get him."

"No," Rand said quickly. "I don't want you to pick him up. At least, not yet. Not until I've had a chance to watch him for a while."

"Watch him for what?"

"He was involved in a train robbery not too long ago," Rand said. "I have reason to believe that there is one more who was involved who is still at large. I think Donohoe can lead me to him. Also, he might be able to lead me to someone who committed a murder in Nebraska a few years ago. Someone I've been looking for, a long time."

"Yeah? Well, I'm sorry about that, Colby, but a murder in Nebraska and that train robbery ain't none of my affair. A murder right here in Laramie is, and since that's what Donohoe done, I'm going to pick him up."

"Sheriff, isn't there any way I could change your mind?" Rand asked. "As long as we keep an eye on him, he isn't going to—"

Rand's words were suddenly interrupted by the sound of gunfire in the street, and Rand and the sheriff moved to the door. A deputy was standing in the middle of the street, holding a smoking pistol in his hand. Men and women were diving for cover.

"What is it, Lenny? What are you shootin' at?"

"It's Donohoe, Sheriff!" the deputy replied. "I just seen him headin' toward the Bloody Bucket, and I took a shot at him."

"Looks like we got no choice now, Colby," the sheriff replied. "We've got to pick him up."

"Sheriff, try and get him alive," Rand requested.

"I'll try," the sheriff assured him. "But I'm not goin' to get my head blowed off talkin' to him."

"Where did he go?" Rand asked the deputy.

"After I shot at him, he cut over there behind that barn," the deputy said, pointing to a large, red barn.

"You wanna help?" the sheriff asked Rand.

"Yeah."

"Then, you go down that way, in case he tries to head down the alley. Lenny, you get over to the railroad 'n make sure he don't sneak into any of the freight cars," the sheriff ordered. "I'll take the barn."

Rand pulled his pistol, then ran toward the alley, cognizant as he did, of the stares of those people who had been caught out on the street when the excitement began.

"You people!" the sheriff shouted, as he started toward the barn with his own gun drawn. "Get off the streets! Stay out of the line of fire!"

When Rand reached the alley, he could see all the way up to the barn. There was no way Donohoe could slip away now without being seen. He hoped that he would see Donohoe first, because he had a feeling that the sheriff and his deputy would shoot first and ask questions later. That would never do, because there were a few questions that Rand wanted to ask him. They were questions that had to be answered.

A low picket fence ran along most of the length of the alley. Rand bent over so that he was no higher than the top of the fence and began moving slowly, cautiously in its cover, headed for the barn.

At the second house a dog rushed toward him, moving quickly and quietly, exploding with a bark only at the last instant as he leaped toward Rand.

The fence separated Rand from the dog, and it actually hit the fence, but the suddenness of its movement, and the tenseness of the moment, startled Rand. His heart leaped and he was unable to suppress a short cry of surprise.

At the next building, a pile of stinking garbage lay rotting in the sun, and a swarm of flies buzzed noisily. Several of the flies moved over to investigate Rand as he crept by, and he slapped at them ineffectively.

Finally, Rand reached the end of the fence. He stood there and stared toward the yawning, black opening, which was the back door to the barn.

For several moments, Rand waited there, poised behind the fence. Sweat rolled down his sides and back and his eyes stung, not only from perspiration, but from the blazing, afternoon sun, which, though now was quite low, was still very bright.

Rand knew that if Donohoe was in the barn, he enjoyed the advantage for the moment. From inside the barn everything outside was clearly visible. No one could approach the barn without being seen. Also, if inside, Donohoe's eyes would be adjusted to the dark, whereas if Rand should rush him, his eyes would still be so blinded by the brightness of the sun that it would take several seconds before he would be able to see anything.

Rand waited and listened, but he heard nothing. Finally, he knew that he could wait no longer. Quietly and cautiously, he began moving toward the barn.

Darting across an open space, he backed up against the barn wall. He crept toward the open door, then stopped and listened. The wind was sighing through the cracks in the boards, while overhead, a rope creaked and groaned in the breeze.

The rope was attached to a pulley, which was used to winch hay into the loft. Rand slipped his pistol back into its holster, then climbed the rope. As soon as he was in the loft, he rolled over behind a bale of hay and lay there for a few moments until his eyes were adjusted to the dark. Then, when he could see what he was doing, he crept to the edge of the loft and looked down. The sheriff was lying on the ground below him, a small trickle of blood coming from his head.

"Sheriff!" Rand called. He looked around to make certain Donohoe wasn't lying in wait for him, then he dropped down to the sheriff's side. He'd been knocked out and was just coming to. "What happened?" Rand asked, helping the sheriff to sit up.

"He was waitin' for me, just behind the door," the sheriff said. "He hit me over the head when I first come in, then he run out that way."

The sheriff pointed to the front door. So, that was why Rand hadn't seen him. He was coming up the back way, while Donohoe, with total impunity, was escaping by the front route.

"Are you all right?" Rand asked.

"Yeah," the sheriff said, touching his head gingerly. "Yeah, I'm all right."

"I'm going after him," Rand said, starting through the front door.

"DID you find out what the shooting was about?" Carrie asked Morton when he returned. It had been the sudden outbreak of shooting in the street, which had interrupted her musing over the strange contents of the letter Professor Heimrod had sent her. Morton, who was still in her office with her, had volunteered to investigate.

"Yes, ma'am, I found out," Morton said. "It was Donohoe."

"Donohoe? Isn't he that awful man who killed Polly?"

"Yes'm," Morton said.

Carrie shuddered. "Did they get him?"

"No ma'am, he got away," Morton said.

"Oh, I hope they get him soon. Someone like that has no right to be running around free, murdering and terrorizing people."

"Don't worry," Morton said. "They'll get him."

Even as Morton spoke the comforting words, the door to the office was suddenly pushed open, and Gilbert Donohoe burst in upon them.

"It's you!" Carrie gasped, raising her hand to her mouth.

"Don't scream, woman, or I'll blow your brains out," Donohoe hissed in a low, menacing voice. He pointed his pistol toward her and pulled back the hammer. The cylinder rotated with a deadly click.

"No!" Morton called, jumping in front of Carrie. "Don't shoot her!"

"Who are you?" Donohoe asked. Then, recognizing Morton, he smiled an ugly evil smile. "I know you," he said. "You're the boy that does all the odd jobs . . . the one they call Mort."

Morton didn't say anything. He just stared at Donohoe defiantly.

"Yeah," Donohoe said. "You're the one that tol' the law 'bout me killin' that whore, ain't you?"

"Yes," Morton boldly confessed.

"Well, ain't this my lucky day?" Donohoe sneered. He had dropped his pistol arm when Morton had stepped in front of Carrie, but now he raised it again, and pointed the gun at Morton. "When you see Polly in a couple of seconds, you tell her I said hello," Donohoe said, laughing evilly.

Carrie grabbed Morton and pulled him down.

"No!" she said.

Donohoe let the end of the gun lower again.

"Well now, what is this?" he asked. "Are you two tryin' to see which one of you can save the other?"

"He's just a boy," Carrie said. "Please don't shoot him."

"Just a boy, huh? Well, on account of this boy's word, they's paper out on me now, for murder. Couldn't no full-growed man have made anythin' any worse for me."

"But the damage is done now," Carrie pleaded. "Why kill him?"

"Why? Because it will give me pleasure," Donohoe growled.

"Oh? Really?" Carrie stepped toward Donohoe, moving her legs so that her dress pressed tightly against her body, in a desperate bid to make herself more provocative to him. "I thought there were other things that gave you more pleasure." Carrie forced herself to smile at him, fighting against the almost overwhelming urge to scream out in terror. But if she could get him interested in her, perhaps she could buy Morton's life.

"What . . . what are you talkin' about?" Donohoe asked, suddenly conscious of Carrie's sensuous curves.

"Polly was my friend," Carrie said. "We used to talk about you."

"Yeah?" Donohoe said. His eyes, which had gleamed with a death lust a moment before, now changed subtly, to another kind of lust . . . but one which was just as frightening. "What did you talk about?"

"We talked about you," Carrie said. "We talked about things you used to do for her. She liked it, you know."

"I know she likened it," Donohoe said. "I tol' ever'one that she likened it, but no one would believe me."

"I believe you," Carrie said. "I'd . . ." Carrie closed her eyes tightly and drew a deep breath to fight against the fear and nausea pulling at her. "I'd like you to do some of those same things with me," she finally said.

"Yeah?" Donohoe said. He was beginning to breathe heavily now, and his tongue flicked out to lick his lips. "Yeah, it'd be good. You'd like it, you'll see. They all liken it."

"But we don't need him around," Carrie said, pointing to Morton, who was standing nearby now. With wide, frightened eyes, Morton was watching the drama being played out before him.

"No, we don't need him," Donohoe said. He raised his pistol again.

"No!" Carrie called out, frightened that her plan was about to backfire right before her eyes. "No, don't hurt him."

Donohoe lowered the pistol again, then he rubbed his cheek.

"If I let the boy live, you'll come with me?" he asked.

"Come with you?" Carrie asked. She hadn't reasoned her plan any further than talking him out of harming the boy. Now he was asking her to come with him. Come with him where? And for what reason? She didn't really want to know the answers to those questions.

"Come with me," Donohoe said. "Come with me now."

"No," Carrie said, taking a step away from him.

Donohoe, who had deluded himself into believing Carrie earlier when she had told him she wanted to be with him, now looked at her in surprise.

"Come with me," he said again.

"No, please, no," Carrie said. "I ... I can't."

Donohoe looked first at Carrie, then at Morton, and he smiled another evil smile.

"Come with me and the boy lives," he said. "Stay here, and you and the boy both die." He pointed the pistol toward Morton again.

"No!" Carrie said. "I'll . . . I'll come with you."

"Good," Donohoe said. He looked at Morton. "You, come here."

Morton stepped toward Donohoe, then without a word of warning, Donohoe brought the barrel of his pistol down sharply on Morton's head. Morton fell to the floor without a sound.

"What have you done?" Carrie asked fearfully.

"Don't worry," he said. "I just knocked him out. He'll come around all right." Donohoe smiled again, and Carrie noticed how ugly and yellow his teeth were. "You didn't think I was going to let him stay awake to watch which way we went, did you?"

"I suppose not," Carrie said. "Where are we going?"

"Don't you worry none about that," Donohoe said, "I got a place all picked out. Me 'n you is gonna have us a fine time, in a place so private no one's ever gonna find us, 'lessen I want 'em to."

"Morton!" Rand called. He saw Morton on the floor just as soon as he stepped to the door of Carrie's office, and he slipped his gun back into his holster and hurried to the boy.

"Ohh," Morton said, coming around slowly. He put his hand to his head and winced when he touched the knot that had been raised there.

"What happened?" Rand asked.

"Carrie!" Morton said, sitting up quickly, then closing his eyes in dizziness. "Rand! He took Carrie!"

"What? Who took her? What are you talking about?"

"Donohoe! He came in here and he took her with him."

"Where? Where did he take her?"

"I don't know," Morton said. "He hit me over the head with his gun and knocked me out ... so I didn't see anything."

The sheriff and his deputy came into the room then, as did half a dozen others, drawn to the office by all the commotion.

"Donohoe was here, sheriff," Rand said. "He knocked out Morton and took Carrie."

"He has to still be in the building," the sheriff said. "We've combed the streets outside. Lenny, you take some men and look back in the kitchen, and all around down here. The rest of you fellas come upstairs with me."

"I'm going to look around outside," Rand said.

"I tell you, he can't be out there, or else someone would've seen him."

"He got in here without being seen," Rand said. "I figure he could get out the same way."

"You do what you want," the sheriff called. "Come on, men, let's go."

The sheriff and a few of the other men ran up the

stairs, their boots clumping loudly on the steps. In the kitchen, as pantry doors and cabinet covers were being banged open, the men shouted back and forth so loudly that it sounded more like a cattle roundup than a manhunt.

Outside, Rand walked all the way around the hotel, his eyes carefully searching the dirt, for tracks or signs. But there were just too many footprints, both human and horse, for him to find any leads.

"I'll get a posse together, first thing in the morning," the sheriff said when everyone returned to the jail after night fell and the search was fruitless.

"I'm not going to wait until morning," Rand said. "I'm going out tonight."

"What good will that do you?" the sheriff asked. "You know you won't find anything out there, in the middle of the night. If he left any tracks, it'd be too dark for you to pick 'em up. The Almanac says there ain't no moon tonight."

"I don't care," Rand said doggedly. "I'm going out there, and I'm not coming back until I find her."

"Her? I thought you were looking for Donohoe."

"I was," Rand said. "But there's something a lot more important, now. I've got to find Carrie before that bastard hurts her."

"Look, Colby, I know you want to save the girl. We all do. It's just that, if you go off half-cocked in the middle of the night, you never know what you're walkin' into. He may have an ambush all set up, just waitin' for you."

"I'm going," Rand said again, just as determined as before.

"All right," the sheriff finally said. "But just so's we don't stumble over one another out there, suppose you tell me where you're gonna be searchin' for 'em. It'll also give us an idea as to where to come to find your body, just in case he's a waitin' for you."

"Have you got any maps?"

"Yeah, I got some maps," the sheriff said. He walked over to a cabinet, opened a drawer, and pulled out a rolled up map. He put the map on a table unrolled it, then held it open with an assortment of books, inkwells, and paperweights.

"He's going to have to go where there's water," Rand said, looking at the map. He traced his finger along the Laramie River. "I'm going to follow this river up into the mountains."

23

CARRIE HAD LAIN, BOUND AND GAGGED, IN EDWARD Steele's room while the sheriff and his helpers searched the hotel. She heard the impatient knocks on the doors, and the doors being opened, one by one as the search party progressed along the hall, and she hoped they would come into Edward's room.

During the search, Donohoe sat on the edge of the bed, alternately pointing the gun at her, then at the door. Suddenly, Carrie changed from praying that someone would open the door, to praying that no one would. She knew that Donohoe would shoot the first person through the door, and afterward, probably shoot her.

"Don't bother with that door," she heard the sheriff say. "That's Edward Steele's room."

Donohoe smiled proudly, as if he had scored a great victory, and he looked at Carrie as if he expected her to congratulate him for his cunning.

Finally, when it grew dark outside, he walked over and stared through the window for a long, long while.

"All right," he said, in a harsh whisper. "We'll go now.

I'm goin' to untie you so as you can walk, but if you try 'n run, I'm going to shoot you down like a dog. Do you understand that?"

Carrie nodded yes, with her eyes reflecting her fear.

"Let's go," Donohoe said.

Donohoe opened the door and peered out into the hall. He looked up and down with quick, darting eyes, and Carrie shivered.

Once, when Carrie was a very small girl, she had gone to the basement of the orphanage to bring up some potatoes. When she had opened the cellar door and started down the stairs, she saw a rat sitting on the top of a barrel of apples. The rat raised up on its haunches and looked at Carrie with black menacing eyes, and Carrie had frozen in fear and revulsion. For an instant, Donohoe's eyes and menacing behavior reminded Carrie of that rat she had seen so many years ago, and she felt the same degree of revulsion and fear now, that she had felt then.

"It's clear," Donohoe hissed. He reached for her, putting his hand on her arm and roughly pulling her out into the hall.

A cold, numbing fear blotted out all other sensation in Carrie. She didn't know if there was a crowd in the Community Room, or if anyone was in the restaurant, or even in the hotel. She neither saw nor heard a thing, while, like a snake's victim, she followed Donohoe's instructions without a word of protest.

There were two horses saddled and tied to a hitching rail behind the hotel, and Donohoe took the animals without a second thought.

"Now," he said, swinging up onto the horse beside her. "We'll just ride out of town real slow, like we ain't in no hurry at all."

A streak of lightning lit up the alley, and for an instant the entire world was reduced to a stark study in harsh white and coal black. A moment after the lightning flash, a peal of thunder roared through the night sky. A gust of wind, damp with impending rain, whipped by.

"We're in luck," Donohoe said, smiling. He pulled a yellow rain slicker off the back of the saddle and handed it to Carrie. "Put this on," he ordered.

Donohoe found another slicker for himself, then with both of them covered by the raincoats, they began to ride slowly down the main street of Laramie.

Carrie saw Lenny, the sheriff's deputy, at the far end of the street. He was leaning against a hitching rail, cradling a rifle in his arms.

"Don't you say a word," Donohoe hissed at her. Donohoe pulled the brim of his hat down and turned the collar of the raincoat up. He hunched down in the saddle so that as they rode by the deputy, there wasn't a whole lot for the deputy to see.

Carrie was desperate to call out, to say something that would attract the deputy's attention, but she knew that if she made a sound it would be her last one. Then, just as they drew even with the deputy, she got an idea. The canteen was on the side of the horse away from Donohoe so, without being seen, she managed to slip it off the pommel and slide it down so she could drop it. She let it go from as low as she could reach, and she hoped the sound of the horses' hooves would cover the noise so that Donohoe wouldn't realize what she had done.

Carrie looked over at Donohoe just as the canteen hit the ground, and she breathed a sigh of relief when she saw that he didn't notice it.

"Hey, you, hold it!" Lenny suddenly yelled.

Carrie and Donohoe both stopped, and Carrie looked over toward Donohoe. Donohoe was holding his pistol under the raincoat, and he cocked it. Carrie had a sudden spasm of fear. What had she done? Had she signed her own death warrant and that of the deputy's?

"You may need this," Lenny said, hooking the canteen back over the pommel. "Sometimes it's a long time between waterholes." He never even looked up.

"Thanks," Donohoe said gruffly.

Across the street, the door to the sheriff's office opened.

"Lenny, get on in here, will you?" the sheriff called.

"Sure thing, Sheriff," Lenny replied. "You folks better hole up somewhere," he said to Donohoe and Carrie. "It looks like a terrible rain's comin' up."

Carrie twisted around in her saddle as the deputy walked away, and then she felt a pain in her heart more severe than anything she had ever felt before, because through the lighted window of the sheriff's office, she could see Rand Colby. She drew in a gasping breath.

"Uh, uh," Donohoe hissed loudly. "Don't you make one sound!"

Tears of anguish welled in Carrie's eyes, but from somewhere she found the strength to choke off the sob which had begun in her throat.

The first few drops of rain began to fall just as they rode out of town. They were large, heavy drops, indicative of the cloudburst about to begin. Donohoe laughed.

"How about this?" he said. "The rain'll wash away all the tracks . . . not even an Indian could find us."

The rain fell in torrents, stinging Carrie's face with its whipping fury. It formed a solid, almost impenetrable wall of water in front and behind them. From horizon to horizon, Carrie could see long, wicked streaks of lightning slicing through the downpour, going from cloud to ground and from cloud to cloud. There was an almost constant matrix of lightning before them, and a continuing roar of thunder like the sound of cannon fire.

Carrie, nearly blinded by the rain in her eyes and the brilliant lightning flashes, pulled her horse to a stop.

"Come on," Donohoe shouted, fiercely. "We've got to make as much distance as we can during the rain."

"I can't see," Carrie complained.

"You don't have to see nothin'," Donohoe said. "Just do what I tell you."

"No, please," Carrie said. "You're out of town now, let me go back."

"So you can tell 'em which way I went?" Donohoe asked.

"No, I won't say anything, I promise."

"And you expect me to believe that?"

"I promise," Carrie said again, sobbing, for now she was free of the restraint against the sound and could hold it back no longer.

Donohoe chuckled and his laugh was all the more menacing, when contrasted to Carrie's bitter tears. "Well, I've got a secret for you," he said. "I wouldn't let you go back, even if I did think you'd keep quiet. I've got plans for you. Surely you ain't forgot what you said? We're gonna have some fun, me 'n you. And you're gonna liken it, too. I promise you, you're gonna liken it a lot."

"Please," Carrie begged. "Just let me—" Carrie's entreaty was interrupted by a quick, and unexpected, sharp pain on her face. She put her hand to her cheek and felt a long, burning sensation. Donohoe, still chuckling, held up a small, leather quirt.

"How about that?" he asked. "I've got a lot more of

that, my pretty. Much, much more," he said followed by a cackling laugh. Then the smile left his face. "Now come on," he said gruffly.

"YOU MIGHT AT LEAST WAIT until this rain slows down," the sheriff said.

"Nope." Rand said. "They're out there in it. I can go out there too. I'm not going to let him get a whole day's head start on me."

"Suit yourself," the sheriff said. "But this is a real frog-drownin' rain, and there ain't gonna be track one for you to follow."

"That might work out all the better," Rand said.

"The better? How so?"

"If Donohoe knows that the rain will wash away his tracks, he might get careless. He doesn't think anyone can find him in a rainstorm like this. All I need is for him to get a little overconfident."

"Well, all I can say is, lots of luck to you, Colby. I hope you find 'em."

"I will," Rand said resolutely. "You can count on it, Sheriff."

The sheriff came out onto the front porch with Rand, while one of the deputies brought his horse up for Rand to use.

"Take ol' Samson here," the deputy said. "He can run down any three horses I've ever known."

"Thanks," Rand said, pleasantly surprised by the offer. The deputy who was lending him the horse was the same one who had seen Rand in the room with Polly and had turned evidence against him.

"I hope you catch him," the deputy said. He looked down toward the ground. "The truth is I kinda liked

Polly. That's why I was so fired up to get you hung for killin' her, when I thought you was the one that done it. Now that I know you ain't the one, I'm still just as fired up to get the one that did do it, and that's Donohoe."

Rand took the reins of the horse and patted the animal on the head.

"He might be just a mite spooked at the idea of a stranger gettin' on him, but he'll settle down fast, don't worry," the deputy said.

Rand climbed into the saddle. As he settled down on the animal's back, the horse began to dance about, nervously.

"Easy, Samson, easy," Lenny said. "That's a friend, you hear? You treat him right."

The horse seemed to calm down at the deputy's easy words. Rand smiled and patted the horse on the neck, then waved goodbye to the sheriff and the others, and rode off into the rain.

Rand reached the Laramie River, just west of town. He didn't need any tracks to follow, he had followed Donohoe enough now, that he knew exactly how Donohoe operated. Donohoe would stay with the Laramie River until he found another stretch of water just as dependable. That would be the Platte River, if Rand remembered right, and that was far enough away that it would not even have to be considered now.

The Laramie River was running higher than usual, because of the rushing rain. It was small and unimpressive, for a river. The Platte, the Snake, the Wind—all were streams of water truly deserving of the name, river. The Laramie just barely qualified. At least the Laramie had a constant flow of water, no matter how small it often got, and in a land where water was prized, and rivers frequently dried up or just disappeared, the

Laramie, despite its size, was a welcome piece of geography.

It was welcome for Rand, because it was easier to follow than any trail, and he knew that it would eventually lead him to Donohoe.

"Laugh about the rain all you want, Donohoe," Rand said under his breath. "I've got you just where I want you, now."

Lightning lit up the countryside, and Rand stared ahead, looking for a lead, but he saw only mountains.

The rain stopped at around two o'clock in the morning, and when it stopped, Rand decided he would stop too. He swung down from the horse and patted it on the neck.

"You've been a good horse," he said. He took a small rope and hobbled the horse's legs together. "I really hate to do this to you, but I don't know you, and I don't know if I can trust you to be here in the morning."

Rand stretched, feeling the soreness in his body, then he found a high, sandy spot, which was not as wet as the other places, and he lay down and pulled the hat over his eyes.

It would not do to blunder on through the dark, now. As long as it was raining, he was somewhat protected. Donohoe would have felt safe, perhaps even overconfident, and the rain would have blocked out any sound. But now, Donohoe would grow cautious again, and Rand might give himself away in the dark.

Rand was exhausted, but sleep was a long time in coming, not only because his bed was uncomfortable, but because he couldn't get Carrie off his mind.

Was she all right? Had Donohoe hurt her in any way? Was she still alive? Yes, Rand was sure she was still alive. He wouldn't have taken her with him, if he hadn't planned to keep her alive. And he doubted if he had done anything to hurt her, yet. After all, he had to move rather quickly, and it would be a lot easier moving with a healthy captive than one who was badly injured.

Even if Carrie was unhurt, she had to be nearly frightened to death right now, and she was certainly going to be uncomfortable. She would be even more uncomfortable than he was, Rand knew, because she was not used to living in such conditions.

The sun rose in a sky as blue as that in which it had set the night before. The rainclouds that had not moved in until after sunset were already gone. When Rand awakened and stood up, he could see from horizon to horizon without the slightest trace of a cloud.

"Where did you go, horse?" he called out. He heard a sound and looked around to see the horse, still hobbled, standing just behind a rock outcropping. Rand chuckled. "Trying to hide from me, huh? You better not do that old horse, you and I have got to become friends. We've got a lot of work cut out for us today."

Rand saddled the horse, then loosened the hobble and swung onto the animal's back.

"I hope you found something to nibble on during the night," he said. "We're not going to take time out for breakfast just yet."

The railroad had been a fact of life in Laramie for over four years now, but every train that arrived was still greeted with the enthusiasm and excitement of the first train. The platform was crowded with people: farmers, ranchers, townspeople, men, women, and children, laughing, shouting sometimes even crying, all drawn by the arrival of the train from Cheyenne.

The sheriff was one of those in the crowd, but he hadn't been drawn by the excitement of the event. He had come to the train specifically to meet Edward Steele who was returning from Cheyenne.

"Mr. Steele, over here," the sheriff called, as Edward stepped down from the train.

Edward nodded toward the sheriff, then picked his way through the crowd toward him.

"The telegram said it was urgent that I return to Laramie," Edward said. "What is it? What's wrong?"

"It's Miss Holliday," the sheriff said.

"Miss Holliday? What happened? Has there been an accident?"

"No," the sheriff said. "There ain't been a accident. But . . ."

"But what, man? What are you trying to tell me?" Edward asked, growing impatient with the sheriff's plodding.

"She's been kidnapped."

"Kidnapped? By Indians . . . who? . . ."

"By Gilbert Donohoe." The sheriff sighed. "Donohoe rode into town yesterday, just as bold as you please. Lenny seen 'im and took a shot at him, but he missed. Anyway, during all the excitement, Donohoe somehow got away from us, and when he left, he took Miss Holliday with him. I thought you might need to know about it, seein' as you're her business partner and all."

"Yes," Edward said. "Yes, I appreciate your telling me. Which way did they go, do you have any idea?"

"No," the sheriff said. "Colby is out trying to follow 'em."

"Colby? You mean Rand Colby?"

"Yeah. Colby's has been trackin' Donohoe all along, and he trailed him right to town. When Donohoe got away last night, Colby went out after him. Colby figures they'll be followin' the Laramie River."

"Did he find signs?"

"No, and like as not there won't be no signs now, not after that rain we had last night. But it makes sense that Donohoe would go to the river when you stop to think about it. Where else would he find water?"

"He won't follow the river," Edward said. "That river doesn't lead anywhere. Why would he go out into the wilderness? He's got to be near some settlement, somewhere. My guess is he'll follow the railroad west. Anytime he needs water he can get it from a railroad water tank, and anytime he needs provisions, he can get it from a store."

"Yeah," the sheriff said. "Yeah, that kind of makes sense. I was gonna take some men up the Laramie myself, to sort of follow up on Colby, but I don't think I'll do that."

"If Colby is following the river, let him look there, and you and your men follow the track. You might send some of them back east and the others to the west. That way everything will be covered—the river and the track —in both directions."

"Thanks," the sheriff said. "That's a good idea. I'm glad you come along when you did. Do you want to join the posse?"

Edward smiled. "Nothing would give me greater pleasure than to see Mr. Donohoe captured and brought to justice," he said. "But I'm afraid I would be of very little use to you in the field. I'm a city fellow, and I'm totally out of my element when I get away from civilization."

The sheriff laughed. "I think I can see what you're a sayin'. I've had help in posses before, who would have been more help, if they'd just stayed at home." The sheriff touched the brim of his hat. "I'd better get the boys goin', Mr. Steele. With any luck, we'll be bringing Donohoe and Miss Holliday back in today."

Edward watched the sheriff return to his office, then he walked over to the hotel. He had a drink at the bar and listened as conversations swirled around him, all pertaining to the excitement of the night before.

"The posse's leavin'," someone shouted from the front door, and everyone hurried out into the street to watch them leave.

"You ain't goin' to ride with the posse, Mr. Steele?" Hal asked, as he wiped the bar. Hal had returned to the Holliday House from the Bloody Bucket, as soon as the Holliday House had begun making a profit again.

"No, I guess not," Edward said.

"If you don't mind my sayin' so, Mr. Steele, I'm a little disappointed," Hal said. "What with Miss Holliday in danger 'n all, I would've thought you'd be anxious to help."

Edward looked at Hal, then he smiled. "I didn't say I wasn't going to look for her," he said. "I just said I wasn't going to ride with the posse. I prefer to go out on my own."

Hal smiled. "Now you're talkin'. Where are you goin' to start lookin'?"

"I've got a few ideas," Edward said. He wiped the back of his hand across his mouth, then left through the back door. He walked down the alley toward the stable, because he didn't want anyone to see him leave. He told Hal he had a few ideas as to where he might find Donohoe. That wasn't exactly an accurate statement. He had more than a few ideas. He knew exactly where Donohoe was.

24

GILBERT DONOHOE STOOD JUST INSIDE THE DOOR OF THE small cabin and looked over toward the bed. There, Carrie was secured to the bed by ropes which held her arms and legs outstretched.

Donohoe chuckled as he looked at her, and he rubbed himself between the legs.

"Are you waitin' for somebody to come find ya, dearie?"

Carrie looked at him with frightened eyes, but she didn't say anything.

"I thought you might like to know your friend, Colby, is out lookin' for us."

"Rand?"

Donohoe laughed. "Yeah, Rand," he said. "But before you get your hopes up too high, I probably should tell ya, I saw him followin' the river north. He ain't got no idea we crossed the river durin' the night and doubled back to this here cabin."

"He'll find us," Carrie said.

"Oh, he just might," Donohoe said. "But it won't make

no never mind to me, cause you and me'll already had our fun. And it is goin' to be good, my dearie. Oh, it's goin' to be so-o-o good. Just wait, you'll see."

"Mr. Donohoe," Carrie said in a weak voice. "Let me go. Please . . . just let me go."

"Oh, no, I can't do that," Donohoe said. "I got plans for you. Such good plans—you'll see."

Picking up his riding quirt from the table, Donohoe walked over and stood beside the bed. He let the leather ends of the quirt rest on her shoulders, then, slowly, he dragged them across her skin.

At that moment, there was a sound outside the cabin. It was a small, almost imperceptible sound, as a rock slid down the side of the mountain. Carrie managed a momentary delight at seeing a quick flash of fear cross Donohoe's face.

"What was that?" Donohoe asked.

"Maybe you aren't as safe as you thought you were?" Carrie suggested.

Donohoe pulled his pistol and walked over to peer through the window. He searched the rocks diligently, leaning around to get the widest possible angle of the country in front of the cabin.

While Donohoe was looking through the front window, Edward Steele suddenly appeared through the back door.

"Edward!" Carrie said, barely able to contain her happiness over seeing him.

Donohoe swung around quickly at the sound of Carrie's voice, but when he saw Edward, the expression on his face changed from fear to relief, and he smiled.

"Oh, it's just you," he said, slipping his pistol back into his holster. "I was afraid it might be Colby."

The gun in Edward's hand roared, and the bullet

caught Donohoe in the chest. He put his hands over his wound, and bright red blood began spilling between his fingers. He fell back against the wall, then slid down it, slowly, until he was in a sitting position on the floor.

"Jay, you've killed me," he said in a disbelieving voice. "Why did you have to kill me?"

Donohoe looked over at Carrie, then he laughed. "Oh," he said. "Oh, yes, this is the best torture of all. You don't know, do you? You really don't know who this man is."

Edward pulled the hammer back on his pistol and pointed it at Donohoe, ready to shoot a second time, but a second shot wasn't needed. Donohoe's head fell forward, his mouth opened and slack-jawed. A line of spittle drooled out with a last death rattle.

"Oh, Edward, thank God you've come," Carrie said. "You don't know what awful things I've been through. He was a—what are you doing?"

Edward was pulling boards away from the wall of the cabin and sticking his arm down inside.

"Ah, yes, here it is," he said, pulling up a white cloth bag. The words "Cattlemen's Bank and Trust" were printed on the outside of the bag.

"What is that?" Carrie asked, seeing the bag. "Edward, what are you doing? Untie me. Get me loose from here."

Edward walked over to the bed and looked down at her and smiled.

"Well, now, I must say I have never seen a prettier picture."

"Pretty? I'm trussed up like a pig for the market. Edward, stop playing games and let me loose."

Edward pulled a pen knife from his pocket and began cutting the ropes. Gratefully, Carrie sat up and began gingerly rubbing the raw areas on her wrists and ankles.

"Have you and Mr. Donohoe enjoyed yourselves?" Edward asked. He went back over to the wall and reached down behind the loose boards again. This time he brought out a packet of money, all neatly wrapped in banker's straps. As Carrie watched him, he pulled out several packets of money.

"Enjoyed ourselves? What a poor joke," Carrie said, wondering at his coldness. "I thought he was going to kill me."

"Oh, I'm certain he would have, if I hadn't happened along," Edward said. By now he had over ten packets of money stacked up on the small table in front of him.

"Edward, what is this?" Carrie asked. "Where did all that money come from?"

"Some of it came from the Cattlemen's Bank and Trust in Rushville, Nebraska," Edward said. "Though most of that money is gone now. The rest comes from banks and rail shipments over the past few years."

Carrie gasped. "You mean Donohoe was a bank robber?"

"Among other things," Edward said. "Get dressed, we're going to be leaving this place, soon."

Carrie got up and started toward her clothes. She was so weak from her ordeal, that for a moment she couldn't even walk, and she had to brace herself on the edge of the bed.

"We can't leave this place too soon to suit me," she said. "You'll never know how glad I am you found me."

"Yes, I'm quite the hero," Edward said. He started stuffing the money into the cloth sack, while Carrie began getting dressed.

"Did you see Rand? He's out there, somewhere."

"He went on up the river," Edward said. "I saw his tracks leading north. He didn't know where to cross."

"How did you find it?" Carrie asked. "Donohoe was very careful not to leave any tracks."

Edward chuckled.

"I didn't have to look for tracks. I knew about this old cabin, and I figured it was the only place he could be. I just made a lucky guess, that's all."

"No, I'm the one that was lucky," Carrie said. "You got here just in time."

"Hurry," Edward said. "We haven't much time. Colby might figure out that Donohoe doubled back on him, and he could show up at any moment."

"What difference would that make?" Carrie asked. "You've already found me."

"I know," Edward said. "But I don't want Colby to find me, any more than I wanted that stupid Professor Heimrod to find me."

"Professor Heimrod? What are you talking about? I thought he was a friend of yours. He came back through Laramie yesterday, looking for you."

"Yes, he wrote me from San Francisco, telling me just what day and what time he would be there. It made it easy for me to avoid him."

"You mean, you avoided him on purpose?"

"Yes."

"Why?"

"I wanted to avoid an embarrassing confrontation," Edward said.

Suddenly Carrie gasped, and she looked at Edward with eyes that were as full of fright as they had been when she had been Donohoe's prisoner.

"You . . . aren't . . . a lawyer, are you?" she asked.

"Oh, yes, I am a lawyer. Disbarred, to be sure, but I am a lawyer."

"But you aren't William Edward Steele."

"What makes you think that?" Edward asked.

"The Professor. There were a few things he said that didn't quite ring true. Then, yesterday, he wrote me a letter in which he gave me your sister's . . . that is, Edward Steele's sister's name and address. You told me your sister's name was Mary, but Professor Heimrod said it was Ellen. And you told me your sister wasn't married, but Professor Heimrod said she was married and had a son, a boy who was your favorite nephew."

Edward tied a knot in the top of the bag, into which he had put all the money.

"Well, now you know about the embarrassing confrontation I was trying to avoid," he said.

"Where is the real Edward Steele? What happened to him?"

"He's dead," Edward said.

"Dead? Did you . . . did you kill him?" Carrie asked in a weak voice.

"No," Edward said. "I didn't kill him. I happened across him out in the desert. His horse had thrown him and run away. He broke his back and couldn't move. I nursed him for a day or two, and we talked a lot. I found out his name, where he was from, and what he was up to. When he died, it just seemed convenient for me to take his name."

"But, why?" Carrie asked.

"Why not? He was a lawyer, an educated man. He had a future ahead of him. I was also a lawyer, but with a somewhat shady past and a need for a new name. It seemed like the sensible thing to do."

"He called you Jay," Carrie said.

"What?"

"Donohoe called you Jay. He knew you weren't Edward Steele, didn't he?"

Edward sighed. "Yeah, he knew. Donohoe was a man out of my shady past."

"He was expecting you here, wasn't he?"

"What makes you think he was expecting me?"

"I know he was," Carrie said. "That's why he wasn't frightened when he saw you. That's why you knew how to find him."

"All right, he was expecting me," Edward admitted. "And I did plan to meet him here. But I had no idea he would have you with him. I was just going to discuss some legal matters with him, in case he—"

"You were in cahoots with him," Carrie said, pointing to the bag of money. "How else would you know where all that money was?"

"He told me," Edward said.

"Don't lie to me. You were in league with this man. You knew about all the robberies, because you were part of them."

"Suppose I was, he's dead now, and it's all behind us. And, there's enough money in this sack to go to San Francisco and start all over again," Edward said as he stashed the sack of money into his saddlebag.

"With another new name?" Carrie asked.

"If need be," Edward said. "Come with me."

"I wouldn't come with you if you were the last man on earth," Carrie said.

"I can show you a life that you've only been able to dream about," Edward said. "We'll go to the finest clubs and restaurants, live in the best houses, travel in luxury. You can't turn all that down."

"I can and I do," Carrie said. "I wouldn't go with you, anymore than I would have gone with Donohoe."

Edward smiled easily. "I hardly think that bears

comparison, my dear. Donohoe was, after all, an evil brute of a man."

"And just what do you call yourself?"

Edward laughed. "What do I call myself? I really don't know. Perhaps I am an opportunist."

"It stands to reason that you don't know what you are," Carrie said. "You don't even know who you are. How ironic, that I've spent a lifetime wishing I knew myself, and you can abandon your identity as easily as changing clothes. Donohoe called you Jay. Is that your correct name?"

"My real name is Jay Bishop."

"Jay Bishop? You're the man Rand is looking for! You were one of the bank robbers."

"That's correct," Edward said. "Now, you can see why it's imperative that we leave this place before Colby finds us. Come on, let's go."

"I told you, I'm not going with you," Carrie said.

Edward smiled an evil smile at her. "Oh, I think you are," he said. "If you don't, you will find that I can be just as unpleasant as Mr. Donohoe. In fact, I can be even more unpleasant, because I'm more intelligent, and I can think of more unique forms of persuasion." The smile left his face. He pulled his pistol out and made an impatient motion toward the door with it. "Let's go," he said.

Rand was on his knees, looking at the ground closely.

"We've lost them, horse," he said disgustedly. "They haven't come this way."

Rand stood up and removed his hat, then ran his hand through his hair as he thought about it. Where could they have gone?

He walked over to the river, now faster and colder than it had been when he first began following it. It roared over the rocks and burst into bubbling white froth as it worked its way down from the mountain sides. Rand dropped down beside it and filled his canteen. While he was stooped there, an elk crept cautiously to the other side of the river and began drinking.

"Well," Rand said quietly, looking at the elk. "You think you're safe, do you? Let me tell you friend, if I needed meat, I could shoot you over there, just as easily as I could if you were over here. Just because you're on the other side, that doesn't mean—" suddenly Rand stopped in mid-sentence. The other side! Donohoe had crossed the river somewhere, and Rand had missed the sign. All right, that made it simple. He would just cross over here. If he couldn't find any sign, that meant that Donohoe had doubled back.

"You gained a little time on me, mister," he said. "But you haven't gotten away."

Rand stood up and closed the canteen, then he walked over to get his horse.

"Come on, boy," he said. "You're going to get your feet wet."

Rand crossed to the west side of the river, then followed it south, searching the ground for any sign that others had been here before him. He rode for half a day, backtracking most of what he had covered earlier, when finally he saw the telltale sign of horse droppings. This was where they crossed!

A small trail led away from the river, and Rand had just started following it, when he noticed something puzzling. Three horses had recently gone up the trail, one of them much later than the other two. He wasn't the only one on Donahoe's trail.

It was late afternoon by the time Rand reached the

cabin. He got off his horse about a hundred yards away, because he didn't want to be heard as he approached it.

"I'm going to have to hobble you again, Samson," he said. "I can't have you wandering around out here, you might give us away."

Rand slipped the hobble back on the horse's forelegs, then he moved toward the cabin on foot.

Darting from rock to rock, always staying low, Rand moved as cautiously and quietly as he could. He waited for several seconds after each movement, just to make certain that he hadn't been seen. Finally, when he was within ten yards of the cabin, he stopped to study it very carefully.

There didn't appear to be anyone inside. Rand listened for a sound, but heard none, and he looked for a sign of movement, but saw nothing. Finally, with his gun drawn and his senses on the keen edge, he moved up to the edge of the cabin and looked in through the window.

"Well, I'll be—" he said. Inside, he saw Donohoe sprawled against the far wall, with a pool of blood on his chest.

Rand stepped onto the porch, then through the door, into the cabin. Except for Donohoe's body, the cabin was completely empty.

Rand walked over to check the body. Donohoe had been dead for at least a couple of hours. Whoever did it had probably rescued Carrie and they would be back to Laramie by now. Rand sighed and stood up. He would have liked to have been the one who'd saved Carrie, but the important thing was, she was safe now.

But, why didn't they take Donohoe's body back with them? That would have been the normal thing to do, wouldn't it?

Unless they didn't go back.

Suddenly, Rand got an uneasy sensation in his stomach. Suppose Carrie wasn't rescued? Suppose she was just taken from Donohoe by one of Donohoe's henchmen? If so, she was still in great danger.

Rand went outside to search for signs again. If the trail led back toward the river, then he would feel all right, because it would tell him that whoever killed Donohoe was taking Carrie back to Laramie. If it led anywhere else, then he would follow it, because that would be cause for worry.

He didn't have to look long. After but a moment's search, he let out a groan of frustration and concern. The trail led away from Laramie and up into the mountains. There were two horses. One of the horses was undoubtedly carrying Carrie. But who was riding the other? Carrie's rescuer or Carrie's abductor?

25

EDWARD ORDERED CARRIE TO DISMOUNT AND WALK HER horse as they approached the summit of Medicine Bow Peak. Now their breath came as loud and as labored as that of the horses just before they had dismounted. It was a long and difficult climb, and still the peak seemed an impossible distance above them.

"Please," Carrie said. "Can't we stop and rest for a while?"

"We'll rest at the top," Edward said.

"I'll never make it."

"I think you will," Edward said. He chuckled, evilly. "Consider the alternative."

"Which is?"

"Staying here," Edward said, "with a bullet in you."

"Why are you taking me?" Carrie said. "I'm just slowing you down."

"I thought it was obvious. I want you to share my fortune with me."

"That is ridiculous," Carrie said.

"Then, let's see. Perhaps there is a more practical reason," Edward said.

"What do you mean?"

"It may become necessary for me to trade you off."

"Trade me off? What are you talking about?"

"If either Colby or the posse finds us, I might be able to strike a bargain with them. Your life for my freedom. The same would hold true with the Indians, you know."

"The Indians?"

"Yes," Edward said. "We'll be going through some Indian country, and they may not be too pleased. If they show any signs of belligerence, I might have to make some sort of an accommodation with them."

"What sort of accommodation are you talking about?"

"One that would be to their liking, I'm certain," Edward said. "Though not to yours perhaps. You see, I would offer you, in return for my own safe passage through their land. The Indians seem to set quite a store by white women."

"You wouldn't really do that, would you?" Carrie asked fearfully.

"Oh, yes, my dear, I certainly would," Edward said. "So, as you can see, you should be thankful for my company."

"I don't know about that," Carrie said, forcing a bravado that she didn't feel. "Now that I think about it, I would rather be with the Indians."

"Oh, my dear," Edward said, faking an injury to his pride. "You do know how to hurt a person, don't you?"

Carrie was quiet after that. Her reticence didn't come from a quiet acceptance of her fate, but rather from the exertion of the climb. It was long and arduous, and any effort to speak merely used more breath.

Finally, when the sun had almost set, they reached the summit. Under any other circumstances, Carrie might well have thrilled to have been here. Medicine Bow Peak was the highest summit around, and from here there was a commanding view of nearly half the state of Wyoming. It was particularly beautiful now, in this light. The sun was a glowing orange in the west, slowly sinking behind the purple folds of distant mountains. There was a stiff wind, and at this elevation, it was as cold as the plains of winter. Carrie walked over to a rock overhang and stared down into the abyss. The towering pine trees in the notches below appeared to be little more than tiny matchsticks from this viewpoint. How easy it would be to step off now and escape whatever fate Edward had in store for her.

"You'd better step back," Edward said. "You aren't an eagle, you know. One false step and it would be all over. That's a long fall."

He removed a coffee pot from his saddlebag and tossed it to Carrie. "Go over into that draw and get some clean snow," he said. "Melt it down and make us some coffee."

Carrie took the pot and started down the draw toward the snow. After a moment, she discovered she was out of Edward's sight.

She could flee!

But if she tried, she would have to go back down the mountain by herself, and without a horse. And if she made it back down the mountain, could she make it back to Laramie on foot?

Well, what if she couldn't? Wouldn't it be better to die trying to escape, than to stay here with this man? Anyway, the chances were very good that he would kill her when he was finished with her. And what about the meantime? Wouldn't he try to make use of her, much as Donohoe did?

Suddenly, Carrie remembered Donohoe's last words. Something about this being the best form of torture, then he had said, "You don't know, do you? You really don't know?"

That hadn't meant much at the time, because Carrie didn't understand. Now, she understood perfectly. Donohoe meant that she didn't know about Edward, and he was intimating that while she thought she was escaping, she was actually in for more of the same.

"Carrie!" a voice called in a hoarse whisper. Carrie gasped and looked around. There, standing just behind an outcropping of rock, stood Rand Colby.

"Rand!" Carrie said. "Rand, it's you!" Carrie dropped the coffee pot and rushed to him, throwing her arms around him in unrestrained joy.

"Well, now, isn't this a cozy picture?" Edward suddenly said.

In her joy at seeing Rand, Carrie had momentarily forgotten all about Edward Steele. Now she was reminded of him in a most dramatic way, because he was standing at the top of the draw, holding his pistol on both of them.

"Edward!" Carrie gasped.

"Come on up here," Edward said, motioning with his pistol. "Both of you."

"What are you going to do?" Carrie asked in a frightened voice.

"I haven't yet decided," Edward said. He stepped back and made another impatient motion with his pistol. "Come on. Get up here."

As Carrie and Rand climbed out of the draw, he

looked at them and smiled rubbing his chin with his free hand.

"I have to admit, you did a fair job of tracking us," Edward said. "I figured we would be safe until at least tomorrow."

"I don't understand," Rand said. "If you saved her from Donohoe, where are you taking her now?"

Edward chuckled. "Think about it," he said. "It'll come to you."

"You were involved in the robberies with Donohoe."

"Quick. Very quick. I was in a good position to plan them," Edward said. "As an honest lawyer, I was privy to certain 'useful' information. I knew when large sums of money were being transferred, when certain banks would be holding an unusually large amount of money . . . that sort of thing. I used the Holliday House as sort of a clearing station for such information. I received a full share from all the jobs, without having to take a risk."

"Why?" Rand asked.

"Why? The answer is as simple as the story of man. Greed. I am a very greedy man, Mr. Colby. I am the original King Midas. I cannot have too much money."

"But you were a respected man, Steele. A lawyer, looked up to by everyone."

"No," Carrie said sullenly. "He even stole his reputation."

"What are you talking about?"

"He stole his name like he stole everything else. Edward Steele was an honest lawyer who was killed in an accident. This man came along and took his identity. What is the old saying? He who steals my purse steals trash, but he who steals my good name? That's what Mr. Bishop did."

"Bishop!" Rand said in surprise. "Is his name Bishop?"

Edward chuckled. "Jay Bishop, to be more specific."

"You are the one—" Rand started, but Edward cut him off.

"I am the one you have been looking for," he said. He laughed. "I must say, it has been quite an enjoyable game with me. I, like everyone else, knew your story. I knew that you were on some blood lust trail of vengeance, tracking down the desperadoes who robbed the bank in Rushville and killed your sweetheart. That was one of the jobs I did take part in, wearing a hood to preserve my anonymity. I must say, that I followed with interest, as you caught each of my partners, one by one, and eliminated them. I was able to observe you, but since you didn't know who I was, you couldn't observe me. It was almost as if I were an invisible man."

"You're not invisible anymore," Rand said.

"Perhaps not, but I soon shall be," Edward said. "Once you two are out of the way."

"You'll never get away with it," Carrie said. "Someone will find you out."

Edward laughed. "How naive you are, my child. That has always been your most appealing aspect, you know. How simple it is to dispose of you now."

Edward pulled back the hammer of his pistol and pointed it at Carrie, then he chuckled.

"I'm going to let you watch me shoot her," he said to Rand. "Then I'll shoot you, but not before you will have had the experience of seeing me kill both of your sweethearts."

"All right, Sheriff, you can come out, now," Rand said.

Edward laughed.

"Really, now, Colby, you didn't actually expect me to fall for that old trick, did you?"

"Believe me, Steele, it's no trick," another voice

suddenly said, and Carrie gasped as she saw the sheriff, one of his deputies, and three other men standing just behind Edward, moving up on him with guns drawn.

Edward's face froze in a look of fear and shock, and then incredibly, he broke out into a wide grin. He dropped the gun and put his hands up.

"Well now," he said. "Fancy meeting you here, Sheriff."

"I thought you might be surprised," the sheriff said. "Especially as you sent all of us on a wild goose chase, up and down the railroad tracks."

"We met at the cabin," Rand explained. "They got there just as I discovered your tracks coming up here."

"The more I got to thinkin' about Rand's idea on where Donohoe might go, the more sense it made to me," the sheriff said. "So, I sent some of the boys on down the rail line, just to be safe, but I cut across to hit the river. The truth is, I just stumbled onto that cabin, because of the way we was comin' to the river, but one look inside tol' the story. We joined up with Colby, 'n here we are."

"Yes," Edward said. "Here you are." He sighed. "I suppose you'll be wanting to go back tonight?"

"No," the sheriff said. "It'll be dark soon, and I don't want to have to try and go down the mountainside in the dark. We'll camp up here overnight and get a start back early in the morning."

"A wise decision," Edward said.

"Cuff 'im, Lenny," the sheriff said, and Lenny started toward him with the handcuffs.

"Stick out your hands," Lenny ordered gruffly.

Edward stuck out his hands as ordered, but just as Lenny started to put the cuffs on him, Edward grabbed him and spun him around. Pulling Lenny's pistol, he put it to the deputy's head.

"Watch it, he's got Lenny!" the sheriff called.

Edward started backing away, slowly, all the while holding the pistol, cocked, ready to shoot the deputy if anyone made a move toward him.

"I'm sorry, Sheriff," Edward said. "I'm afraid I can't stay around." Edward backed toward the rock precipice where Carrie had enjoyed her view a moment earlier.

"You'd better look out, Steele, you're getting close to the edge, you're going to go over," Rand said.

Edward laughed. "You never give up trying, do you?" he said. "If you think I'm going to fall—" his words were stopped in mid-sentence, because at that moment he took one step too many. One instant he was there, and the next instant he was gone, disappearing over the side without a sound.

"What the . . . ?" the sheriff asked. "What happened to him?"

"Lenny! This way—quick!" Rand called, and the deputy, now free of restraint, wasted no time getting away from the sheer edge of the rock.

Rand and the others rushed up to the edge and looked down. There was a sheer drop of more than two thousand feet. The canyon was dark, and, though they looked hard, they could see nothing except the tops of trees, muted in the shadows, far below. Somewhere down there, with his body broken and torn, lay the remains of the man they had known as Edward Steele: Jay Bishop.

"He ... he never made a sound," Carrie said, with a shiver.

Rand put his arms around her and pulled her to him. "It's all over now," he said.

Carrie looked up at him and smiled. "Rand, you are free of your vow, now."

"No," Rand said.

"No?" Carrie asked, puzzled by the strange statement.

"I freed myself of that vow long before this," he said.

THREE WEEKS LATER, Mr. and Mrs. Rand Colby were about to board the train. As Carrie started toward the steps being guarded by the conductor, Rand pulled her back.

"No, this is our car, back here," he said, pointing to the last car of the train."

"Our car?"

"That's right," Rand said. "It belongs to my grandfather, but he gave it to us as a wedding gift."

Once they were aboard, Carrie looked around the opulent trappings of the private rail car. Instead of the usual seats and aisles, there was a large, overstuffed davenport, two huge chairs, a dining table, a bookshelf stocked with books, and in a separate bedroom at the rear of the car, an enormous bed.

"When we came out, I thought the parlor car was impressive, but I've never seen anything as luxurious as this," she said, running her hand along the upholstery of one of the chairs.

"It is rather nice," Rand said.

"Rather nice. It's . . . it's fabulous!"

Three hours after they boarded the train, they ate their evening meal brought to their private car by one of the porters.

"This last three weeks have been like a fairy tale," she said. "Being rescued by a knight in shining armor, marrying a prince, and now travelling in a private, luxurious car. And I can hardly wait until we're in Boston. I've always wanted to see Boston. Tell me about it. Is it beautiful?"

Rand smiled. "Look through the window," he said. "What do you see out there?"

Outside the train, there was nothing but wide-open space as far as one could see. They could have been at sea, for there was no more accurate description of the plains of Nebraska than that.

"I don't see anything," Carrie said, puzzled by his comment.

"What can be more beautiful than that?" Rand asked. "Out here there's room for a man and woman to be free, to love and live as they like. Boston is too crowded and too close for me. I like this country."

Carrie looked at the empty earth, graying now in the twilight, and she smiled.

"I have to confess, that I have come to love it too," she said. "But there is one thing I love even more."

"Oh? And what is that?" Rand asked, teasing her.

"You'll have to guess," Carrie said. She walked over and sat on the sofa, and Rand moved over to sit beside her.

"I think I know," he said.

"Rand, are you happy?"

"Happy?" Rand replied. He put his hand on her face, with his fingers teasing her jaw line. "I've never known what happiness could be, before now."

Rand moved his lips to hers and kissed her.

Outside the train, the passing countryside remained unchanged, and the rush of the train over the track penetrated Carrie's senses. Carrie smiled an unseen smile in the dark.

All was right with her world.

A LOOK AT: ON THE OREGON TRAIL

A five-star masterpiece from best-selling author Robert Vaughan.

When sixteen-year-old Matt Logan and his friend Danny Duggan run away from an orphanage, they go west. There, they meet Jim Bridger, among other mountain men, and become fur trappers. But the market for beaver plews dies out, and the two friends take on jobs as wagon train guides, where they separate.

One of the trains Matt picks up in Independence began its journey in St. Louis, led by widower Cody McNair. Cody was a well experienced leader, having once been the captain of an ocean-going sailing ship. His adult son and daughter, Jared and Ellen and their daughter Emma Joyce, make the trip with him. Also a part of the wagon company is the Baker family, Lon, his wife Norma, and their eight-year-old daughter, Precious.

On the journey west, they rescue two travelers from other trains: Nonnie Hughes, a widow who had been going west with her brother and nephew when their wagon train was attacked by a gang of white outlaws, known as the "Hood Raiders", and beautiful, young, Darci Clinton, who had been captured by Indians after her family was slain.

Tension develops with some of the members of the train, but Cody keeps everything in check as the train endures the rigors of travel. When the train is hit by the Hood Raiders, the Raiders, including their leader are killed, and the others run off.

Five months and ten days after leaving St. Louis, the train reaches its final destination of Oregon City, Oregon.

AVAILABLE NOW

ABOUT THE AUTHOR

Robert Vaughan sold his first book when he was 19. That was 57 years and nearly 500 books ago. He wrote the novelization for the mini series Andersonville. Vaughan wrote, produced, and appeared in the History Channel documentary Vietnam Homecoming.

His books have hit the NYT bestseller list seven times. He has won the Spur Award, the PORGIE Award (Best Paperback Original), the Western Fictioneers Lifetime Achievement Award, received the Readwest President's Award for Excellence in Western Fiction, is a member of the American Writers Hall of Fame and is a Pulitzer Prize nominee.

Vaughan is also a retired army officer, helicopter pilot with three tours in Vietnam. And received the Distinguished Flying Cross, the Purple Heart, The Bronze Star with three oak leaf clusters, the Air Medal for valor with 35 oak leaf clusters, the Army Commendation Medal, the Meritorious Service Medal, and the Vietnamese Cross of Gallantry.